D1522641

Love, CANTER, ACTION

KATIE GILBERT

**UNION
SQUARE
& CO.**

NEW YORK

UNION
SQUARE
&CO.

NEW YORK

UNION SQUARE & CO. and the distinctive Union Square & Co. logo
are trademarks of Sterling Publishing Co., Inc.

Union Square & Co., LLC, is a subsidiary of Sterling Publishing Co., Inc.

Text © 2025 Katie Gilbert
Cover art © 2025 Maeve Norton

All rights reserved. No part of this publication may be reproduced,
stored in a retrieval system, or transmitted in any form or by any means
(including electronic, mechanical, photocopying, recording, or otherwise)
without prior written permission from the publisher.

This is a work of fiction. Names, characters, businesses, events, and incidents
are the products of the author's imagination. Any resemblance to actual persons,
living or dead, or actual events is purely coincidental.

ISBN 978-1-4549-5717-1 (hardcover)
ISBN 978-1-4549-5718-8 (paperback)
ISBN 978-1-4549-5719-5 (e-book)
ISBN 978-1-60582-493-2 (galley)

Library of Congress Control Number: 2024041773

For information about custom editions, special sales, and premium purchases,
please contact specialsales@unionsquareandco.com.

Printed in Canada

2   4   6   8   10   9   7   5   3   1

unionsquareandco.com

Cover design by Marcie Lawrence
Interior design by Kevin Ullrich

Dedication TK

CHAPTER 1

The horses know something's wrong.

That probably explains why Ethel has four hooves fully planted on the ground, refusing to take the last step into her stall, no matter how hard Jess pulls at her lead.

I bite down a smile while I watch Jess struggle.

"Come on," she says, her voice thick with irritation.

She thinks Ethel can't hear it—can't tell how much she hates her. But horses can sense irritation and anxiety. And today, there's enough of that around here to power a small village.

"Move, you *big. Stubborn. Monster.*" Jess yanks the lead after each word, like she thinks if she pulls hard enough, her tiny five-foot frame can overpower the horse. Hell, even at five-eight I wouldn't be able to do it. A grown man couldn't force Ethel somewhere she didn't want to be.

I let her pull for another thirty seconds, enough time to suffer for calling my favorite horse a monster. Then I walk over and hold my hand out, eyebrows raised.

Jess huffs—sending her long bangs flying up in the air then back down on her forehead—before she hands the lead over.

"Good luck. She's stubborn as can be today. Swear she knows I have a date and wants to make sure I don't have time for a shower."

"She's nervous. They all are."

Jess rolls her eyes. "No she's not, Nora. She doesn't know we're all out of a job or that the ranch will be empty next week. The only thing she knows is if she plants her feet long enough, she'll get a sugar cube before going in for the night."

Ethel's ear flicks at the word *sugar*. I run my hand along her favorite spot, the one on her neck. She nickers and nudges my chest.

"Long day, huh?" I ask Ethel. She lets out a little sigh and nudges me again. "Why don't we get you in your stall so you can have some rest?" I pull gently at her lead and she follows right along. I'm proud of myself for resisting the urge to stick my tongue out at Jess as she steps in front of us to open the stall door.

I get Ethel settled, slipping her a sugar cube from the front pocket of my jeans. Once her lead is off, I take my time brushing her, hoping that if I take long enough, Jess will leave. But despite the fact that she was whining about being late five minutes ago, she leans up against the side of the stall and watches me.

I'd already told Ethel goodbye this morning, mainly because I was only supposed to work until noon and thought I'd be gone by the time they took her in for the day. But I couldn't bear to leave, knowing it'd be the last time I set foot on Shep Farm, the last time I got to help new riders in and out of the saddle, watch as they went from terrified and stiff to relaxed and amazed. If Jess wasn't here, I'd say another, better goodbye. A longer one. But with her watching, I simply finish my brushing, rub Ethel once more on her neck, and whisper, "Be good."

Jess follows me out, locking the door behind us. The horses sigh and whinny as we walk by, some sticking their heads over the stalls as we pass, hoping for a quick scratch or pet. I don't stop, knowing full well if I do, I'll spend another ten hours here.

Without speaking, we both walk straight to Mrs. Shep's office. The AC hits us when we walk through the door and I realize how hot I've been all day. I wipe at the hair stuck to my forehead, and, with the dirt all over my hands, it's probably more black now than dirty blonde.

Mrs. Shep looks over her cat-eye lenses at us. Those glasses and the chain attached to them—the kind that keep you from putting them down somewhere and losing them—are the only things about her that look old. I mean, her skin is wrinkling around the eyes, and she's slower than she was ten years ago when I met her for the first time. But she once mentioned she married her husband in 1980-something, which was a *long* time ago, so she has to be old. Still, she doesn't have any trouble hopping up in the saddle or cleaning the stalls.

But she does have trouble paying to run the ranch, which is why she's been selling it off little by little over the years. And even though she tried real hard to keep it from happening, she finally let her son sell off all the rest. He convinced her to leave Georgia and live in Nevada with him—putting me out of a job and costing me the only place that had ever felt like home.

She smiles a little when she sees me, and I crumble at the thought that it may be the last time I get to see the lines that pop up around her mouth when she grins. Her eyes dart down to the desk she's standing behind. She licks her fingers, combs through a stack of envelopes, hands one to me and then to Jess.

"Thanks," Jess says. I wait for her to say more, to tell her how sorry she is that the ranch is gone, how much she'll miss it. But she waves, sticks the envelope in her back pocket, and walks out the door we came in through.

I raise my eyebrows and look back at Mrs. Shep, who's sporting a full-blown grin now.

"Devastated, isn't she?" Mrs. Shep says. I snort.

"I found her trying to wrestle Ethel into the stalls. She was here almost a year, and I don't think she learned a thing."

"Well, we can't all be the horse whisperer."

"I wasn't expecting her to take over for you one day," I say, grabbing a candy from the bowl in the middle of the desk and sticking it in my front pocket for later. "But she could have at least learned all the horses' names."

Mrs. Shep shakes her head and slips her glasses off her nose. They fall to her chest. "Not everybody has the kind of passion you do."

"What you really mean is—other people have a life outside of this place."

She smiles. "Have a seat. There's something I've been meaning to talk to you about."

I settle into the leather chair that sits opposite her tiny walnut desk. It's worn and faded in some places, but beautiful. She told me once that her husband made it for her, before he passed. I never got to meet him. By the time Mama and I showed up on Mrs. Shep's doorstep, he had been gone for three years.

She rifles through a pile of papers on her desk, squinting a little at the words on each one before she remembers to slide her glasses back on. Once she comes to whatever she's looking for, a small smile creeps back onto her face. She folds the paper. Her chair squeaks a little as she leans back in it.

"Now," she says, settling into whatever it is we're going to talk about. "You're sure you haven't changed your mind about going to college?"

I force myself not to roll my eyes. Mrs. Shep thinks that because my mama's gone now, she has to take over the college talk. Mama never went, and she wanted me to be the first in our family to go. I never wanted anything more than what I had found here at the ranch—horses and fresh air and hard work. After Mama died, I realized there wasn't anyone around to disappoint if I didn't go. So, I won't.

I had planned to spend the rest of my life here, helping Mrs. Shep.

That plan, unfortunately, has gone to crap.

But I still know I don't want to go to college. I just have to figure out exactly where I'm going next.

"I'm positive," I say, making sure not even a single note of doubt creeps into my voice. I really don't want to have to talk about this again after today.

I brace myself for an argument, but surprisingly, she nods.

"And your daddy's all right with that?"

I bristle. "*Daddy's* a strong word."

That's a lot milder than what I want to say—that the man who didn't know I even existed a year ago would never really be a father to me. I don't know how the courts found him after Mama died, when I was a ward of the state there for a hot minute, but they did. And both he and I have regretted it ever since.

Not as much as his wife, Cecelia, though.

They think I'm just taking a gap year, that I'll see my friends leaving for college and change my mind.

I won't.

"Well, he *is* your father, Nora. How does he feel about you not going to college?"

I shrug. "He's okay with it."

She stares at me until I give in.

"Fine," I say. "He wants me to go. But I'm seventeen. Almost eighteen. The man has known me a total of five months. He doesn't get a say. So I told him I was taking a gap year."

"I think you're more stubborn than the horses sometimes."

"Thank you."

She purses her lips and takes another deep breath in through her nose. "It wasn't a compliment, Nora. But if you haven't changed your mind about college, then that makes what I'm about to tell you a little less complicated."

I lean back in my chair and watch as she fiddles with the folded paper in her hands. She's looking up at the wall behind me, her lips pursed, small wrinkles appearing around the outside of them. "I've done something. And I think it's a good thing—I hope you will, too. But you might not. And if you don't, feel free to tell me to go to hell."

"You're headed to Nevada. That's the same thing, isn't it?"

Her eyes narrow at me, but I see the whisper of a smile playing around her lips.

"You know there's a world outside of backwoods Georgia, don't you?"

"Of course I do.

She stares at me, the hint of a smile gone. "And would you ever be willing to leave Georgia? Or are you set on staying in this tiny town for the rest of your life?"

I freeze, breath caught.

Is she asking me to come with her?

"I—" My voice catches. Is that what I want? "Well . . ." I hesitate. "Yeah. I've thought about it."

She relaxes, her shoulders dipping an inch. When she leans forward to hand me the paper she's been toying with, I take it. But I don't open it.

Is it a plane ticket? Apology tickets to Disney World?

Sorry I'm abandoning you here, but at least you can ride the teacups and throw up overpriced popcorn afterward.

"Good," she says. "I'm glad to hear it. Because there's a big world out there, and I think you need to see a little more of it." She nods at the paper. "Open it."

I still don't, fiddling with it instead, trying to sort through my thoughts.

Do I want to go to Nevada? I look at Mrs. Shep's face, trying to remember when she became more like a grandmother than an employer to me. My heart skips, because even though I love her, and appreciate everything she's done for me since Mama died, I do *not* want to tag along with her as a charity case.

"Mrs. Shep—"

"Open it, Nora, before I die of old age."

I grit my teeth. How much did she pay for this ticket? Maybe it'll have the price on it and I can reimburse her. My bank account is embarrassingly low after I had to repair Mama's old, half-rusted pickup last month, the only thing she had left to give me when she died. But I can probably scrape together enough—

My mind stalls when I finally open it and read the words embossed on the top of the page. There's no barcode, no destination or departure city. No gate number or price, because it's not a plane ticket at all. It's—

"What is this?"

7

I read the words EQUINE STUDIES—DIRECT PATH PROGRAM, BILL-INGS, MONTANA on the top of the page over and over again, like they'll tell me something new. I skip down to the first paragraph, the words *We are pleased to accept you* jumping out at me, and I fold the paper in on itself again without reading anymore.

"I don't want to go to college," I say reflexively. But the words *Equine Studies* are stuck in my head, begging me to open the paper again and see what else it says.

Mrs. Shep holds her hands up. "Calm down. It's not a college."

"Then what is it?"

"It's a program, out in Billings."

"A *program*?" I ask, and even I can hear the skepticism lacing my voice.

"Yes, a *program*. It's a one-year advanced course on how to care for horses. How to break them, how to deal with small injuries, that kind of thing. It is *not* college," she says, eyebrows raised, waiting for me to interrupt. I don't, so she goes on. "It's not in a classroom. It's hard work and hands-on and all outside. I know that's important to you."

I thumb the paper again, and I want to read the whole thing so badly I can barely stand it. But I don't.

Not yet.

"I didn't apply for this."

"I know," she says, steepling her fingers and looking down at the top of her desk. "I did it for you."

I'm speechless for the space of three breaths.

"Why?"

Her eyes travel my face before she answers. "I know you thought you'd be working here forever. I thought so, too. When things started to go downhill, when the payments got harder and harder to

make, I held off on selling this part of the ranch as long as I could."
She sighs. "Once I saw the truth, that this place was too big and too
expensive for me to keep on forever, I started looking for a contin-
gency plan for you. This was what I found."

I meet her gaze, hearing what she doesn't say. That she's worried
about what might happen to me after she's gone. That she wishes it
didn't have to be this way.

That she loves me.

"It's a very prestigious program," she says, leaning forward,
her arms on the desk. "I wasn't sure my recommendation would be
enough, so I didn't want to say anything. You were wait-listed at
first." She gestures at the paper. "But someone dropped out, and you
were next on the list. Figured it was high time to let you know."

I push at the feeling that's welling in me, one that I haven't felt
in so long I almost don't recognize it. Hope. But hope is dangerous
as hell—it builds you up and takes you higher and higher. Then it
disappears, nowhere to be found as you fall and fall with nothing
there to catch you.

The paper is heavy, expensive, and opens stiffly as I unfold
it once again, a large crease running down the middle. There's a
congratulations. A start date. An address. Notes about the housing
on site.

And a price.

I almost choke.

"I can't," I say, my voice coming out strangled. "This is—" I fold
the paper and push it back toward her. "There's *no* way."

She puts her hand down on the paper and pushes it back. "I've
already paid half of it. Called and put down a deposit when the letter
came in."

"You *what*?" I all but shout. "How? Where did you find the money?"

"I finally sold Ethel."

"And instead of using the money on something useful, like moving across the country, you spend it on *me*?"

"She was your horse as much as mine," Mrs. Shep says, waving me off. "You and I both know you spent more time raising her than I did. You were there when she was born. And I've got enough money to be going on with." I try to interrupt, but she beats me to it. "Just because I don't have enough to run a ranch doesn't mean I don't have enough to live off of. Now, do you want to go or not?"

I stare her down, prepared to kick up a fuss until she calls and begs for the money back.

But after a second, I can see clear as day that she's made up her mind and there's no talking her out of it. So, I sit back, letting the fight drain out of me.

I think for a minute before I answer her. No, I don't want to go to college. But this *isn't* college. It's spending all day outside with horses, learning how to care for them. It's training that will make me invaluable on a ranch somewhere else, somewhere far away from my father and Cecelia.

That last thought makes my decision for me. I swallow once before answering.

"Yes. I want to go."

She smiles, pleased with herself and my answer. "Good."

"But there's no way I can pay for the rest of this. Not by the start date they put on the letter. And how am I supposed to get myself out to Montana? And—"

"That's the second thing I wanted to talk to you about."

"I'm not taking any more of your money."

"I don't have any more to give. If I did, I would pay for it today. But I can't." She looks me over before going on. "I assume your daddy can't help?"

"Can't or won't?" I ask, but before she answers, I go on. "It doesn't matter. I wouldn't take his money, either. It's bad enough having to live with him." The perils of having a late summer birthday—I had to wait until I was eighteen to move out, according to the state.

"Well, I think I've got a solution to that, too. You know how they filmed that TV series here a few years back? The one about the vampires? Well, there's another crew coming in, for a movie this time. A man in a suit showed up with a check and took all the horses we had left, including Ethel. Overpaid, if you ask me. But I wasn't going to tell him that."

"Okay," I say.

"They need someone to wrangle horses on set. Asked if I knew anybody." It takes me a second before I realize what she's saying.

"I don't know anything about working on a movie set," I say. "I'm sure there's someone more qualified out there."

"More qualified to work with Ethel? Who else knows when she's irritated or upset or about to buck off a rider who hasn't done more than watch somebody mount a horse on television?"

"I guess not," I say reluctantly.

"You could say I'm right, you know. It wouldn't kill you."

I smile. "It might."

She rolls her eyes. "You should take the job, Nora. It's a big-budget film. They're paying enough to cover the rest of your tuition."

My breath catches. "That's . . ."

"A lot of money," she finishes for me.

"A lot."

"I'll email you the location and time. I've got it around here somewhere." Someone knocks on her office door. "Be with you in a minute," she hollers, then looks back at me. I stand as she walks around her desk, mortified to feel tears creeping at the corners of my eyes.

"Don't," Mrs. Shep says, her calloused hands rubbing up and down my arms. I look up at the ceiling to keep the tears from falling, a trick I learned after Mama died. The tears would come out of nowhere, then, and I had to find a way to keep from breaking down ten times a day at work. It helps. A little.

When I look back at Mrs. Shep, she's only a little blurred around the edges. I blink away the few rogue tears, and she's clear again.

"Take the job," she says, her face serious and concerned. "Take the job, take the money, and get out of here. Your mama would want more for you than this town. *I* want more for you than this town. Don't make me spend my golden years floating around a pool worrying over you."

I nod once.

"So you'll take the job? And the spot in Montana?"

"Yeah. I'll take it."

She smiles. It's happy and sad and excited all at once. "Good."

"Thank you," I say. My voice trembles, making it clear that I'm about a second away from crying, *again*. "For doing all of this. Arranging the spot and paying for so much of it. The job. All of it."

I think of all the things I want to say: that I love her, that she's the only thing close to family I have left, that she saved me from floundering around, looking for somewhere to be other than in a home that suffocates me more each day. But before I can find the words to say, someone knocks on her office door again.

She pulls me into a fierce embrace. I tense when her arms wrap around me, but after a breath, I hug her back. When Mama and I showed up here, Mrs. Shep didn't just give us jobs, she gave us a home. We lived in one of the guest suites for free, no privacy and no space, but a roof over our heads and a safe place to stay. She was like family, and I'm not sure where I'd be without her.

"Be good," she says. "Don't embarrass me out there."

"No promises," I say, pulling away and smiling. I follow her out of the office and nod at Charles, one of the ranch hands. Then I'm outside again in the scorching Georgia sun, and when the heat hits me like a ton of sun-soaked bricks, so does one question:

What did I just agree to?

CHAPTER 2

Charlotte has asked me to come to dinner approximately twenty billion times in the last two weeks.

Before Mama died, it would have taken a single text message and the promise of fried okra and I would have been out the door in less than twenty minutes. Now, it takes an act of God (or not-so-subtle threats from Charlotte who, despite being one of my best friends, terrifies me a little) to get me out and around anyone I might have to interact with.

Horses are easy. People? Not so much.

"What happened to that blue dress I gave you?" Charlotte asks. Her chin sits daintily on her manicured hand, elbow on the table while she studies me. "I haven't seen you wear it lately."

I raise an eyebrow. She's judging my outfit? Really? I mean, I showered. Levi's and a blouse that's rubbing my armpits the wrong way is about as fancy as I get.

"The one I borrowed for homecoming?" I ask, taking a bite of the most delicious hamburger I've had in months. It's real red meat, something we don't eat much of at my father and Cecelia's house.

She rolls her eyes. "You were underdressed."

Even though we're at the fanciest restaurant within fifty miles, everyone around us is still in blue jeans and blouses. One of the many perils of living in a small town—not much choice when it comes to restaurants. Despite knowing that no one would be in anything fancier than a button-down and khakis, Charlotte sits in front of me in a red spaghetti strap dress, her strawberry-blonde hair tumbling down her bare shoulders. She leans back in her chair in a way that makes her long legs look even longer, and I'm trying not to feel inadequate across from her.

My hair is just as long, but it's a dull, dishwater blonde. We're both taller than average, but working on a ranch for years has shaped me in a way that's wholly different from the soft, gentle shape of Charlotte.

"I wasn't underdressed," I say, but then I take a bit of a french fry (Parmesan and garlic crusted—not bad) and remember Char wore a floor-length, vintage '90s Badgley Mischka to the same homecoming.

"When are you leaving for Athens again?" I ask, knowing good and well when she's abandoning me. Charlotte's older sister has been at UGA for two years already, and she's spending a few weeks with her before the semester starts, "getting to know the town." That's absolutely code for learning which places don't look too closely at your ID.

"Two days," Charlotte says. "Mama insists on bringing half of the Amazon warehouse in the car with us. She's planning on loading it to the top with purple rugs and flower trash cans and enough lamps to power the entire campus. 'You need to be able to see, Charlotte. You can't study if you can't see.'" Her accent gets heavier when she impersonates her mama, the southern twang almost comical. "It's ridiculous."

"She wants to make sure you've got everything you need," I say, toying with the last few fries on my plate, trying to keep the bitterness out of my voice. It's not Charlotte's fault that I don't have any parents (my father doesn't count), but she constantly complains about hers, and it's rubbed me the wrong way for months.

This is why it's easier to not answer the phone. Easier to make up excuses for missing dinner and hang out in the stalls instead. I can't even have a conversation with my best friend without wanting to pull her hair like I'm a freaking ten-year-old, angry she got a better toy than I did for Christmas. Except, instead of a toy, she's got a living, breathing mother.

She stops tying the ends of her hair in little loose knots, a habit she's had since we were middle schoolers, and gives me an apologetic look. It's worse than the complaining.

"It's fine," I say before she can actually apologize. Once you join the dead parent club, the pity gets old, fast, especially from your friends. "I'm in a mood."

"Bad day at work?"

"Last day at work, actually."

"What?" Charlotte says, a tiny line popping up in between her perfectly shaped brows. I rub between mine, trying to remember when I actually tweezed them last.

"It was super weird, seeing the ranch that empty. Only a few horses and goats waiting to be picked up."

Charlotte's looking at me like I'm speaking a different language.

"And Mrs. Shep randomly told you today that you wouldn't need to come back? That doesn't sound like her."

I shake my head. "No. She let us all know a few weeks ago."

"Did you tell Bree it was your last day? I didn't see anything in the group chat."

"I don't think so. Never really came up." Charlotte stares at me over the table.

"What?" I ask.

She presses her lips into a little line, then shakes her head. "Nothing."

Charlotte won't look at me.

"It doesn't seem like nothing."

She shakes her head a little. "I mean, in the past week, Bree's detailed the decoration, comfort level, and cleanliness score of every bathroom she's used on the Amalfi Coast. That didn't exactly come up organically. But you've known for weeks the date of demise for the ranch and you didn't think to tell your best friends?"

The Parmesan on my tongue is replaced by something sour.

It isn't like I haven't thought about it. But it never felt right. Charlotte's going to UGA, Bree's touring Italy with her family. What, I'm supposed to be all *hey, glad your lives are perfect! Mine is falling apart again!*?

Anyway, I didn't even need to text them to know exactly what they'd say. Bree would have sent me a list of jobs, organized alphabetically. Charlotte would have told me to trust the Universe to bring an opportunity my way, that I only had to wait until the stars aligned and then things would start looking up.

"I'm sorry," I say, even though I don't fully get why she's this upset over me not saying anything about it. "I should have told you."

She shrugs, wiping the hurt look from her face, trying to seem normal. We never had to try before. But things have been off for months.

"It's fine—now that I know, I can fix it. Hey," she says, leaning forward, her hair brushing the top of the table. "We should manifest tonight. Figure out exactly what you want to come your way and then speak it out into the Universe. Let the Earth bring the opportunity to you." She grabs my hands over the table, gripping them tightly. "Let's figure out your mantra. Maybe 'I will find a job I love'? Or 'I will find a cute, rich boy to sweep me off to Europe and feed me grapes'?"

I try not to smile, but fail miserably. The weirdness is gone and bright Charlotte is back in full force.

"Thanks, but I don't need to manifest. I got some good news today."

She quirks an eyebrow. "Spill it."

Determined to fill her in on everything after not telling her about the ranch closing, I spare no details about the program in Montana, or how Mrs. Shep arranged all of it, even a job to help me pay the rest of the tuition.

Charlotte waits until I'm done talking and then squeals so loud that the man at the table next to us flinches and drops his fork. It clatters against his plate, calling more attention to our area of the restaurant.

"I don't believe it!!" she says. My eyes widen and I look around the room, blushing.

Most of the people here are over sixty, which is probably due to the fact that we're eating dinner at five p.m. since Charlotte has to get back home to babysit her brother before seven. But I lock eyes with a couple our age when I turn around to see how many people noticed her outburst. The girl is smiling, but the guy she's with looks like he wants to throw a hunk of bread our way and tell us to stop making such a scene. I don't blame him.

Charlotte pulls her chair over to my side of the table, sidling up next to me, and I turn back around. "We have to document this and drop it in the group chat. Brianna is going to *flip*."

I smile when we come up on her screen, my flushed face staring back at me. Charlotte hesitates, then runs her fingers through my hair before holding up her phone again and snapping half a dozen photos.

She leans her shoulder against mine when she's done, and I watch her type out a message in our group chat, add the photo, and press Send.

My phone dings and the message pops up on the screen, our picture attached.

> Our Girl is moving to MONTANA!!!!

It only takes a second for my phone to vibrate again. Then again, and again, and again as Brianna starts asking for details.

B:
> WTF?

B:
> When?!?!

B:
> Why??

"You fill her in," Charlotte says, standing. "I've got to run to the bathroom."

"You've dragged me into the lion's den and now you're leaving me here to handle it myself?" I say, holding my phone as it lights up again, vibrating almost nonstop now.

Charlotte smiles.

"Oh, come on, Nora. You can break a wild horse but you can't handle Bree?" She walks off before I can respond.

My phone vibrates again.

B:

You can't drop something this big and not give details! Huge friend code violation.

I smile, taking a second to pity anyone who ends up on the receiving end of Brianna's sharp tongue in the courtroom one day. Then I type out a message explaining everything.

B:
OMG.

C:
Right?

Me:
Char are you texting from the bathroom?

C:
You don't?

Me:
No, that's disgusting.

C:
I totally don't believe you. Everyone takes their phone into the bathroom.

B:

Can we get back on track here? You're working on a freaking movie set? And moving to
MONTANA?!?!

Me:

I'm not really working on a movie set. I'm wrangling
horses. It's not as exciting as it sounds.

C:

Yeah right.

B:

What movie is it?

Me:

No idea.

C:

Who is starring?

Me:

No clue. Mrs. Shep didn't say.

B:

What if it's someone smoking? Like Avery Grantham!

C:

Or Elizabeth Bartlett! 😅

Me:

Who?

C:

🤪

B:

Me:

Give me a break. You know step-monster dearest is queen of the Anti-Screen Crusaders. I only get to watch my ancient DVDs in the privacy of my own room.

B:

When do you start?

Before I can type out my answer, the chair next to me shuffles.

"That was fast. You definitely didn't wash your hands." She doesn't answer. "I'm going to sprain a thumb texting her back. She's freaking out and it's your fault."

"My apologies," says a deep voice, decidedly not the high falsetto of Charlotte. I look up to find a man in her seat. No, *man* isn't the right word. But neither is *boy*. A guy, my age. Maybe a year or two older. Deep, auburn red hair half hidden by a beanie, which is weird, because it's ninety degrees outside. He's in a worn Metallica T-shirt, and his faded jeans probably cost more than my mom's truck. He could be handsome, except for the fact that he just scared me half to death, and he's looking at me like he wants to make me the star of a new Netflix documentary about a missing girl, found chopped up and thrown into the Chattahoochee.

It takes me another beat to realize why he looks vaguely familiar. He's the boy I saw scowling at us earlier.

My face flushes. "Uh, hi."

"Hey," he says, leaning back in the chair with the same casual elegance Charlotte held. If I have to keep sitting next to people this attractive and confident, I'm going to develop a complex.

We stare at each other in silence for a few beats, me awkwardly waiting for him to explain why he crashed my table, and him watching me, apparently in no hurry to say whatever he came over here to say.

"Can I help you with something?" I ask, my voice laced with polite confusion. Normally, I would have had a harder time asking without biting his head off, but as we've interrupted the dinner of everyone here multiple times, I manage to keep the bitchiness leashed.

He cocks an eyebrow, leaning back farther in the chair, making himself more comfortable. "Just wondering how your photo turned out."

"Our photo?" I ask, more confused by the second. He's not smiling, which is unsettling.

He's got this supremely irritated look on his face, like he's holding himself back from throwing a glass of water in my lap. Were we really *that* annoying?

"Did you think no one saw you take it? The entire restaurant noticed."

My face flushes; half from embarrassment at realizing the entire restaurant *was* in fact watching us, and half in anger at this boy for clearly making fun of us. Sure, we had been a little over the top, but it hadn't been *that* bad.

"Look," I say, pasting on a smile, "we're excited. We didn't mean to—"

"And you being excited is a reason to invade other people's privacy?"

"I— What?"

"You think you're so clever," he says, leaning forward, arms folded over his knees. I suddenly realize how close we are and wish

Charlotte had left her chair on the other side of the table instead of dragging it next to me. "You thought I wouldn't notice you 'accidentally' catching me in the background of your photo?"

I stare at him, mouth open, trying to process what he's saying.

"You think we took a photo of *you*?" I ask, making sure I understand. All the polite confusion has drained from my voice, and there's a little more venom on the last word than I meant to let out. He bristles.

"Don't play stupid," he says, his face inching closer to mine, voice low. "You took a photo that happened to include me and, judging by how your phone has been lighting up like a Christmas tree, you sent it to someone." He raises his eyebrows. "Who did you send it to?"

"That's none of your business."

"I think it is my business, actually."

I shake my head, trying to process the absolute absurdity of this interaction. "Look, is this some weird ploy to get me to give you my friend's number? I can promise you, she's not interested."

"Don't flatter yourself. I don't want her number, and I don't want yours. What I want is to know who you sent the photo to."

"I didn't send the photo to anyone," I say, hoping if I tell him he'll leave before Charlotte gets back. She'd cause a hell of a scene telling this guy to screw himself in ten different ways. "My friend did. She sent it to our group chat."

He stares at me, disbelief written all over his face. "Do you think I'm an idiot?"

"I think you're a creep," I hiss, thankful that we've inched closer and closer together as we've argued, so no one overhears my outburst. "We're out celebrating because I got a new job, not that it's any of your business," I snap. "But apparently, you won't leave me alone until you know that we were not, in fact, so enamored by you that we engineered a photo specifically to catch you in it and send to our friends." I laugh once, hard. "You really think you're so good-looking that girls can't help but sneak you into the backgrounds of their photos? Give me a break."

Now it's his turn to blush. His face flushes the slightest shade of pink, and he looks so angry you'd think I'd killed his dog. For a second, I think actual fire might burst out of him. A hand lands on his shoulder and he tenses.

"Darling, I've paid and the car is outside."

I tear my eyes away from his furious face and look at the girl next to him. She's at least twenty, and her raven black hair flows down past her shoulders, framing her face in long layers. She smiles at me and I swallow down pieces of the anger that had built up inside. I look around to find that half of the restaurant is covertly looking our way again, and my stomach twists. There are a few phones pointed at us, like people think we're about to break into an actual fight and they have the next viral video. How loud were we? My eyes flit back to the boy still sitting in front of me, He's noticed the phones, too, and they finally draw his attention away from me.

"Come, Alec," the girl says, her hand sliding down to his arm and tugging gently at his shirt sleeve. "We shouldn't keep Mark waiting."

Alec, the colossal jerk who just did his best to ruin my last evening with Charlotte before she leaves, gives me one last scathing look before he gets up. All eyes in the restaurant are trained on him as he and his friend turn and leave without a glance backward.

I watch as they walk out the front door, blood pumping in my ears. How did that happen so fast? I couldn't remember the last time I'd been that angry, much less at a *stranger*.

Before I can think any more on it, Charlotte sits back down next to me.

"Knew not to order the pasta; the cream sauce gets me every time." She settles into her seat. "Why'd you stop answering our texts?" she asks, staring down at her screen, typing furiously.

I look back at my phone to twenty-three unread notifications on the screen. I turn my phone over.

"Can't deal with it right now."

She looks up from her phone, brows furrowed. "What's wrong?"

I hesitate before telling her. "Some guy came over while you were in the bathroom and accused us of taking photos of him. It was super weird." I look around the room and see eyes still flitting our way, people glancing over as they lean toward each other to whisper.

"What?" Charlotte asks, a little grin on her face.

"I know," I say, shaking my head. "It sounds funny, but he was such a jerk about it. Really intense."

She picks up her phone again and scrolls up past all the messages in the group chat from tonight. When she finds the photo of us, she presses it, making it full screen. I watch as she zooms in on a man taking a bite of chicken fried steak, his eyes half closed. "This guy?"

"No," I say. "But I wish I would have thought to pull it up and show him." I shake my head. "What a freaking weirdo."

Charlotte nods, picking up my unfinished garlic bread and nibbling on it. "We're surrounded by them." She shrugs. "I'll kind of miss the weirdos in this town when I'm gone. But especially you. You're my favorite weirdo." She smiles at me and winks.

Charlotte, thankfully, talks my ear off for the rest of dinner. After promising three separate times that I won't go more than a day without texting, she leaves me alone in the parking lot with nowhere to be but home.

Well, not home. But the place I currently live.

On the drive there, I can't help but think about the first time I showed up at my father and Cecelia's house four months ago. I had spent so much of my life wanting a dad. I mean, Mama had been the Ginny to my Georgia. The Lorelai to my Rory. We were best friends, and she was more than enough.

But still, I wondered. I thought about my dad all the time— pretended he was a doctor or a writer or an engineer. Thought about how much he missed me or what he would do if he knew I existed. Because he couldn't know. If he did, of course he'd visit or write or *something*.

Then Mama died. And I found out that he already knew about me. And instead of seeing me or calling me or writing to me for the last seventeen years, he sent money. Money to keep Mama away and quiet, and to keep Cecelia in the dark. But apparently, he never terminated his rights. So when Mama died, he got a phone call from the state. And Cecelia learned he cheated on her eighteen years ago. And my father learned if he didn't take me in, it would be considered child abandonment. And I learned I'd have to live in a house with people I barely knew, because I'm still technically a minor.

I'm in the driveway when I realize I don't remember any of the ride home.

For a second, I think about sleeping in the car, but summer in south Georgia means it's hot even when the sun isn't out. So I go inside.

The sounds of Vivaldi meet me at the door. I stifle a sigh, but really, would it kill her to play some Noah Kahan once in a while?

I put my keys on the ring by the door and kick my shoes off. My father and Cecelia never had kids of their own, so they're not used to any amount of clutter. There was never a three-year-old running around, throwing handfuls of flour all over everything and then pouring red Kool-Aid on the couch. Everything has a place and it stays there, nothing out of order.

They also never had to sit a kid in front of the TV for half an hour to have time to take a shower, so there isn't one in the house. Cecelia is militant about TV and how it affects the young brain. She's principal over at the private school, the one Mama never had enough money to fill out an application for, much less send me to. Every single behavioral issue kids have these days is due to TV, iPads, and early cell phone use, she says. Anything that has a power source and a connection to the internet is enemy number one in her eyes.

I didn't care much for TV anyway, Mama and I never had time for it. Maybe when I was younger, but after we moved here, back to her hometown ten years ago, we were too busy for it. She worked at the ranch all day, and when I got out of school, I'd join her. We'd have dinner with Mrs. Shep and then play cards or ride the horses while the ranch was free of customers. I'm not addicted to screens or anything. But it'd be nice to catch an episode of mindless TV every once in a while, and not have to depend on Mama's ancient DVD collection to do it. If I get desperate enough, I'll text Charlotte and get her Netflix login info, but for now, the DVDs are enough—and as an added bonus, they remind me of Mama.

I can hear something sizzling in the kitchen, and I know if I don't go say hello, they'll come upstairs and find me later. I walk in and try to force a smile.

Cecelia's at the stove, pushing something around with a wooden spoon. My father is behind her, arms wrapped around her waist, whispering something in her ear. He smiles when he sees me, but he doesn't step back. Well, at least I didn't *completely* ruin their marriage. Maybe the news that my father had a love child would have destroyed them when I was a kid, but since it had been so long, Cecelia was able to come to terms with it.

Whatever. Doesn't affect me. I'll be gone soon, anyway, and they'll never have to hear from me again.

"Hi, Nora," my father says, smiling at me over Cecelia's shoulder.

"I'm making pork chops," she says, and when she meets my eyes, she does try to smile. I have to give her credit for that. I guess. "Real meat this time."

"Smells good," I say.

"We cooked plenty. And I made those mashed potatoes you like," she says.

"Thanks, but I already ate."

Her face falls. Dad lets go of her waist, grabbing the bottle of merlot on the counter next to them and pouring a large glass. He hands it to her.

"All right, then," she says, giving me a tight smile.

"Sorry," I say, though I don't really know what I'm apologizing for. "I went to dinner with Charlotte."

My father nods. "We understand. You can still sit with us if you want, tell us about your day."

"That's all right," I say, taking a step back, readying my retreat to my room. "I'm tired, and I've got work tomorrow."

"Work tomorrow?" Cecelia says before she takes a long drink of wine.

"Yeah."

"But Lottie Mason told me she went to pick up eighteen goats from Shep Farm today. Said it was finally closed down, which I was sorry to hear about."

"She's right," I say, wondering if it's as weird as Charlotte made it out to be that I didn't tell anyone about the ranch closing. "It was my last day. But Mrs. Shep lined up new work for me. With the horses."

"On a farm?"

"No," I say, fidgeting with the edge of my shirt. I'm ready to get up to my room and stop pretending we're a family. It's exhausting. "She got me a job on the set of some new movie they're filming outside of town."

Cecelia perks up. "Well, that sounds fancy." Her brows furrow. "How did she get you a part in a movie?"

"It's not an acting job. I'm wrangling the horses for them."

"Just you?" Dad says.

I hesitate. "I'm sure there will be someone else." But when I think over what Mrs. Shep told me about the job, I start to wonder if maybe it *is* just me.

"Well, I'm sure you'll do great," he says, now pouring himself a glass of wine. "You're magic with those beasts. Just like your mama always was."

The almost-normal-this-isn't-too-awkward feeling that was in the room vanishes, and I watch Cecelia stiffen. Dad's eyes cut over to her as he realizes what he's said, and my nails dig into my palms. Of course we can't talk about Mama. Under this roof, mentioning her is something like invoking a curse. I'm only allowed to think of her in one tiny corner of the house, locked away in my room. I can whisper her name there, but God forbid someone brings her up out here, in the open.

"I should probably head up," I say, more desperate than ever to be upstairs, alone. "Early morning."

Cecelia smiles her tight, stressed smile again, and nods. Dad takes a step toward me, like he might cross the room and give me a good-night hug or handshake or pat on the back. But he realizes almost immediately that I am not his daughter in any way that counts, and decides to wink at me instead. "Night, kiddo."

I ignore his awkward words and rush up the stairs and into my pajamas. Once my teeth are brushed and my face is washed and I'm sure I've got all my clothes laid out and ready for tomorrow, I set three alarms on my phone so I'll definitely wake up. It's too early to actually go to bed, despite what I said to my father and Cecelia, so I read and answer the million text messages in our group chat, which of course causes another avalanche of them to come through.

As soon as they stop texting, the excitement of my possible move to Montana and my fancy movie set job dampens a bit, so I pull up my Audible app and press Play on *Percy Jackson*, listening for the millionth time.

But as I start to drift off, the voice of the narrator fading further and further into the background, my defenses fall a little. As I drift off to sleep, I let myself dream of a new life in Montana. One without a dad who showed up too late or a stepmom who tries way too hard. One with horses and snow and fresh air. I dream and dream, and promise myself that I'll make this dream come true.

No matter what.

CHAPTER 3

The email Mrs. Shep forwarded me only had two things—a time and an address. No instructions, no salutation, no get-to-know-you questions. Only a place to be and a time to be there.

The sun still hasn't quite come up, but the sky in front of me is a pale blue, the clouds an electric pink, so I know it won't be long now. My hair whips around as the wind finds its way in through the open windows, and I shift into fifth gear, watching for a second as the dust from the dirt road kicks up in my rearview mirror.

The address they gave me is the Stewart farm. I've been out here at least a dozen times with Mama or Mrs. Shep to look at one animal or another. Mrs. Shep bought a pair of horses from out here about five years ago when things started looking bad and the Stewarts realized they needed to downsize. Everyone was struggling then. Still are, really. But the Stewarts managed to sell off enough to keep their heads above water. Never got rid of any land, but did sell off the luxuries like pet horses. Their daughter, Amanda, had been about my age—homeschooled. She was heartbroken, but Mrs. Shep had told her to come ride anytime out at the ranch. She had meant it, too. Didn't say a word when Amanda showed up every week to brush or ride or feed them until she got too busy.

I hit the brakes as the silo comes into view, and once I'm a little past it, I take a right and drive the three miles down to the stables.

They didn't say where exactly I needed to go, but I'm assuming as I'm here to wrangle horses, I should head that way.

The stables are still right where I remember them being, but there's also a massive white tent across from them, dozens of long gray tables spread out underneath it. Four trailers are lined up a few feet back. I slow down, not wanting to bring a cloud of dust in with me and make a bad impression on my first day.

There still isn't enough light to see every detail, but people mill about around the tables and outside the tent. A man in a red baseball cap is talking to a middle-aged woman standing behind a camera. They're looking out into the field, and she nods while he points in different directions.

A half dozen cars are lined up across from the tent. I park next to an audaciously bright Mustang and wonder if it belongs to whoever is starring in the movie. I want to kick myself for not messaging Mrs. Shep to see if she had any more information on who exactly I was going to be working for. Would I spend the next few weeks embarrassing myself around big Hollywood producers and actors, or were the actors and directors and crew all from around here?

I'm a good thirty minutes early, but I still get out and make myself walk toward the tent.

Once I'm past all the cars, I see a man in a blue uniform sitting on a fold-up chair a few feet away from the tent. He looks up from his book when he hears my footsteps and smiles. "What can I help you with, young lady?" His mouth is kind, but tight, like he thinks he's about to have to shoo away an adoring fan. I smile as I walk up, wondering if maybe I should have thought to email back and ask for some kind of proof of employment.

"Hi. I'm supposed to be starting a job here today?" I say, the words coming out like a question.

He gives me a skeptical look. "Is that right?"

"Yes," I say, fidgeting with the end of my shirt. "I wasn't supposed to be here until six, but I'm a little early."

"Name?" he asks, pulling out a clipboard from under his chair.

"Nora Green."

He takes a pencil from his front pocket and slides it down the edge of the paper. Once he gets to the bottom, he goes back up to the top and starts again. When he gets to the bottom again, he shakes his head.

"Sorry, no Nora Green on the call sheet." He looks up at me with raised eyebrows. "We get a lot of kids on these sets hoping to come sneak a peek at the celebrities. I know it's exciting, especially in a little town." He shrugs. "Sometimes they let locals watch the filming from a specified place, but this is a closed set." He leans forward. "I'm under strict orders not to let anyone past here who isn't on the extras list."

"Extras?" I ask.

"Background actors. I've got a special call sheet for them, and you're not on it."

"That's probably because I'm not a background actor. But I *am* supposed to be here. I'm working with the horses."

"You're the wrangler?" he asks skeptically.

I nod. "That's me."

"You look a little young for that."

"Thanks," I say. He looks at me a little longer.

"Crew is on a different list."

"That explains why you didn't find my name, then."

But instead of looking at the clipboard, he keeps staring at me.

"What?" I ask.

"I'm trying to figure out how you're pulling one over on me here. Because if I look on that list and find your name, I'm going to have to let you in. But if I let you in and you're not really supposed to be here, I'll lose my job. I like my job." He leans back in his chair a little. "Never been on a set where it's this locked down. They're serious about nonessential people. But it's quiet, it's easy, and it pays well. I need a job that pays well."

"So do I," I say, exasperation in my voice. "And you're in danger of making me late for my first day of a job that pays so well I near about can't believe it. So can you check the list, find my name, and let me through?" My eyes flit down to the little name tag above the pocket on his uniform. "Please, Sebastian?"

He looks at me for a second longer before he turns the page on his clipboard, then runs his pencil down the side of it. This time, instead of making it all the way down the paper, his pencil stops halfway down. He stares at something for a beat, then his eyes flick back up to me.

"You have some ID on you?"

I roll my eyes and hold up a finger before digging through the belt bag Bree gave me last Christmas. As much as I was sure I'd never wear the baby blue fanny pack, as my mom used to call it, it *has* turned out to be super useful.

I slip my license out of the little compartment in the back and hand it over to him. His eyes dart from the license to my face a couple of times before he finally makes a little check on the paper and hands it back. He breaks out into a smile, and despite how annoyed I am at being held hostage here for five minutes, I find I kind of like him. So I smile back.

"Sorry. Just doing my job."

"I understand," I say, putting my license back, anxious to get over to the stalls and check on the horses. "But I do need to get to work."

He nods. "Go on in." He points over his shoulder toward the stable. "Somebody should be in there after a bit to check in with you and let you know what they need. And your assistant should be here at some point."

"Assistant?" I ask, confused.

He looks back down at his clipboard. "They've got you listed as wrangler, and another person here as your assistant." His eyes flit back over my face again. "Might be a mistake. Still think you're too young to be doing this job on your own."

"Apparently I won't be," I say, wondering who they brought on to assist, and if they knew the first thing about wrangling. Was I going to spend half my time here making sure some greenie who thought horses were pretty didn't get their head knocked off by a rogue kick?

Another car pulls up behind us and parks beside mine. Sebastian's focus finally leaves me as he watches the person get out. "I'll send the assistant your way once they're here," he says, sparing me one last glance and a small smile.

"Thanks."

I walk past him and onto the set of a movie for the first time in my life. It's not nearly as exciting as Charlotte and Brianna made it sound on the group chat. The fact that it's taking place on a farm I've been to before may be dulling the novelty a little.

Inside the stable, the first rays of sunlight are peeking in through the wide, open spaces up and down the length of the hall. There are twelve stalls, most are occupied. Ethel and Jack are housed right next to each other, and I'm genuinely surprised by the rush of joy that runs through me at seeing Ethel. Mama and I had been there for her birth, had watched the ranch hand guide her out. I had seen her take her first steps, been the first person to ever ride her. She's always been stubborn as hell and spent a good few months refusing to let anyone but me on her back. In fact, when she gets in a mood, she's still finicky about who can ride her. Even when she wouldn't let anyone else on, she'd always make an exception for me.

She nickers when she sees me, and I smile. My feet suddenly feel planted on much more stable ground than they did five minutes ago. We may be on a movie set, but it's still just me and Ethel. I've cared for her since she was born, and she did a great deal of caring for me after Mama died.

Ethel steps closer to the stall door and sticks her head through the opening. I laugh, the sound breaking the quiet in the stables, and run my fingers along her favorite spot. Jack notices and moseys over, trying to nose Ethel out of the way from his stall. He can't quite reach, and stops trying when I run my hand along the side of his neck.

I give myself a few minutes to enjoy seeing them again before I pat each of them once on the neck and walk through the rest of the stables, past the rest of the horses. I don't recognize any of them, and I try not to balk at the idea of working with eight other horses whose temperaments I don't know.

The gentle sunlight catches the dust in the air, making the walk through the stable almost ethereal. It reminds me of early mornings with Mama, doing our chores hours before the riders would show up, making sure the horses were cared for and well fed before a hard day's work.

The last stall holds a stockpile of pellets and electrolyte powder. There are bowls and some measuring cups to scoop out the food. There's an envelope on top of it all, my name across the outside. I walk in and grab it, smiling when I see the handwriting. It's from Mrs. Shep, letting me know that they had bought the last of her food supply, not wanting to upset our horses' stomachs by changing brands. She walks me through what's included, and then ends the letter with a reminder that I can do this.

I believe her a lot easier than I did the first time she said it.

After a few minutes of wrestling with them, I got the bags open and the food measured out for all the horses. I put a scoop of electrolyte powder in each, and pick up a bucket for Ethel. There may or may not be a little more in hers than the rest, but since there's no one around to see, it doesn't really count. I think about slipping her one of the peppermints I was sure to put in my pocket this morning, but I may need it later if she's not cooperating. No doubt she'll smell it on me the minute she's out of the stall, though.

When I'm back out in the hall, it takes me a minute to figure out why I feel a spike of fear.

Her gate is open.

My heart drops and I pick up speed. She's not hanging her head out of the opening, and all I can imagine is her wandering wild through the movie set at six a.m. on my very first day.

When I round the stall door, I expect to find it empty. But Ethel is standing in the middle of the enclosure, someone in front of her.

She takes a small step backward and he follows.

When she raises her back leg slightly off the ground, deep fear grips me.

The guy in front of her inches forward a little more, his hand outstretched like he doesn't even realize how close she is to kicking him.

"Uh, can I help you?" I ask, trying to figure out how to politely tell him to get out. He turns around, a smile on his handsome face. We stare at each other for a beat, and my smile slips away the same second as his. It's the guy from last night.

In the space of a heartbeat, his expression goes from polite, open, and kind to downright furious. I'm sure mine does the same.

"You," he says.

"What are *you* doing here?" I ask, all pretenses of being polite gone. If *this* is who I'm dealing with, then there's no need to beat around the bush. He had no problem being a total jerk to a stranger in a restaurant. I'm happy to return the favor.

"*I'm* supposed to be here," he says, like I should magically know he belongs in the stables. "What are *you* doing here?"

I'm tempted to tell him it's none of his business. But right before I do, I get this sick feeling in my stomach.

Sebastian had told me an assistant was coming.

It's him. He's the assistant.

I laugh once, hard and unkind.

Just my luck. Piss someone off the first time I meet them, and they turn out to be my coworker.

I bite down my angry retort.

"I'm here to feed the horses." I lift the giant bucket of food I've got for Ethel a little higher, and he looks at it for the first time. Ethel sees it, too, her attention drawn from the strange guy in her space.

She slowly moves past him and makes her way over to the food. I put it down even though I wasn't planning on letting her eat in the stall. Unfortunately, the redheaded boy with a temper to match drew me in here before I could set the food outside in the paddocks.

While she nibbles, I look back up at him. He's staring at me like I'm a pile of horse crap sitting in the corner of the stall.

"What do you want?" he asks.

"For you to get out of the stall so my horse can eat in peace," I say, even though what I really want to respond with is *For you to go to hell*. But I bite my tongue. I've done that so much this morning that I'm liable to start tasting blood soon.

He doesn't move. Ethel takes another mouthful, then her eyes roll back to where the boy is standing. Her leg twitches again.

"Look, you do realize you're standing at the ass end of a twitchy horse while she eats, right?"

He looks over at Ethel, surprised to find himself standing right where I said he was.

"And that's a bad thing, I guess?"

"Uh, yeah. That's a bad thing." I shake my head. "Come out of the stall and let her eat before you get kicked through the stable wall."

He looks a little nervous at that, but irritation is still the dominant expression on his face.

He must believe me, though, because he slips past and leaves Ethel's stall. He waits right outside, watching me as I step out and close the door, sighing. She's going to want to eat in there every morning, now. It'll be a pain to get her stubborn butt outside for breakfast.

"Dude, what are you doing here?" I ask, turning around to face him. He's leaning against the door of an empty stall, his arms crossed. When he hears my words, his face goes from irritated to astonished, and a small spot of red spreads across his cheeks.

"Did you seriously just call me *dude*?"

I ignore him, unable to stop my tirade. "You walked into the stall of a horse you didn't know, backed her into a corner, tried to pet her *on her face*, and didn't even notice that she was about to kick you to high heaven while she was eating." I shrug. "You're the worst stable hand I've ever seen. Is this your first time working with horses? You know somebody in the movie or something, and they got you a job? And don't try to tell me you're from around here. Not after the way you acted last night. Only entitled people from out of town act the way you did."

His irritated expression falls away little by little, a confused one taking its place.

"You're not serious," he says.

"Look, it's *painfully* obvious that you don't know a damn thing about horses. So, what? Are you sleeping with the director?"

His mouth quirks up at that, and I realize that with his angry expression gone, he's devastatingly handsome.

Too bad I can't appreciate it, what with wanting to punch him right in one of those perfect cheekbones.

Perfect cheekbones.

Something about the observation lingers in my mind for a moment too long. Objectively, he's handsome as hell. As a casual observer, I mean. Not that *I* find him attractive.

I feel the nagging wrongness again.

Perfect cheekbones. Face that would get him a date in under thirty seconds flat with any girl from my high school. Hands that look like they've spent more time signing autographs than holding a horse's reins. An extreme reaction when he thinks someone is sneaking a photo of him in a restaurant.

"You're not here to help me with the horses."

"No," he says, his lips turning up at one end. "Of course I'm not."

"Because you're an actor."

My teeth are clenched, my mind working overtime trying to place his face. The girl had called him Alec, but the name doesn't do anything to help me. He could be an A-list star, or a barely known minor actor. One would cause me a lot more trouble than the other.

He rolls his eyes and I have the almost unbearable urge to throw a bale of hay at him.

"So this is where you pretend like you had no idea who I was yesterday when you snapped that photo with me in the background? I'd respect you more if you just owned up to it and apologized, Horse Girl."

"Don't call me that," I say, bristling.

He smiles, and I realize my mistake.

"Sure, won't happen again," he says. "Who knows how much longer you'll be around anyway, so I wouldn't worry about it."

Fantastic. He's famous enough to get me thrown off set after all. I cannot lose this job.

"I had no idea who you were." I'm embarrassed by the hint of pleading in my voice.

He stares at me in silence for a few moments, like he's trying to glean the truth from my face.

"So it was just a coincidence that your friend squealed loud enough to deafen the whole restaurant and then took a selfie that was perfectly angled to catch me in the background?"

"She squealed because I told her I had good news for the first time in months. And the photo didn't even have you in it."

"Too bad you can't prove it," he says. The smugness radiates off of him.

My hands shoot to the belt bag at my hip. I don't miss the amused look that crosses his face when he notices it. But it melts away faster than lightning when he sees what I pull out.

"Those aren't allowed on set."

"Says who?"

I step over to him, though I'm reluctant to get any closer than I have to. It pisses me off to find he smells delicious. Almost as good as he looks.

Too bad his personality is so repulsive.

"Who wears cologne to work with horses?" I mutter, disdain in my voice.

"Obviously not you," he retorts, his breath tickling my neck.

I scroll as fast as I can through the group chat while I mentally hurl insults his way, but it's taking me way too long to get to the photo. They've sent ten million messages since then. Alec sighs impatiently and I suppress a shudder when his breath runs down my neck.

"Here," I say, tapping the picture and making it full size the way Charlotte had. "See for yourself."

His arm brushes against mine as he leans down.

He stares at the photo so long I swear he almost *wants* to find himself back there. After another awkward second, Alec hands my phone back and steps away from me, meandering into an empty stall.

"That proves nothing," he says, turning back to face me. "You could have taken a dozen other photos that did have me in them." But he sounds like he's starting to doubt his own words.

"You know," I say, unable to stop myself from laughing, "I'd respect you more if you just own up to being wrong and apologize." I slide my phone back in my belt bag. "It's simple, you say something like, *I'm so sorry for being such a major ass-hat, ma'am. Next time, I'll make sure someone is being a creepy stalker before accusing them of taking my photo.*"

I expect him to lash out again—to say something equal measures irritating and sharp. But before he can, a girl walks through the door. She's in the middle of throwing her long, curly brown hair into a ponytail, and her flannel is buttoned wrong.

"Sorry," she breathes, finishing her hair as she crosses the distance between us. She's in such a hurry that she rushes right past Alec. He watches her from the stall, eyebrows raised.

"Nora, right?" she asks, sounding winded, like she ran here.

"Yeah," I say, trying to place her very familiar face.

"Amanda," she says, smiling. "We met a couple of years back? When we sold those horses to Shep Farm."

"Right. Yeah, of course I remember."

"You and your mama took away my two favorite horses that day. But don't worry, I won't hold it against you," she says, tightening her ponytail. Then she gets this look on her face that I'm way too familiar with—the one that lets me know we've crossed over into your-mom-is-dead-here's-some-pity territory. I'm all too aware of Alec still standing behind her, probably watching my face for another weakness he can exploit. Before I can stop her, Amanda says it.

"I was real sorry to hear about your mama."

"Thanks," I say, hoping that's the end of it and she'll move on.

"I'm surprised you're still working with horses," she says. "What with . . . everything that happened." She hesitates a little, realizing halfway through her sentence that she's gone too far.

"It wasn't the horse's fault," I say, not wanting this conversation to go any further with Alec still watching. My eyes dart to him without my permission. There's something on his face when our eyes meet, and for a second, I'm worried it's pity. But it's not. Curiosity is written all over him, plain as day.

I stare just a beat too long, and Amanda, wondering what's got my attention, turns to find a boy in the stall behind her instead of a horse.

A shriek that makes Charlotte's sound like a whisper pierces the stables.

I jump.

Alec's eyes fly wide.

Ethel snorts a few stalls over.

"No way." Amanda squeals. She slaps her hand over her mouth, belatedly realizing how loud she was.

Alec's face, open and curious before, shutters. He slips on a smile, a different one than any he's shown me. Those were sharp and mocking. This one looks like something he practiced in the mirror way too many times. It's fake as can be.

"Alexander MATHIS?!" Amanda's voice goes up ten octaves on the last word, and I cringe.

His smile gets wider, but it's stilted. He's no longer leaning against the wall; instead, he's standing straight, tense. "Hello, Amanda. Pleasure to meet you."

"You know my *name*."

"Do you prefer Mandy?"

"You can totally call me Mandy if you want," she says, breathless.

"Then I will," he says, stepping forward to shake her hand. "Pleasure to meet you, Mandy."

I think she might faint.

I think *I* might vomit.

"When Dad told me people from Hollywood would be filming here, I *never* for a second thought it might be *you*! Weren't you in Sweden a couple of weeks ago? Only, I saw that picture of you and Elizabeth Max in Stockholm. So sorry to hear about the breakup, by the way. Is that why you cut your trip short? I saw it all over TikTok. I totally don't believe what everyone is saying, by the way. I'm fully team Alexander."

She doesn't look sorry at all. In fact, she looks like she's ready to kick off her cowboy boots, forget about the horses, and run off to whatever country he's visiting next. He, however, is starting to look *very* sorry. I wonder why Amanda didn't notice how his face fell when she mentioned Elizabeth whatever-her-name-is, and why she didn't stop. Probably for the same reason she didn't realize I wasn't keen on talking about my dead mother with a girl I barely remembered.

"I thought your name was Alec," I say, unable to stop myself.

"Only my friends call me Alec." The look he shoots my way tells me that under no circumstances am I to call him that. I am completely unable to suppress a smile, and he notices with irritation. He turns his attention back to Amanda, fake face pasted back on. "When *the* Ashton Jacobson offers you a starring role in his latest production, you say yes, no matter where you are."

Amanda opens her mouth to respond, but a soft voice says from the stable entrance, "Alec." The three of us turn in unison to see the gorgeous girl from the restaurant last night. She's standing in the entryway, dressed more casually today, and somehow even more beautiful for it. "Ashton's ready for us." Her gaze lands on me and immediate recognition lights her face. "I knew it was a small town, but this is quite a surprise." She walks over to our group and reaches her hand out to me. "I'm Diya. Pleasure to meet you properly this time." She glances at Alec. "Hopefully Alec's behaving himself better today than he was last night."

"Of course I am," Alec says.

"Hardly," I say at the same time.

"Last night?" Amanda says.

We collectively ignore her inquiry.

"Well, give him time. He's always cranky after a flight. A couple of days, and he'll be his usual sweet self."

I snort.

Alec's jaw twitches.

"Mandy, it was lovely to meet *you*," Alec says. His smile morphs when he looks at me, turning into something less shiny but more believable. "Horse Girl. Maybe I'll see you around. Maybe not."

My stomach lurches. Surely, the photo was proof enough. No one would be so cruel they'd get someone fired over a misunderstanding—not even Alexander Mathis.

Diya looks confused, but Alec quickly places a hand on her upper back and leads her toward the stable exit.

"All hands meeting in five minutes, under the white tent," Diya says over her shoulder. "Don't be late. Ashton's a stickler for punctuality."

"Holy crap, Nora! That was Alexander freaking *Mathis!*" Amanda says the second they're out of sight. "Can you believe we get to spend every day on the same set as him? Breathing the same air?"

"No. I can't." Because he's probably going to go straight to the director and tell him to get rid of me.

I sigh and pick up the bucket of food I'd made for Jack. Might as well do the work while I can. "Come on. We've got five minutes to finish feeding the horses."

"Alexander Mathis," she breathes, following behind me as I walk to the stall. "This is going to be the most incredible two weeks of my life."

Well, I think, sliding the bucket in front of Jack, *at least one of us will have a good time.*

There are a few stragglers in front of us, headed toward the significantly larger crowd that's now here. Amanda grabs my arm way too tight for my liking when we join the others, and she bounces from one foot to the other.

"I can't believe this is really happening here, on the farm I grew up on," she says for the millionth time. She has been talking about him nonstop since he left the stables. Thanks to her nearly encyclopedic knowledge of him, she had a lot to say. From what I caught during her raving, Alec is the rising star of the moment. He had gotten his break when he was discovered on YouTube and hadn't stopped making hits since. He also happened to have just gone through a very nasty, very public breakup. Of course, I don't care about any of this. I'm here for the horses. That's it.

A man in a red baseball cap whistles three times.

The chatter that had been going on around us dies down. Amanda stops whispering nonstop in my ear, but her grip tightens. I gently pry her hand away. She smiles apologetically and mouths, *Sorry*.

"Welcome to the first day of filming for *Never Say Neigh*," he says. The crowd laughs. "Don't worry, it's a working title. We'll make sure you don't have to put something that embarrassing on your résumé.

"Most of you have worked with me before—I keep my cast and crew lists pretty familiar. For those of you who haven't, I'm Ashton. Glad to have you here."

"We're welcoming back our full crew from *Summer in December*. Mike is still head of lighting—wave to everybody, Mike." A giant, burly man that looks like he walked out of a catalog for lumberjacks waves. "Jacob is still head of wardrobe. Luciana is in charge of the makeup artists, and she'll be assigning someone from her crew to each cast member soon. Same goes for Brandon in hair.

"Martín is in charge of the animals, and no, I don't mean the cast." Another laugh. "He'll make sure the horses and livestock all cooperate. Martín, you had something you wanted to share with cast and crew, right?"

"Yeah," someone says from the other end of the group. A man with dark, wavy hair parts from the crowd and comes to stand beside Ashton. He bows, gesturing for Martín to go ahead.

"Hey, everybody. I wanted to quickly say that I know that horses are pretty, but I need you guys to remember they aren't as docile as they look. We've done what we can to make sure the ones we brought in are well trained." He shrugs. "Still, that doesn't mean they won't get temperamental. And it definitely doesn't mean you should let your guard down around them." He eyes the cast. "Horses don't care if you're famous, so don't walk in there unannounced or unaccompanied."

Ha, I think, wishing Alec was beside me so I could whisper *I told you so*. I scan the crowd for him reflexively and find him next to Diya. I start when we lock eyes, surprised to find him already staring at me. I raise my eyebrows, trying to convey my gloating without any words. He rolls his and looks back at Martín.

"In general, don't do anything stupid, and if you have any questions, find me or"—he pulls a piece of paper from his pocket and opens it—"Nora Green?" He scans the crowd, and I raise my hand.

"Right here."

A few dozen heads turn my way, and I try not to think about the fact that I'm holding the attention of actual celebrities. I may not be as enamored with it all as Amanda is, but I'd be lying if I said I didn't have a few butterflies right now.

Martín smiles. "If you couldn't tell before, I'm sure that accent gave her away. Nora's our local expert. The woman I bought the horses from says Nora raised a couple of them. So don't let her age or the accent fool you—she knows what she's doing."

I smile back at him, thankful when the eyes turn away from me one by one. And, even though I hate myself for it, mine travel straight back to Alec's, like a moth to a flame. He's whispering something into Diya's ear. He looks at me as they laugh.

"In short, everybody stay away from the horses unless you know what you're doing," Ashton says. "Ladies and gentleman, boys and girls—here's the part you've all been waiting for. Drumroll, please!"

One by one, the people around me start to slap their hands against whatever's nearest. Thighs, scripts, the back of the person standing in front of them. Amanda joins in, but before I can bring myself to do it, too, Ashton makes the same motion as a conductor telling his orchestra to quiet and the sound dies away as quickly as it started.

"I present to you, your leading man and woman—Alexander Mathis and Diya Yadav!"

Alec and Diya both smile and wave at the now clapping crowd. Diya's like a princess in front of her people, gracious and stunning. And to anyone else, I'm sure Alec looks just as regal. But to me, all I can see is a mask over the real him—the one that yells at strangers in restaurants for taking photos. I'm not letting my guard down around this guy, no matter how bright and charming his smile is.

"Thank you," Diya says as the noise dies down. "I'm so happy to be here with all of you, and I'm excited to see what we can create together. It's been a while since I've been able to do something fun and light and lovely. This will be a nice change of pace."

Alec nods. "Cheers to that. It'll be a fun couple of weeks." He looks at me, his careful facade slipping the tiniest bit. "Ashton, would you mind if we did a quick reminder about phones on set?" His eyes never leave mine.

I bite down on my tongue so I don't stick it out at him. I hold his gaze, refusing to be the first one to back down. We stare at each other until Diya clears her throat and elbows him gently in the ribs. He glances at her, his face softening.

Ashton looks like he very much does mind making an announcement about phones, and I wonder if he and I are the only two around here not utterly charmed by Alec. "Yeah, forgot to mention that. I know most of you have your phones on you this morning—normally we ask that you just keep them on silent or in your pocket. But we're going to be a little more locked down for this production. There are lockers near craft services and—"

Ashton is interrupted by the sound of a hundred different vibrations traveling around the crowd of cast and crew. The notification goes through the group like a wave, two short vibrations here, a long one there, a rouge beep from the one phone not on silent.

Even Ashton grabs his phone from his back pocket, brows furrowed as he reads whatever notification everyone in the production seems to have received at the same time. Amanda gasps softly beside me.

Everyone in the crowd looks up from their phone to stare at Alec. Then, after a beat, they all turn to stare at me.

CHAPTER 4

A shton doesn't even try to regain everyone's attention. He gives a brief dismissal and Diya's hand is on Alec's arm before anyone else moves. They walk off toward a row of trailers in the distance—Alec's head bent down looking at the screen of the phone she holds up for him to read.

People are buzzing as the crowd starts to disperse, and I don't miss the way their glances shoot over at me with way too much frequency.

Something is very wrong.

I turn to ask Amanda what's going on, but she's buried in her phone, fingers moving lightning fast over the screen.

"He's even hotter in person," a blonde girl says to someone as they brush past us, voice low. She stops and bends down to tie her shoe.

"Yeah, but . . ." Her friend shrugs.

"But what?" the other one asks, looking up as she loops her laces around each other.

"Elizabeth keeps saying he's a cheater. I mean, why else would he be out with another girl while her parents are in the middle of the most embarrassing divorce ever? And did you *see* that TikTok her dad put out? So mortifying. I'd delete the app from my dad's phone while he was sleeping if I were her."

"Didn't Elizabeth live stream their breakup or something?"

The other girl stands. "Supposedly it was an accident. Do you think Alexander's really with—"

She looks up to find me watching her, clearly eavesdropping. Instead of looking embarrassed at being caught gossiping, she stares at me, like she's trying to figure something out.

Martín steps in front of me, pulling my attention away.

"Nora," he says, smiling. He's older, I'd guess mid-thirties, and his face is so open and kind I automatically smile back, despite my apprehension. "Nice to finally meet you. Mrs. Shep had a lot of nice things to say. You've got quite the reputation to live up to."

"That's . . ." I trail off, unsure what to say. "Terrifying?"

He laughs. "No worries. If you're half as good with horses as she says you are, this should be a piece of cake. And you must be Amanda," he says, reaching out to shake her hand. She takes it, finally looking away from her phone.

"Hi." Her voice is wispy, like she's having trouble breathing.

"Your family has a nice place here. Thanks for letting us use it."

"Anytime. Whenever you're filming a movie, you know. Feel free." She trips over the last few words and blushes. Martín is nice enough to pretend that he doesn't notice. He looks back at me.

"Sebastian told me you came in pretty early. I'm assuming you got the horses fed? Sorry I wasn't there to meet you. We had an incident with the cattle."

I nod. "Fed, but not brushed."

"Right," Martín says. "For today, we need to get the horses assigned to riders. Ethel's the one you're most familiar with, correct?"

"And Jack."

"Great. You'll need to have them all ready by call every morning, which will be announced at the end of shooting every day. They'll need to be brought in after their work is done and—well, from what Mrs. Shep told me, you know what to do with a horse who just finished hours of hard work."

"I do."

"Good. Walk with me." He gestures toward the stables, and Amanda and I follow him through the lingering crowd. Once we're away from the noise, he starts again.

"Part of your job is to be an advocate for the horses. I know that sounds kind of ridiculous, but it's not. If it were up to some directors, they'd work the animals until their legs gave out, then replace them with another one."

He glances at me, and must be able to see the shock on my face. "Glad to see you understand. Don't worry." We reach the stables and he walks us halfway in before stopping again. "Ashton's not like that. I've worked with him before and he's never been anything but fair. To everyone, not only the cast. Makes sure the crew is taken care of and cares about the animals, too. But it happens. And it's your job to tell somebody if the horses need a break, or if the conditions they're working under are wrong, or anything else. Tell me, or tell Ashton. But tell somebody, all right?"

"All right," I say, and Amanda nods.

"Today, let's get an idea of the horses we've got here, what size they are, the kind of rider they'd hold best, learn their temperaments. Then we'll pair them off later this afternoon. The leads will have a horse they stick with throughout shooting, but the extras can trade out as needed."

He looks at Amanda, then back at me, like he's trying to decide something.

"Amanda," he says finally. "Can you handle brushing and saddling the horses? I need to have a word with Nora."

"Of course," Amanda says. I can *feel* the impatience radiating off of her, like she can't wait another second to tell me whatever it is she saw. But there's no way for her to do it with Martín standing here. So instead, she gives me a wide-eyed look when he turns around. I shrug at her and follow behind him.

He leads us outside of the stables over to the giant pen holding the half dozen cows that will be used in the background of a few scenes.

"Excited to be on set?" Martín asks.

"It's fine so far," I say. "The location doesn't really matter, though. Ranch, farm, movie set. As long as I'm working with horses, I'm happy."

He nods. "Some people can figure out how to work with horses, like putting a puzzle together. They can make the pieces fit. But for some of us, it's like breathing. The animals can tell the difference. According to Mrs. Shep, you've got *it*."

"What's *it*?"

He shrugs. "Not really sure. Don't have a name for it. But whatever *it* is, she says you've got it. Despite your age." He pauses. "You're heading to Montana after this, right? I've heard of the program out there. It's good."

"Yeah," I say. I don't tell him that my entire future hangs on this job to actually make Montana happen.

"Have you thought about what you'll do afterward?"

I laugh. "I had no idea I was even going to Montana until yesterday. Had no idea I'd be working here, either. So, no. I haven't really thought about it."

"Well, you should. A lot of doors could open for you once you graduate from a place like Montana Equine. You could have a bright future."

"I—" The words don't come. I have no idea how to respond to something so big. Up until now, Montana had been an escape from my current home, a way out. But Martín makes it sound like it could be more, a way to make working with horses a viable career.

"The thing is, Nora—if you're going to work in film again, you have to learn how to separate yourself from the cast. It gets messy. We're in the same world as celebrities, technically. But it's more like . . ." He pauses, his face pinched. "Like, we're orbiting them instead of occupying the same space. I mean, that's not exactly right, but does it get the picture across?" He looks at me questioningly.

"Uh, sure," I say, utterly confused by the turn the conversation is taking.

"Good," he says, nodding. "It's not even Alexander—he's a great kid. The bad press should slow down and other directors will be willing to work with him again. But that's not really how you want to start off your career in the movie business, all tangled up in a high-profile mess. If a kid like Alexander, with all that star power, is having trouble getting work . . . well, you wouldn't stand a chance if the public turned against you. They love you today, but they'll hate you tomorrow. I don't know how serious you two are—"

A strangled cry jumps out of my throat.

"What?" I gasp.

He looks at me again, eyebrows raised. "You and Alexander? The picture—I mean, maybe I'm wrong—hell, maybe the entire internet is wrong," he says skeptically. "But you two looked awfully cozy." He holds up his hands. "Like I said, I don't blame you. He's a good kid. Just be careful, okay?"

What. The. Hell?

His walkie-talkie beeps.

"Go for Martín."

"We've got a rogue sheep at craft services."

Martín rolls his eyes. "Copy." He sighs. "Listen, just think about it. Not really my business. Just thought I'd give you some advice, you can take it or leave it. I'll be in the stables later to help you match riders, but have someone walkie me if something urgent comes up."

I can't even bring myself to say anything to him—I just nod and watch as he leaves.

My hands curl around the metal gate that's pinning the cows in, fingers turning white from my grip. For one second, I think about going back to the stables and asking Amanda to explain everything to me. Then a guy carrying a light bigger than my head does a double-take when he walks past me, and I realize Alec has no right to hide away in his trailer while I have to sit out here and deal with the fallout of whatever's going on. I let go of the fence, all of the blood painfully rushing back into my fingers.

Then I turn and walk in the opposite direction of the stables.

My righteous indignation fuels me as I pass the giant tent, ignoring the crowd of people that look up when I pass by. The grits I had this morning roil in my stomach when a middle-aged woman turns to her friend the second she spots me. I make myself look away as she points me out to the man sitting beside her. This happens more than once as I walk the path that leads to the trailers, and I have to bite my tongue to keep from shouting at them to mind their own business.

I walk through the maze of trailers, reading the signs taped to the doors as I pass by.

MAKEUP. HAIR. WARDROBE. DIYA.

The last one is the biggest, of course, and the sign reads, ALEXANDER.

Before my anger can lessen, before I can talk myself out of it, I stomp up the stairs and pound the door with my fist. I notice the music coming from the trailer for the first time right before it cuts off. Alec's footsteps sound slowly inside, so I bang on the door again and feel a deep stab of satisfaction when his pace quickens.

"What—" he starts, opening the door with a wrinkled forehead. The mild annoyance on his face changes to full-blown irritation when he sees me.

"You've got some nerve," I say, venom lacing my words. "Kind of cowardly to hide away in your trailer while I can't even do my job without being stared at, *Alec*." I stress his nickname and feel a thrill of pleasure when his eyes narrow. I swear he thinks I should address him as Lord Alexander.

"Get inside."

Alec walks back into his trailer, not waiting to see if I'll follow.

I almost leave without another word, just to irritate him, but I do want to know exactly what's going on, and I want him to be the one to tell me. So I walk into his trailer and slam the door behind me.

It's giant and roomy, somehow even bigger than it looks from the outside. Alec's already down at the other end, sitting on a couch with a computer on his lap.

"Come look," he demands, without even glancing my way. Everything inside of me grates at doing what he says, but the curiosity burns stronger.

I sit down beside him on what I now realize is more of a love seat than a couch, but I wasn't going to stand there and wait for him to order me to sit, too. I'm not a dog. And now I can't get up without looking like an idiot, even though this "couch" is barely big enough for the two of us. He moves his arm when mine brushes against his, equally repulsed by the idea of touching me as I am at sitting next to him. This close together, his cologne is stronger, all woodsy pine and clean sweat, though I'm sure he's never done a hard day of work in his life. The smell of new leather dampens the scent of *him* a bit, making it bearable.

The distance between us is so small I can see the smattering of freckles across the bridge of his nose, and the small white mark at the edge of his lip. It almost looks like a tiny scar.

"You reek of hay, Horse Girl."

"And you smell like pretentious jackass."

His mouth twitches, the tiny scar moving slightly upward.

If I didn't know better, I'd think he was trying not to smile.

"Here," he says, turning the laptop screen toward me. I make myself look away from his irritating mouth and at whatever he's trying to show me.

Everything inside me turns to ice.

There's a photo of us on his computer screen.

I'm sitting at a dinner table, staring intently at Alec.

My hair is flowing down my back, perfectly tousled from Charlotte's attempt earlier in the night to tame it. Pieces frame my face perfectly from the layers Bree cut into my hair a week before she left on vacation. Alec's in the chair next to me, sitting almost as close then as we are now. I'm staring straight up at him—the polite confusion on my face reads as doe-eyed and dreamy. He's smirking down at me, all judgmental and assuming—but in the photo, it looks like he's studying a painting he's obsessed with.

Every bit of our anger and frustration reads like angst and desire. We look like we're about to embrace. Like we're about to *kiss*.

Without thinking, I lean over Alec and grab the computer. My arm presses into his, and our legs are forced closer together. Even the annoyed chill that runs through me at having to be so close to him, bringing goosebumps to the surface of my skin, can't bring me out of the utter shock of seeing our picture on his screen. The e-magazine name, *Seville*, runs across the top of the page in pink, followed by the words *Alexander Mathis and His New Southern Lady Love—Did TikTok Get This One Wrong?* And in tinier letters underneath: *How Will Elizabeth Respond?*

Alexander Mathis was spotted in south Georgia hot spot Fern Bank last night having a lover's quarrel with his new, heretofore unknown, girlfriend. An unnamed source says the two shared a quick bite before Alexander left in a hurry—and our source also reports they heard a whispered promise to meet up later.

But what does this mean for TikTok sensation Elizabeth Max's claims that America's down-to-earth boy next door is secretly a Hollywood snob who looks down on the public that discovered him and shot him into stardom? Max, whose cult-like following has more than doubled since her infamous breakup live stream, has dedicated fans who once worshiped Mathis now ready to boycott all of his movies. The backlash was so strong that Mathis was dropped from the cast of what is expected to be next summer's blockbuster hit, *U UP?*, the much anticipated and star-studded remake of Sleepless in Seattle.

Was the public perhaps too hasty in taking sides? This messy breakup even convinced yours truly to follow Max on TikTok and binge-watch their relationship from beginning to end in three-minute bursts. But if Mathis is dating a Georgia peach with no star power and a singular private Instagram account with forty followers (John Cena's parakeet has more), could Max's claims be wrong? A misunderstanding between the former couple—or worse, an intentional misleading of the public who was ready to console her with open arms? This reporter might end up #TeamAlexander after all.

My breaths are coming in shallow waves. The internet. I'm on the internet. My (nonexistent) relationship with Alec is *on the internet.*

"Everyone on set has seen this?" I meet Alec's eyes, and the look I saw in them earlier, when Amanda brought up my mama, is there again. For the first time since we've met, I don't see any anger or irritation in them. Just raging curiosity and something else I can't quite place.

Then he smiles. Not the Hollywood one—a tiny, apologetic one. "The entire world has seen this."

I stare at him, shocked.

"Well," he says, shrugging, "maybe not the entire world. China should be heading to bed about now. Maybe they won't know until morning."

"Oh no," I whisper, looking back at the screen. Every inch of my body feels exposed each time I see the photo, like I'm naked in front of a crowd of people. I mean, sure, I look great. It's a good photo. But no one asked *me* before taking this picture. No one told me they were going to plaster *me* on the front page of some website.

When I look up at Alec again, he's staring at me like he knows exactly what's running through my head.

"Who did this?" I say, my voice finally coming out right again.

He studies me before answering. "I don't know. I thought . . .

It only takes me a second to catch his meaning, and then I'm angry all over again. I'm on my feet in a flash and he stands, too, inches away from me.

"You thought I engineered a fight in a restaurant at exactly the right time so some creep could get a picture of it and plaster my face and body all over the internet?" I toss the laptop onto his couch. "What is wrong with you, Alec?"

He bristles, all of the openness gone, his typical irritated-with-Nora face back. "I don't know you, Horse Girl. People do this kind of stuff all the time. They want to be in the spotlight, they want their pictures all over the internet. And they do whatever they need to get there." His phone starts vibrating on the counter next to us, but we both ignore it.

"*You* came up to *my* table. All I wanted was a nice night out with my friend, not to get verbally accosted by some random guy I had literally never seen before. And to make matters worse, while you and I were having a private moment, someone took a *photo* of it. Then they showed it to the world. I've been through some crappy things, but this is pretty damn close to the top of the list.

"So let me make this crystal clear for you: I don't care who you are, I don't care that you're famous, I don't want to ride your coattails into the spotlight. That's not why I was at Fern Bank yesterday, and that's not why I'm here now. I know you can't understand this, but I need money. I need this job. That's what I'm here for. *I. Don't. Care. About. You.*"

I reach out and poke him in the chest as I say the final word, emphasizing my point. As my finger connects, I realize how close we are, near enough that I can see the gold flecks in his green eyes.

We're so locked into our staring contest that it takes us a minute to hear the vibrating again.

Alec notices first.

He glimpses at the screen before sighing. *Sean.* Alec turns his back to me while he talks. I think about leaving while he's distracted, but that feels like conceding. "Yeah, of course I saw it. No clue. You starting damage control?" There's silence on Alec's end while he listens.

"What?" The word is clipped, irritated. "Wait—who called?" More silence. "Because of one picture? An article?" He turns back to face me again, still listening. Alec *hmm*s and *yeah*s, staring at me the entire time.

He looks like he ate a bad bowl of boiled peanuts. Whatever he's hearing on the other end of that phone is making him sick.

"I don't know." Another pause. His lips purse and he closes his eyes, massaging the bridge of his nose. "Can you think of literally anything else that will get me off the blacklist so you don't have to keep coercing your friends into giving me parts in Netflix original movies?" Another pause. "Then I guess I don't have a choice," he spits. Alec ends the call, muscles in his jaw tightening as he looks over at me again.

I raise my eyebrows as he studies me, his jaw twitching. As curious as I am about the call, I refuse to ask about it. That goes directly against the "I don't care about you" declaration I made less than three minutes ago.

"That was my agent," he finally says.

"So?"

"I thought he was calling to drop me. That the *Seville* article was the last straw."

I shake my head, letting him know how uninterested I am in his relationship with his handlers.

He takes this deep, slow breath, like he's a second away from snapping at me. It gives me more pleasure than I care to admit that I can get under his skin so easily.

Once he's done trying to inhale every bit of air in the room, he continues.

"But he wasn't calling to drop me. He was calling to let me know that a director I've been dying to work with finally responded to our emails ten minutes ago, after radio silence for the past week and a half."

"Congratulations," I say, not meaning it in the slightest. "But as this has nothing to do with me, I think I'll get back to the horses. They're better company, anyway."

I turn to leave, but he grabs my arm gently. Before I can even look down, he drops it, like one single second of touching me was enough for a lifetime.

"It does have something to do with you. A lot, actually."

"How?"

"TikTok is starting to turn on Elizabeth. My ex." He runs his fingers through his hair. "I mean, nothing big. They're not revolting. But they're starting to wonder if maybe they're not hearing the full story. Apparently, I have you to thank for that." It looks like it makes him sick to say it.

"All because someone took a photo of us? That doesn't make sense."

He shrugs. "It's enough to make them hold off on the pitchforks for a second. Elizabeth said I'm turning against the people who made me who I am. Being pictured with a nobody from nowhere goes directly against that."

"Wow. I wonder why it was *so* easy for them to believe you're a stuck-up, egotistical snob."

I wait for him to quip back. But he stares at me, his mouth doing that thing again where it looks like he's chewing his thoughts before he says them.

"Sean wants me to take you out."

I hear the words, but it takes me a minute to *hear* them. When I process, my answer is a resounding, deep-chested cackle.

Alec doesn't join in, watching from where he leans against the kitchenette counter, waiting for me to get a grip on myself.

I laugh longer than I usually would, the irritated impatience on his face making it so, so difficult to stop.

When I finally collect myself, he speaks. "Are you done?"

"Laughing? No, I'll be cracking up over that one for the rest of the day. Sean's a trip. Maybe he should do stand-up."

"Could you be serious for a *second*?"

"Oh, I'm serious. Seriously shocked I didn't hear you tell him to go screw himself."

"Do you think I *want* to do this? Usually my dates have Birkins, not knockoff Lululemon belt bags. But Sean thinks we should run with the good press. Get some photos of us out, doing normal things. Hammer home the down-to-earth image while the public is still watching. He's a shark—but he's a shark in my corner. He'd do anything for my career. And if he says this is a good idea, it is."

"Great. Have Sean find you another townie, then. What's the difference? A nobody is a nobody, right?"

"Maybe if our photo wasn't all over the internet, and if a million people hadn't spent the morning stalking every picture of you that exists online, then sure. But it's *you* they love. It's too late to find another stand-in."

"Well, let's hope the public falls out of love as quickly as they fell in love. Because there's no way I'm going anywhere with you."

"I don't think you understand how much of a game changer this is. One photo, and doors are opening again! If we were seen out together, if we went on just half a dozen dates, I'd be golden."

"Great. I guess I missed the part where any of that benefits me."

"I can't go out in public without someone throwing themself at me, but you act like being seen with me is the most distasteful thing you've ever heard of. Most girls would give their college savings to go out with me once." He looks genuinely confused, like he can't fathom my reluctance.

I roll my eyes. "You think I should do it for the honor of being by your side?"

"You'd be infamous, Horse Girl. When people google you, they'd see something more than a hit on the local newspaper's website about a horse-riding competition you won junior year."

"You googled me?" I say, my voice shrill.

"In my defense, there wasn't much to google. I'm not sure it really counts."

I stare at him and imagine throwing the bowl of dried apple slices on the counter at his stupid, perfectly coiffed head.

"A few dates," he says. "Then your name goes down as the normal girl who got the chance to date Alexander Mathis. You could have a million followers on every social media outlet by tomorrow."

I shake my head. "Are you listening to anything I say? Fame, even fifteen minutes of it, is my *nightmare*. I don't want people watching me, asking me what I'm wearing, refreshing their pages for an update on what kind of coffee I drank that morning."

"To be fair, I don't think anyone would ever ask who you were wearing. It's pretty clear your wardrobe comes from Target."

"Are you seriously roasting me while asking for a favor?"

He starts to answer, but I wave him off. "Whatever, forget it. The answer is no. A resounding, absolute no. I don't know when you'll finally get it through that Prince-Harry-ass head of yours that I'm not interested in you, or your fame, or any fame of my own. You are offering me the last thing on Earth that would have convinced me to help you. Even if I liked you, I wouldn't do it. And I don't like you, Alec. Not one bit."

I turn and open the door, stepping out into the sun before he can say anything else.

CHAPTER 5

My phone rings the entire walk back to the stable.

Just when I think whoever it is calling has given up, the ringing starts back up again.

I snatch the phone out of my pocket and accept the call without looking at the number.

"What," I snap, irritation at Alec's arrogance making my fuse shorter than usual.

There's a pause. "Nora Green?" The woman's voice is politely confused.

"Yeah, this is Nora," I say, trying to control the impatience in my voice. If this is a reporter, I might actually explode.

"This is Sherri calling from the bursar's office of Montana Equine. Is this a bad time?"

Shit. Great day to answer the phone with an attitude.

"No, not a bad time," I say, squeezing my eyes shut and leaning against the outside wall of the stable. "How can I help you?"

"Well, we did receive the partial payment on your tuition last week, securing your spot."

The payment Mrs. Shep had made before she even told me about the program. Lord bless that woman.

"Right—if this is about the rest of the tuition, I'll have it in a few weeks, I promise."

What I don't tell her is that I'll have it down to almost the penny. Enough money to pay the tuition, and if I'm extraordinarily lucky, a one-way ticket to Montana. Who needs silly things like food or bedding anyway?

"No, it's not about the tuition. You have until the first day of classes to pay that. I'm calling today because we haven't received your housing deposit."

"What housing deposit?"

The woman pauses again. "Students are required to live in the cabins on site. There's a housing fee, due at time of acceptance. It was all detailed in the email we sent." She rattles off an email address I recognize as Mrs. Shep's. If she had seen it, she would have tried to help me pay it.

"How much is housing?"

"Fifteen hundred dollars."

I shut my eyes tight and rub my forehead with my free hand. "When do you need it?"

"It was due at your time of acceptance." She pauses. "But if we didn't have a conversation today—if maybe you didn't pick up the phone and I left a message—I could try to call again. Say two weeks from now?"

I appreciate what she's doing. But I'm not sure how two weeks is going to help me.

"Two weeks," I say confidently, like it won't be a problem to come up with almost two thousand dollars before then.

"Sorry I couldn't reach you today," she says with a smile in her voice. "Hopefully I'll have better luck next time."

"Thanks," I say, and hang up.

It might as well be a million dollars. My predicament is exactly the same as when I took this job—I need money, and I have no way to get my hands on it. Filming is scheduled for three weeks. Even if the money wasn't going to tuition, I wouldn't be paid in time to take care of housing.

I feel like I'm trying to climb out of a hole that just keeps getting deeper.

Amanda's in the stable when I walk in. There's nothing I want more than silence and a few moments alone with Ethel. I need to clear my head, and I can't do that with my feet planted on the ground.

Amanda spots me before I can sneak Ethel out of her stall.

"Why didn't you tell me?" she hisses, her face elated.

"Tell you what?" I ask, my mind swimming in deposits and tuitions I can't pay.

"About you and Alexander," she says, like it's the stupidest question she's ever heard. "How did you two even meet? What's he like? Is he a good kisser? Never mind, that's a stupid question. Of course he's a good kisser. Those lips . . ." She looks off behind me, eyes wide and dreamy.

"Did you get all the horses ready for riders?" I ask, hoping she'll drop it if I don't answer.

"The horses are mostly ready," she says, waving a hand in the air. "When exactly did this start? My theory is that he's been here for weeks and you two had some sort of meet-cute in town. Was it Stephanie's Coffee Shop? I bet it was. He seems like someone who drinks fancy espresso or oat milk lattes."

"When you say the horses are *mostly* ready, what does that mean?"

She sighs in frustration. "We've got ten horses. You know Ethel and Jack, right?"

"Right," I say.

"Daddy's letting them rent Apricot, Lucy, and Sawyer. I saw two of the three being born, so I'm good there. That leaves five horses, which I feel like is manageable between the two of us. We can spend the next couple of hours taking them out, seeing how they ride. But I suspect that Martín knew they needed horses that were comfortable with inexperienced riders, and we'll really only be worrying about who fits on which horse."

I walk over to the nearest stall and cluck at the horse inside. He looks up, mouth full of hay. He leans his head toward me and I run my hand along his neck, watching to make sure there are no signs of irritation. No flinching or twitching, and he doesn't have whale eyes, so I know he's comfortable with strangers.

"I'll take this one out and see how he does," I say, though I can already tell he'll do fine.

"I can come with you," she says—but I don't plan on riding at a talking pace. There's no way I can listen to Amanda go on and on about Alec, not with my mind on the new financial deadline.

"No, that's okay. You stay here and check out the last four horses. Let me know how they react to a stranger, and we'll talk when I'm back." The look on her face lets me know she has badly misinterpreted my statement. "About the horses, Amanda. We'll talk about the horses."

She deflates, but nods, finally seeming to get the picture.

Once I've got the horse (Chestnut, according to the name burned into his bridle) saddled, I take him out on the farm, starting with a slow walk. When we pass by crew members and cast, he holds steady, no signs of irritation or nerves. Once we're pretty well clear of everyone and we're closer to the fields than the tent, I take him up to a trot, then to a canter. His hooves hit the ground in a rhythmic motion, *ta-ta-ta-thump*, *ta-ta-ta-thump*, *ta-ta-ta-thump*, and I start to feel relaxed and at home for the first time all day. I give a gentle squeeze to let him know it's okay to head into a gallop, and he does it willingly. My braids bounce against my back, and suddenly I'm twelve again, Mama riding beside me.

Mama's hair flew behind her, like a yellow scarf caught in a gust of wind.

I giggled at the sight, knowing she'd spend at least an hour working the knots out of her hair later. My braids kept mine from tangling, though with how fast Ethel carried me, they were liable to come loose.

Mama glanced at me, riding Jack in a way that was so regal, I wouldn't have been surprised if she told me she was secretly a runaway princess, in hiding from an evil queen. I was so sure I'd never look like that on the back of a horse, like I was born on top of it and hadn't stopped riding since. She saw me studying her, and stuck her tongue out at me before slowing Jack to a canter. I followed her lead and Ethel and I slowed beside them.

"You ready to go back?" she asks. We've been riding for so long that the sun had started to lower behind the pine trees.

I shook my head and she smiled.

"If we don't head back now, we might be late for dinner. You know how Mrs. Shep gets when we're not washed up and ready. We won't have any dessert if we're late again."

"That's true," I said. "Maybe we should go back."

She watched me for a second, seeing my reluctance. After a breath, she shook her head. "I've got some Twizzlers under my pillow. Five more minutes won't hurt."

The wind whips through my hair and tickles my cheeks. The smile that breaks over my face isn't reserved. I don't do anything to temper it or hold some of it back. Usually, thinking about Mama causes a wave of sadness to crash over me. I don't let it today. Instead, I focus on the joy of that moment with her, and the joy of *this* moment. Out here where no one can see me, where I'm in a world all on my own, just me and Chestnut. I let myself breathe. And for the thousandth time, I'm so glad I didn't give in—didn't say yes all those times Mama and Mrs. Shep pressured me to go off to college. Because nothing—no degree, no campus, no "job security" could make me feel anywhere near as alive as I feel now, anywhere near as good as I feel when I'm on the back of a horse.

Montana started as a way to get out of my father and Cecelia's house. But now, it's more than that. It's a path that leads to me working with horses forever, a way to add legitimacy to my years and years of experience with them.

By the time Chestnut and I are back at the stables, I know exactly what I have to do.

We pair off five horses over the next three hours.

It's not really scientific, matching horse to rider based on how they respond to each other. Amanda had been more worried once I came back from my ride with Chestnut. But she knew how to do it, even if she didn't realize it. Making sure your loud friend didn't ride a horse that was skittish was essentially what we were doing here. It was just relying on a feeling you got when you were around horses for so much of your life. You can tell when they don't like someone, and you don't want to put somebody on the back of a horse that can't stand them. I'm glad for the work, it gives me time to think. So much time to think, in fact, that when Alec finally shows up for his pairing, I'm almost relieved to see him.

Apparently, the feeling is not mutual.

"How long is this going to take?" he says, refusing to meet my eyes.

Great, he's in a terrible mood.

This whole situation is delicate as hell. I can't be the one to bring up his earlier proposition—it's imperative that I have the upper hand. I've got to figure out how to get Alec to ask me again, organically.

"It takes as long as it takes," I say, shrugging.

"Can't I just hop on one?" he says, impatience in his voice. "I'd rather get this over with."

And before I can stop him, he stomps right up to Sylvie's stall. "How about this one?"

"Alec, don't!" I hiss, and reach him in time to grab his arm as he lifts it to pet her on the nose. She startles back, huffing, her head shaking back and forth.

"You can't just walk up to a horse and touch her on the nose," I snap.

His face is pink. "The article I read said—"

"Stop," I say, forcing myself to take a deep breath. "Do you go to the doctor and tell her she's wrong because you got a different diagnosis online?"

"Okay, Dr. Horse Girl," he says, rolling his eyes but his cheeks are still pink.

"Mock me all you want, but if you don't want a bitten hand or a kicked face, you should listen to me. At least when we're in here."

A muscle in his jaw flickers. "Fine."

"Okay," I say, forcing my voice to come out even and calm.

"Amanda's been working with people all day. Five of our horses are assigned. One is out now. The time it would take to repair your relationship with Sylvie, who you scared half to death, is more than we have. Diya already claimed Chestnut. So that leaves . . ." I sigh, standing in front of the last two horses. "Jack and Ethel." Of course.

"Right. So how do I decide which one of them to ride?"

"*You're* not picking one to ride," I say, trying to keep the irritation out of my voice. With anyone else, I wouldn't mind this part at all. But with Alec, it grates on my nerves to have to explain it to him. "You're partnering with them." He looks at me skeptically. I try to figure out a way to explain it to him that he'll understand.

"Okay, so imagine you show up on set the first day. You take a giant pair of those metal drum things, whatever they're called—"

"Cymbals," he says, and the little white scar at the top of his lip twitches again.

"Yeah, cymbals. You take a pair of them and you go up behind the guy who makes all the food."

"Craft services."

"Not important," I say, waving him off. "But whatever, craft services guy. You slam the cymbals behind him and scare him. Then you follow him around, poking him in the back with a butter knife. It doesn't really hurt, but it's super annoying. Or maybe he's got a really big bruise there, but you don't know because you didn't take the time to get to know him."

"I know Gary pretty well, and I still don't think I can tell you where his bruises are."

"My point is, after all of that, he brings you lunch. Are you going to eat it?"

"No," he says, sighing. "I suppose I wouldn't."

"Because you don't trust each other."

"Sure."

"Horses are the same, okay? You have to get to know them. The relationship is built on trust. And it's really dangerous not to know their triggers or where they're hurting. Because then *you* can get hurt."

I almost stumble over the last words. My stomach drops as I remember what it was like to stand there and watch Mama fall. I wasn't able to save her, but I sure as hell could make sure Alec understands how serious this is. He may not be my favorite person in the world, but I wouldn't wish what happened to Mama on my worst enemy.

"You're concerned about me?" he asks, and the scar above his lip almost disappears when he smiles.

"I'm concerned about my horses," I lie.

He laughs, but it's quiet. At least he's listening enough to know he doesn't want to startle the horses with a loud noise.

"So how do I figure out which one I can work with?"

"Slowly," I say. I take him by the arm and he looks down in surprise at my hand against his skin.

I pull him gently toward Jack's stall. "Don't walk head-on, like you did with Sylvie. They can't see you right when you do that." His arm is warm under mine, the skin soft against my calloused fingers. I make him stop when we're a few feet away. Jack's head swivels over. "Give him a second to look at you."

Alec sighs, and his muscles tense under my fingers. "You have to do this every time?"

"No, these horses trust *me*. It's only this slow the first few times."

We wait for another couple seconds as Jack surveys him. Then I slide my hand down from his bicep to his forearm and gently guide him forward.

"Now," I say, loosening my hand so my fingers are barely touching his skin. "Walk up the rest of the way and gently put your hand out for him to smell."

"Like with a dog?"

I look over, ready to snap at him for being smart. But his face surprises me. He's staring intently at Jack, the irritation that's ever present around me erased.

"Yeah, like with a dog," I say, something in my heart softening.

Alec walks forward, slowly, and raises his hand, making sure Jack can see his every move. For a minute everything seems perfect.

Then Jack's ears pin to the back of his head.

I take a quick step forward and try to grab Alec's arm, but my fingers wrap around his hand instead. He doesn't hesitate when I guide him backward. Once we're far enough away from Jack's mouth and I see his ears flick back up, we stop.

"What did I do wrong?"

"Nothing," I say, watching Jack as he backs away from his stall window. "But did you see his ears pin back? That means he's upset. It could have been anything, though. The way you smell. Something he heard. A feeling he got. Horses are finicky."

When I look at him, the clear, open expression he was wearing while he looked at Jack is gone. His smile is wry again, his eyes slightly crinkled.

"What?" I snap.

"Has the danger passed?"

"We're fine," I say.

"Then maybe you could let go of my hand now."

He's right. My fingers are still laced around his.

I drop his hand like it's a hot coal.

The look on his face now makes my blood boil.

"Next time, I'll let him take a bite out of you."

He laughs like he thinks I'm joking.

I slowly and methodically pop all of my fingers, hoping it helps me calm down.

When I feel like I can talk without yelling, I say, "Okay, let's try again. We'll do it a little differently this time."

I pull him to a spot in the middle of the stable, right near Ethel's stall. I put a hand on each of his arms.

"Stay here."

I go to the last stall, the one that holds all the feed. It takes a second for me to find what I'm looking for, and I grab a small handful.

Alec is, thankfully, in exactly the same spot I left him in. If nothing else, at least he's learned that the horses don't care if he's famous.

His eyes stay trained on me as I walk back over. They flick down to my boots. Run over my Wranglers. Slide up my shirt. For a flash of a second, I wonder what I look like to him, all rough edges and worn clothes. Then his eyes settle on my braids, and he smirks.

At least he keeps whatever snarky comment he's thinking to himself. When I stop in front of him, his lips are pushed tight together, like he's afraid if he so much as breathes, the words will slip right out.

"Here," I say, ignoring his face and handing him the sugar cubes.

He takes them without hesitating.

"This feels a little like cheating, but desperate times call for desperate measures." I turn and stand beside him, facing Ethel's stall. Then I click my tongue a few times. Chestnut and Toffee both stick their heads out of the stalls around us. After a second, Ethel does, too.

"Walk up the same way you did with Jack. Make sure she can see you. Put your hand out, let her smell the sugar. But don't give it to her at first. Talk to her a little."

"About what?"

"It doesn't really matter." I shrug. "Introduce yourself. Tell her your name, and call her by hers. Then talk about whatever you want. After a minute, let her have the sugar. Then gently rub her neck."

He looks at me for a beat like he's searching for a sign that this is all some kind of ploy to get him bitten by one of the horses, but he must not find anything nefarious in my expression, because he turns and starts slowly walking toward Ethel.

I make myself take steady, controlled breaths while he makes his way to her. Everything inside of me wants to walk beside him, to guide his every movement and breath. But if this is going to work, they'll have to figure this out together.

When he finally makes it up to Ethel's stall window, I slowly inch back, far enough away that I'm not right on top of them, but close enough to make it there in seconds if something goes wrong. He reaches his hand out to let her smell, and I make myself lean against the wood of the stall and at least attempt to look relaxed. She lets out a little huff onto his hand, and Alec smiles.

His eyes dart up to her ears, looking to see if she's reacting the same way Jack did. When he sees they're still relaxed, he reaches forward and gently runs his hand along her neck. I wait for a twitch of her muscles, the flick of her ears. But she's relaxed as ever. More relaxed than she is meeting most people, which is saying something for stubborn, irritable Ethel.

"Hello, Ethel. I'm Alexander. Pleasure to meet you." His voice is calm and sure, and Ethel reacts well to it. "But, as we're meant to be friends, I suppose you can call me Alec." She nudges him with her nose, and he smiles again, his face open and kind. "Yes, well. You should be flattered. Very few people call me Alec. Even fewer horses." He slips her the sugar cube stashed away in his palm, and she sniffs it once before licking it up.

There's this moment that happens sometimes, right when I introduce a horse and rider.

Most of the time, they decide to tolerate each other for the duration of the thirty-minute ride—the horse doing their job and the rider cashing in on the experience they paid for. But sometimes, there's this magic, where something inside of the horse and something inside of the rider just connects. A little piece of them recognizes the other, a part of their soul that whispers, *I'm not sure how, but I know you.* It's something not many people get to see, but each time I have, it's been breathtaking.

Alec looks at Ethel. She sniffs his face gently, savoring the last bits of sugar. Something that's been there in his face since the moment we met melts away, and his expression—relaxed and honest and genuine—seems to say, *I'm not sure how, but I know you.*

And I think, then, that maybe he is handsome. When his eyes move from Ethel's to mine, still sparkling and clear, I feel a shiver pass through me. But there's no air-conditioning to blame, no winter wind. Only Alec's sharp, bright eyes. We're frozen like that, suspended in a moment I have no desire to rush through, until someone walks into the stable.

It's Diya. She smiles when she sees us and walks over.

When Alec looks back at me, the magic of the moment has dissipated. I'm back to being a crew hand, the girl he can't seem to shake. It happens so fast, it almost makes me wonder if I imagined the way he was studying me before.

Diya comes to stand beside him, gently patting Ethel on the neck.

"Hello, Nora. Has Alec behaved himself long enough to be paired with a horse?"

"He's capable of behaving himself?" I say before I can think better of it. But Diya doesn't seem to mind my smart mouth. On the contrary, she laughs, soft and sweet.

Alec is less appreciative of my wit.

"Can we get to the part where I actually sit on the horse?" he snaps.

"Cranky already," Diya says. "I'll wait by the paddock for you." She glances at me. "Good luck, Nora."

I turn, intending on getting Ethel saddled. But Alec's right in front of the stall. I wait a few seconds, but he doesn't budge.

My teeth clamp together.

"I need to get Ethel ready."

But he just stares at me, looking like he's a bored cat and I'm a mouse he wants to toy with before he kills.

"Move."

"Hmm," he sounds, shaking a finger. I force my hand into a fist so I don't do something stupid like reach out see how far I can bend that stupid finger back. "That's not how you ask, is it, Horse Girl?"

"Stop. Calling. Me. That," I say through gritted teeth.

His face lights up. "I knew it bothered you."

Perfect. Now he'll never stop.

Still through gritted teeth, I force myself to say, "Move. *Please.*"

"There's that Southern charm everyone told me about." He steps aside.

I ready Ethel as quickly as I can, ignoring the feel of Alec's eyes on me as I lift and place the saddle. I work efficiently and quietly, letting my rage and embarrassment fuel me.

Stupid, stuck-up movie star.

Alec walks beside me as I lead Ethel out of the stables. Mercifully, he keeps his mouth shut on the walk over. I open the wide gate and lead Ethel into the paddock, though I should let Alec do that part. He needs to get used to her. But I can't bring myself to see his smug face before I have to, so I wait until I've got Ethel smack in the middle of the clearing. Then I make myself look up at him.

The worry, sharp and clear on his face, stalls me. He meets my eyes and worry morphs into embarrassment.

"Are you just going to stare at me, or are we going to get started?"

I cannot lose this job. I cannot lose this job. I need the money for Montana. I cannot lose this job.

Deep breath.

"I need you to get up in the saddle so I can make sure the stirrup length is right."

"How?"

"I'll be able to tell by how your legs look."

"No," he says, voice harsh "How do I get *on* the horse?"

"You . . . you've never been on a horse? Like, ever?"

"No," he says, lips pursed.

That makes absolutely no sense.

"Why would they cast you in this movie, then?"

He fidgets. "I may have . . . fibbed a little about my experience."

"*Fibbed?*" I say, more mocking his word choice than asking for clarification.

"All actors do it. Diya lied about knowing French once. Sean basically had to sell his future firstborn kid to get me this role in the first place, I couldn't tell them I've never ridden."

"And you expected to be able to hop on and ride around like an expert?"

"I expected I'd be able to ask the wranglers for help."

I bite down a smile.

"So why don't you?"

He looks at me, eyebrows raised. "That's all it would take?"

"Of course." Ethel impatiently kicks at the dirt beside us while Alec studies my face.

"Fine," he says. "Will you show me how to get on the horse?"

I grin. "I think you forgot something."

"What—" His voice cuts off abruptly as he realizes the trap I've laid for him.

Alec's jaw ticks, scar twitching when he purses his lips. His mouth works, and I swear it's like he's about to choke on the word rather than give me the pleasure of hearing him say it.

"Will you show me how to get on the horse, *please*?"

"My pleasure," I say, flashing him a bright, satisfied smile. Then I turn and, exaggerating every movement, I work my way into Ethel's saddle. It feels as natural as breathing.

I look down at Alec, ready to talk him through what I just did. But his eyes are trailing up my leg, and my breath catches when they stop on my thigh. They stick for a few seconds, and when his gaze finally meets mine, what I see there both annoys and warms me.

A second later, it's gone, and he's all broody irritation again.

"It's simple," I say. "Left foot in the stirrup, hand on the saddle horn, step up, swing your right leg over. Do you need to see it again?"

"No," he says, and the answer is so immediate it startles us both. He clears his throat. "No, I've got it."

I dismount and take a few steps back, gesturing at him to have at it. I watch closely as he replicates me exactly. He's in the saddle in a blink.

"Good," I say, looking over his form clinically, definitely not noticing how the muscles in his legs look so much more pronounced from this angle, even through his jeans. I adjust the stirrups so they're the right length. Once I talk him through correct posture and make sure he and Ethel are both calm and ready, it's time for him to ride.

"Grab the reins, hold them softly." I walk him through how to get Ethel to start and stop.

He nods along, and I'm relieved to see he's taking it seriously. It only takes a second of not paying full attention for something to happen. The image of my mom crumpled on the ground flashes through my head for the second time today, but I push it aside, forcing myself to concentrate as Alec signals for Ethel to start walking. They take it slow, so I'm able to follow alongside them.

Technically, he does everything right. But he's obviously anxious and has no confidence whatsoever.

"You have to relax," I say, and he has no problem hearing me, because even though he's been riding for ten minutes he still hasn't been able to work up to a trot.

"Thanks," he quips. "Telling me to relax will definitely work." His eyes snap to the people passing by, like they've done every time someone comes near. It's like he can't get over everyone watching him, which is hilarious, seeing as that's his job.

I bite the inside of my cheek.

Diya waves sympathetically, catching my attention, and for the first time, I see Ashton, the director, standing beside her. He gestures for us to come over to where they're leaned against the paddock fence, watching.

"Great, "Alec says. "How do I get off of this thing?"

I decide not to snap at him for calling my favorite horse a thing. Instead, I tell him quietly where to place his hands and how to get down without hurting himself or Ethel.

We walk up to Ashton and Diya. She looks apprehensive, and Ashton looks *pissed*. I hold Ethel's reins, wondering if I should use her as an excuse to get out of whatever is about to happen here.

"What was that?" Ashton asks, his voice firm and annoyed. There's none of the warmth he had earlier in the meeting.

"That was a horse," Alec says.

It's a terrible joke.

Ashton agrees.

"Not funny, Alexander. Did you or did you not tell us you were experienced in horseback riding?"

"*Experienced* is such a broad term." He's trying to give off an air of unbothered calmness, but his hands are in fists and his back is ramrod straight. He's nervous.

"I'm glad this is a joke to you. Especially after Sean pulled every single favor I owe him to get you an audition, and Diya put her name on the line to help you get this role." She shifts uncomfortably beside him. "I trusted her when she told me you were worth the possible backlash for casting America's most hated celebrity." He glances over at me for a second, then back at Alec. "Not that I care what's going on in your love life. But I risked the success of my movie by bringing you on. And now I see you out on the paddock, not even able to handle a trot. If I find out that you lied—"

"It happens sometimes," I interrupt. My palms immediately grow sweaty. What am I *doing*?

I swallow hard while Ashton stares, waiting for me to continue. "With new horses. It takes a little bit to click." He raises his eyebrows skeptically. "With Ethel especially. She can be real particular. But we can get there."

Ashton rolls his eyes. "Your riding scenes start Monday, Alexander. The horse better be a hell of a lot less *particular* in six days. Because if you can't ride that horse, I *will* recast your part. The world knows you're working here. Can you really handle the bad press when news gets out that you were cut the first week of production?"

Alec's face is white as a sheet.

"Good luck finding work once you're labeled a publicity risk *and* too unreliable to work with. By Monday, Alexander. I mean it."

He turns and walks off.

I study Ethel's ear, refusing to look at Alec. If I look at him, he might ask why I got involved.

I'm asking myself the same question.

My worries are unfounded, because Alec immediately pushes through the paddock gate and stomps over to the stables.

Awesome. Just what I need around temperamental horses—a pissed-off movie star.

"He's going to be a pain at dinner tonight," Diya says, turning to look at me with her wide, honey-colored eyes. She studies my face. "I've been meaning to ask, how are *you*? At least Alec is used to all of the pressure this career can bring. But I know seeing yourself everywhere can be . . . startling."

Her genuine care catches me off guard.

"I'm fine," I say reflexively.

She gives me a knowing look. "Well, I'm here if you need to talk. And it might not seem like it, but Alec is, too."

I snort. Ethel touches her nose to my head.

"I know he seems prickly at first," Diya says. "But it's all show. Alec has been there for me through my worst moments as an actress. And he understands better than anyone what you're going through. This role, the breakup, the media attention over the past few weeks—it's all been hard on him. He's had to hunker down and stay silent while the entire internet speculates about his integrity. As his friend, it's been torture to stand by and watch what they're all saying. I can't imagine how hard it's been for him." She sighs. "It's amazing what the media can spin out of a single innocent photo, isn't it?"

"Yeah," I say, trying not to feel sorry for Alec. But if they made our photo look like something it wasn't, what else had the media lied about?

"Anyway, my trailer is open anytime if you want to chat." She smiles before she leaves. I lead Ethel through the gate and back to the stables.

She nudges the front of my shirt, looking for a sugar cube. Once she's in her stall, I slip her a quick treat.

"I have an idea," Alec says behind me.

"First time?"

"Hilarious," he snaps. "Look, you know how to ride a horse—"

"You're especially observant today."

"—and I have money."

Finally.

I know exactly where he's going with this, and I'm ready to shout *yes*, make him sign a contract in blood, and send a deposit to my bank account. But casually, I say, "Good for you," and push against the gate, forcing him out of the way. I walk to the supply closet to get everything prepped for tomorrow while I wait for him to keep going.

"I'm not bragging," he says, following me, watching while I check the stock.

"You said you needed this job for the money. I have money. I need to learn how to ride a horse, fast. You can teach me."

I laugh and turn to look at him, hoping I can hide my desperation. "That would *never* work," I say, and part of me worries it's the truth. "We'd fight the entire time. Nothing would get done."

"It's not like you're my first choice. Or even my tenth. But you're good, right? That's what everyone keeps saying."

"I'm great," I say, because I am. "But you wouldn't listen to a word I said."

"I cannot lose this job," he says, the unbothered look leaving his face. He's earnest. Open. "Ashton's right, my reputation can't take the hit right now. He kicks me from the movie, then Sean drops me, then no one will touch me. I . . . have people depending on me. I can't lose this job." He swallows hard. "Agree to teach me, and I'll listen to anything you say. You have my word."

His sincerity catches me so off guard I can't even manage a snarky response. I study his face, waiting for the mask to go back up. It doesn't.

"How much?" I say.

He hesitates.

"Three fifty."

"Seven hundred," I counter.

"Four fifty."

I almost agree. Almost take it. It's a lot of money, and would put a huge dent in what I need for housing. But at the last second, I say, "Five hundred dollars."

He nods.

"Fine. When?" I make myself ask it casually—like the money isn't a huge freaking deal.

"I have fittings tomorrow and table run Thursday. We'll do it Friday afternoon, after filming wraps for the day."

I laugh. "Friday *afternoon*? You can't learn to ride a horse in half a day."

He purses his lips. "Fine. Friday afternoon and Saturday, too. And half of Sunday if we need it."

"And if I have plans?" I ask. Sunday is my birthday, which I don't really want to celebrate without Mama, but turning eighteen means I can legally leave my father and Cecelia behind. If we have to practice on my birthday, I will for five hundred dollars.

He smirks. "*Do* you have plans?"

I don't respond, and his grin grows wider.

"What if we make it an even fifteen hundred?" I ask, my mouth dry. My plan had been to wait until Alec asked again. But maybe the dating thing was so far out of his mind, he wouldn't consider it again. Maybe by the time he does, it'll be too late for me.

"What if I pay you triple the price we *just* agreed on? Yeah, I don't think so."

"Fifteen hundred dollars. I teach you how to ride . . ."

"And?" he says.

"And . . ." I hesitate, then say the next words so fast I almost can't understand them myself. "I go on two dates with you. Fake dates," I add at the end, just so there's no confusion.

He smirks. "I don't usually have to bribe women to go out with me."

I roll my eyes. "Look," I say, and I hope he can't hear the tinge of desperation in my voice, see it in the way I step closer. "I don't want fame. But you're right. I need money. You need an image boost. The internet loves me. It's mutually beneficial. You win, I win."

I chew on my lip, giving my words time to sink in. The mutually beneficial part irritates me. In a perfect world, I'd be the only one winning.

But fifteen hundred dollars? That's so much money I can barely breathe when I think about it. And it covers the housing deposit *exactly*.

"They'd take pictures of you again," he says seriously.

I nod.

"And they'd be all over the internet." His eyes are soft when he looks into mine. Like he knows exactly how I feel about the publicity, like he hates it, too. But if that's the case, why doesn't he walk away?

I nudge the hay covering the floor with the tip of my boot.

"Five dates," he says. I'm so relieved he's not negotiating the price I almost blindly agree.

"Two."

The muscles in his jaw tighten. "Three."

I bite my lip so I don't smile. I would have gone on ten dates to get to Montana.

"Fine."

"Fine," he says. "I'll pick you up tonight at eight. Leave your address with Sebastian."

"Tonight?" I exclaim. "Seriously?"

"Tonight," he confirms. "We need to capitalize on the good press. There's no time to wait."

"Fine," I say again, teeth gritted. "Where are we going?"

"Seeing as I know nothing about this town, I'll leave that up to you. No square-dancing, though."

"Not only do I have to spend my small amount of free time with *you*, now I have to plan the dates, too?"

He smirks. "Well, if we were really dating, no. You wouldn't have to plan them. I'd take care of everything, from the outfit to the dessert. But seeing as this is a job, I'll let you do your work. Earn your keep and all that."

"You're such a jerk."

"Yeah, I've heard," he says, finally turning to walk out of the stables. "Oh, and Horse Girl?" he says over his shoulder. "Make sure you leave yourself enough time to shower. The rest of us aren't as fond of the barn smell as you seem to be."

I grab the brush before I can think and hurl it at him, narrowly missing his shoulder. His quiet, amused laugh echoes in the stables.

Fifteen hundred dollars, I remind myself. Three dates and some riding lessons. I could stand him long enough to make the money.

I hope.

CHAPTER 6

My phone has been vibrating all day.

I almost threw it into the water trough an hour ago, but I can't afford a new one, so I just silenced all notifications instead. Probably the more reasonable of the two options.

Now that I'm in the truck, all I want to do is put on the Vibes: Relax and Release playlist Charlotte made for me and zone out on the way home, but before I can, Bree's name pops up on my screen.

She and Charlotte are the only ones who can bypass my notification settings by calling twice in a row.

"Bree!" I say, excited despite my exhaustion. I take in her face, her hair, her smile.

"How's Italy?"

"Amazing. And terrible. The most gorgeous men I have ever laid eyes on are on every corner, but it's hard to stop and talk to them when my parents are on either side of me. It's torturous," she says, beaming.

I laugh, wishing desperately I could reach through the screen and wrap my arms around her. I drink her in, noticing the smattering of freckles across her nose and under her eyes, a few shades darker than her brown skin.

"Tell me more," I demand, putting my phone in the dashboard-mounted holder so I can undo my braids. They're giving me a headache.

Bree rolls her eyes. "No. We can talk about me later. I want to hear about *you*. Specifically, I want to hear why you were at Fern Bank with Alexander Mathis when you were *supposed* to be having dinner with Charlotte, and why you didn't say shit about it! You're supposed to be my best friend, but I find out from someone's Snapchat story?" She watches my face intently through the phone. Even though Charlotte has technically been my best friend the longest, Bree was always the one who knew me best. "Well? Why are you on the front page of every website I've visited today?"

I sigh. "I was hoping you guys wouldn't see it."

"Ro, my grandma called me about it. *Everyone* has seen it."

"It's not what it looks like."

"I know. I'm assuming you would have told me if you had dinner with someone more famous than the pope. That's why I'm calling."

I groan. "And *I'm* assuming that's why I've got a zillion unread text messages."

"Well, at least three dozen of those are courtesy of yours truly and Charlotte yelling at you in the group chat. Who else messaged?" she asks.

I pull up my messages and sigh. "Apparently everyone I've ever spoken to." I scroll down, looking at the names. "There's one from Ms. Hester."

"The PE teacher?" Brianna asks.

"She wants to know if I can get her granddaughter an autograph." Brianna's bell laugh sounds in my truck. I start up the engine, relishing in the air-conditioning. "Ninety percent of these are asking for the same thing," I say, deleting the messages as quickly as possible. But the next one I open isn't anyone I know. And they're not asking for an autograph.

Is this Nora Green?

I think about deleting it, but I don't recognize the area code. It could be someone from Montana. Or what if it was my potential roommate?

Yes, I type back. Who is this?

"Earth to Nora," Brianna says.

"Sorry," I say, closing the app. Bree's face fills the screen again. "So many messages." I sigh.

"Ignore them for the next three minutes and tell me exactly what's going on."

When Bree says three minutes, she means it, so I quickly recap everything, even the fake dating, because I don't know how to keep something like that from my best friends.

"Anyway, that's the story," I finish lamely.

"So you managed to pick a fight with the most handsome man to ever step foot in south Georgia, and now you're dating-but-not-dating him?" She shakes her head. "I can't believe you didn't know it was him. I mean, I get it," she says, before I can defend my ignorance. "Warden Cecelia has that house on such serious screen lockdown, and you haven't exactly had an easy five months. I know why you didn't recognize him. I guess I forget sometimes how much you miss out on."

A door opens behind Bree and she turns away from the camera. "Coming. Hey, Ro—I gotta head out. It's midnight and we're going to San Severo at like the butt crack of dawn and then we're catching a flight back. But text me, okay? And get me an autograph before I'm home Saturday, or I'm coming to get one myself!" Then she's gone.

I throw the truck in reverse, smiling. Bree is always like that, a flash in the pan, a quick bright spot in your day before she flits on to the next lucky person she's going to shower her attention on. Before I can back out, my phone vibrates again. Foot on the brake, I read it.

This is Elizabeth.

Elizabeth who? I type back.

I start home, my phone on the seat beside me. I don't look until I'm parked in my driveway twenty minutes later.

Elizabeth Max.

My breath catches. There's more.

Alexander's ex.

I mean, I'm assuming you know who I am. And that he told you about me.

Or not.

Or maybe he did. And that's why you're not responding.

Look, I'm just warning you. Girl code. He doesn't care about anyone but himself. Enjoy it while it lasts.

I take a deep breath, car idling in the driveway.

How did you get this number?

Three bubbles pop up immediately.

> Seriously? It was scary easy. You should really lock everything down now that people are looking into you. That's tip number one.

> Looking into me?

> Tip number two? Don't date Alexander.

As soon as the text comes through, the three bubbles are at it again.

> Tip number 3—if you're going to date him, which like -obvi you are- then at least make it worth your while. He'll move onto someone else next week and you'll be history. So if you're looking to date a celeb, live your fanfic dreams, then enjoy, I guess. But if you're just looking to get your name out there, then forget him. You have like literally 40 followers on Instagram. Go live with me once, and you'll have thousands.

I stare at my phone, stunned.

> Thanks for the tips. But I'm happy with my 40.

She immediately texts back—a singular eye-roll emoji.

No bubbles this time, so I head inside. I'm tempted to roll around in the dirt for a few minutes instead of showering, just to piss Alec off. But I do smell like horses and I don't want to hear him complain about it all night long. I take a viciously hot shower, letting the water relax my exhausted muscles.

I'm drying my hair when my phone vibrates again.

> Then what do you want?

I think while I finish drying my hair. This thing with Alec, it isn't real. He's been nothing but a colossal jerk from the moment we met. Still, this whole conversation feels weird, and my stomach tenses up every time she texts me. I decide not to respond.

Elizabeth keeps messaging, though.

> Everyone wants something. I want the name of the girl in this picture. You get that for me, and I'll get you anything you want. If you don't want followers, I can send money. $5,000 there in Hicksville five mins after I have a name.

A picture comes through. I've seen it before. It was the first result when I googled Alec during my lunch break today.

> Find out who he was with in this photo. Get me a name and I'll pay.

I hesitate, a pit forming in my stomach. Elizabeth hates Alec, that's clear. But Diya vouched for him, hard. She seems to think the cheating accusation isn't true. I don't know which one of them is right, but I *do* know this entire conversation feels slimy.

I had done gross things for money, including cleaning up horse crap for the better part of the last ten years. But this feels more disgusting somehow.

This isn't my business, I finally text back. I'm sorry about what happened, but maybe you should just let it go.

The three dots pop up instantaneously.

> Let it go? In the past two weeks, my boyfriend has abandoned me and my parents have lost their minds. I can't even make a smoothie without interrupting one of the desperate live streams they're constantly running to cling to the tiny sprinkle of fame my breakup got them. Do you know what it's like to not even feel comfortable in your own home? Like you can't trust your own parents?

I swallow and stare at the screen, struck by just how much I *can* relate to that. I mean, minus the part where her parents are embarrassing her in a very public way, I know exactly how she feels. Something tugs inside of me, a little thread of sympathy that makes it almost impossible for me to write her off completely.

> If you post these texts anywhere, by the way, I'm suing the shit out of you.

I roll my eyes, but it sucks that the thought even crosses her mind. It must be an exhausting way to live.

> I don't know anything about the girl in the picture, I'm sorry.

She reacts to the text, giving it a thumbs-down.

Elizabeth doesn't text again.

I'm getting dressed when I hear the telltale sound of the garage door, letting me know my father is home. Twenty minutes later, Vivaldi announces Cecelia's arrival, violins blaring through the built-in Bluetooth speaker that came preinstalled in every house in the all-new cookie-cutter neighborhood. I never liked classical music before. Now, I despise it.

The doorbell rings and I find a small amount of joy in the way the music pauses, the tentative steps toward the door, the mumbling as Cecelia and my father take turns asking if the other is expecting anyone.

Alec's voice carries to the top of the stairs as I close my bedroom door behind me. I take my time coming down, not at all ready for this night to start. Cecelia's the one talking as I finally enter the "receiving room," as they like to call it.

"Oh, there she is. Nora, look who's here!" She's not at all annoyed or put out like I had hoped. She looks over the moon at the simple fact that there's a boy here to pick me up for dinner.

"I can see. Hello, Alec." I look him up and down and then have to bite the inside of my cheek to keep from laughing. He's dressed to the nines. Some kind of crap you'd find on a Banana Republic mannequin at the outlet store. His brow is furrowed as he takes me in—scanning my jeans and cropped Rooney shirt that I stole from my mom's closet before . . . well.

Before.

The way he scowls simultaneously pisses me off and delights me. It pisses me off, because despite my casual clothing, I look fantastic.

My hair has a wave to it, my accessories are on point. My makeup is the perfect blend of flawless and barely there.

"You look . . . nice," I say, a small giggle forming deep in my chest. I swallow it down, but Alec must hear the hint of it in my voice because his eyes dart to mine, and I swear I see a spark in them.

"You too." His voice is careful and soft, not a hint of anger. Really, if nothing else, the guy is a phenomenal actor.

But good enough to fool Diya?

"Nora," Cecelia says, brow furrowed. "Would you maybe like to go up and change? Try something a little more festive?" She shakes her hips when she says it and the room collectively cringes. My father clears his throat. Cecelia turns pink and scrunches her nose. "I thought . . . well, what I mean is, where are the two of y'all off to tonight?"

"Addie's," I answer, grabbing my purse off the hook by the door mounted specifically for me. Directly to the left are a pair of hooks that were built-in, grouped together. Cecelia's purse hangs next to my father's work coat. The hook stuck on for me, apart from the rest and added years after the others, is another sign that I'm an afterthought in this house. I wonder what they'll do with it when I leave.

"Oh, Addie's!" she says with a smile. "That explains the jeans." Her questioning glance at Alec's outfit must be easy to read, because now *he's* turning pink. "I heard the special is catfish this week. Though I *also* heard they're charging an arm and a leg for it."

My father huffs. "You can get fried fish at any restaurant in town."

"I'm sure it's artisanal, dear," Cecelia says, patting his arm.

"Artisanal catfish?" my father asks. "What, did they catch it with a paintbrush?"

I don't realize I've laughed until they both look up at me, surprised.

Well, Cecelia's surprised.

My father looks pleased. Like I've given him one of those **#1 DAD** mugs or something.

Maybe if he'd actually been around, he would have gotten one.

He sees something change in my expression, and his face falls.

"Have her back by ten," my father says, trying to dispel the awkward air. His words come out fuddled and unsure. He glances back at me and adds a late, "Please."

This family is so *weird*.

"You got it," Alec says. Then he reaches his hand out to shake my father's. The play-acting of it all is so cringey that I don't even wait around for them to finish, I just walk right out of the still open door and assume Alec will eventually follow.

I open my truck door, getting ready to hop in the driver's seat, but before it's even halfway open, Alec steps behind me and pushes it shut.

"We're taking my car."

"That wasn't part of the deal," I snap.

"It wasn't *not* part of the deal." His stupid smirk is back. I watch as his eyes drag down me again from head to toe, the smile slowly slipping away. "Thanks for letting me know the dress was dirt-road casual, by the way."

"Oh, you thought it was pre-law chic?"

His mouth tightens. "Get in the car, Horse Girl. Let's get this over with."

"I'm happy with the getting-this-over-with part," I say as I hop into the front seat of the flashy convertible. *Of course* this is his car.

"Where are we going?" he asks. The Mustang's engine roars to life. It's embarrassingly loud.

I open my phone and plug the destination in, for his benefit. I know exactly how to get there, but I don't want to have to give him step-by-step directions.

I use the drive to daydream about seeing mountains in the rear-view mirror instead of an endless line of pine trees.

"The directions were wrong," Alec says, pulling me out of my made-up world.

I look up. "No, they weren't."

"There's no way this is right," he says, gesturing toward the tiny building surrounded by trees. It's so small and so far back from the road that you'd miss it if you weren't looking for it.

"Pull around back," is all I say, and to my surprise, he doesn't argue. He does sigh, though. It's long-suffering.

"What the hell," Alec says as the parking lot comes into view. Well, it's less of a parking lot and more of a square of dirt where people haphazardly park their pickups. There's not a single space left, which seems about right for eight on a weeknight. I direct Alec to a spot of grass that probably wasn't meant for parking, but it'll make do.

"You wanted to be seen, right?"

He nods.

"Well, then it's this or the Piggly Wiggly parking lot. And you're not really dressed for that." I am fully incapable of stopping the snort that comes out as I finish my sentence.

"Did you seriously snort?" he asks. He looks like someone trying really hard to be irritated, but the way his lip quirks up on one side gives him away.

Why the hell does he work so hard to be unhappy around me? And what would happen if he stopped trying?

"I did," I say, owning it. "Look—this is the busiest place in town. Well, outside of town, technically. You want people to notice us together? This is the place to do it."

He doesn't move.

"Roll down your window, Alec." His jaw ticks when I say his name, but he listens.

I watch as it hits him.

His eyes close and his head falls back on his seat.

"What. Is. That. Smell?" he asks, breathing in again, deeply this time.

"*That* is Addie's famous chicken-fried steak."

His brow furrows and he rolls up the window, looking at me questioningly. "How do you chicken-fry a steak?"

"Oh, Alec," I say, opening my door. "I'm about to introduce you to the most beautiful part of living in the south. Chicken-fried *everything*."

"Even the vegetables?" he asks. The gravel crunches under our feet as we walk the path to the front door.

"*Especially* the vegetables."

The smell is multiplied inside. Even I have to take a minute to appreciate it, as accustomed as I am to the scent of heart-attack on a plate.

There's a crowd at the front of the restaurant, families sitting patiently on worn red leather couches. People lean over one another

to catch up with third cousins and coworkers and friends they graduated high school with twenty years ago.

Nostalgia mixes with dread, a feeling I've come to know so well
I almost don't register it, like the feel of my heart beating under my
skin. Mama and I came here twice a week, minimum.

I haven't stepped foot inside since she passed.

I'm so caught up in the space between remembering and trying
not to remember that it takes me a second to sense the hush.

The back of my neck prickles and the sick feeling in my stomach intensifies. One by one, people my mama went to school with,
people I went to school with, her friends, my acquaintances, they see
us. There's quiet. Then the quiet turns into hushed chatter.

"That was fast," Alec says.

I laugh once, quiet and short. "They haven't noticed you yet.
Give it a second."

"Then what—"

"Nooooora." I cringe at the sound. There's a new way people
have of saying your name after someone you love dies. Every syllable
is drawn out and laced with sugar, sweet and syrupy and sickening.
Deanna Webber pushes through the crowd of people milling by the
front door and wraps her arms around me.

Magnolia blossom seeps off of her like it's coming straight out
of her pores. I have to hold my breath while she finishes her painfully long hug. When she finally releases me, she does that thing old
people do where they push you away from them, their hands on your
shoulders, and they look you up and down.

"Boy, but you sure do look like your mama, don't you,
dear-heart?"

I manage a smile. "Thanks, Mrs. Webber."

"Now, darlin', why haven't we seen you over at First Baptist? I know it's probably hard to come back again after your mama's service was there. But there's a pew with your name on it." She finally looks up at Alec. "Bring this handsome one with you if you want."

I stare in shock as she reaches up and pinches Alec's cheek softly.

The look of utter surprise that crosses his face is enough to make the horror of the last five minutes dissipate. We lock eyes and a silent *Help* emanates from him.

Before I can intervene, someone else does.

"Nana," a breathless voice sounds from behind us. A wide-eyed girl rushes up next to Mrs. Webber. It's Tara, a rising senior at the high school. She's smart as hell—I remember seeing her in a few of my senior-level classes last year.

"Nora, I'm so sorry," she says as she grabs her grandmother's arm. She looks at me for a second, her eyes darting to Alec so fast I'm surprised they don't go flying out of her head. "I'm so sorry."

"What in the world are you apologizing for? I was just inviting her to church." She looks back at me. "You can still sit in our pew if your friend won't come. Right, Tara?"

Her face goes bloodred. "Nana, please. That's . . . Nana, it's . . ." She looks at Alec again, at a loss for words. He smiles.

"It's fine, Tara." Her face goes absolutely still, and her hand falls from her grandmother's arm.

"She j-just . . ." Tara stutters, and then starts again. "She doesn't know who you are."

"That's quite all right," Alec says, slipping into that Jane Austen way of talking. "A pleasure to meet you both regardless." Then he winks.

I try not to vomit.

People start to look, then. Really look—past the illegitimate, unwanted daughter of one of the town's most upstanding members. And apparently, they've finally looked long enough to see *Alexander*.

The feeling that rushes through the crowd then is different than the one that went through them when they saw me. It's electric this time. Phones appear, picked up from where they were discarded on the table while everyone dug into the mashed potatoes and homemade bread.

They try to be discreet.

They are anything but.

Alec stiffens, but otherwise, nothing in his manner changes. When a waitress comes to grab us from the group of people who've been waiting for a table much longer than we have, Alec gently places his hand on my lower back, guiding me forward.

It makes for a perfect picture.

She seats us in a corner booth. It's much harder now for everyone in the restaurant to watch us, but they still do. I think about hiding my face behind the giant menu, but when I look across the table at Alec, he's watching me intently. There's no way I'm going to let him see me rattled, so I straighten my back and put the menu down.

"That was weird," he says.

"Thought you'd be used to it by now."

"Not what I mean."

I sigh. "I know. Part of the benefits package when you join the dead mom club."

He stares at me, mouth working in that way he has.

I lean forward a little, arms folded on the table. The ambient noise is ratcheting up and whatever it is he's going to say, I have a feeling I won't want to miss it. I watch his face as he finds the right words, leaning in a little closer, too.

"Do you think—"

A flash goes off to our right and we snap away like magnets repelling. My back hits the worn leather seat. A teenage girl sitting with her parents has the decency to look ashamed when we look over.

I remind myself that this is what we're supposed to be doing. We need them to take the pictures.

It still feels terrible.

When the waitress comes, I order for Alec. We eat what looks and smells like a delicious meal—but I don't taste a single bite. It might as well be hay. Every second passes by slowly, and I'm hyper aware of each move I make and how it's all being documented.

Fifteen hundred dollars, I remind myself every time I see someone take a photo out of the corner of my eye. The noise increases as people pile in, the doorway more and more crowded as word spreads.

I feel like I'm watching from a space inside my body, going through the motions. Alec smiles and laughs and takes small bites that don't leave any food in his teeth. Every once in a while, he looks at me with what I think might be concern.

His hand is on my back again as we try to leave the restaurant. No fewer than two dozen people ask for selfies, and Alec says yes to every single one.

The minute the door closes behind us, my shoulders slump. It's dark outside now. Cicadas chirp in the woods around us, and I let the sound numb my brain. Alec's hand stays on my lower back the entire walk to the car.

I'm not sure what drains me more; the cameras, or having to pretend like I'm not seconds away from crumbling every time someone mentions my mama.

In the car, we sit in silence for a few minutes, recovering.

"That was—" I start, but I'm not able to find the words.

"Draining? Exhausting? The worst hour of your life?"

"Yes to the first two," I say. My phone vibrates. It's Charlotte. I have no idea what to tell her, so I let it go to voicemail.

I have long enough to put in the directions home for Alec before the group chat lights up.

I sigh and open it. There's a photo of Alec and I, sent by Charlotte.

C:
WTF NORA!!!

B:
???

B:
I know the dating part is fake and all, but you could let us know when you and redheaded McDreamy are gonna be at Addie's, basically kissing over the table.

C:
WTF is he wearing? Does he have an interview or something after dinner?

B:

Lmao

"How are there pictures of us out there already?"

Alec laughs. "Welcome to the world of being famous."

"It sucks here."

"Yeah," he says. "It does sometimes."

I look up from my phone. His face is lit by a streetlamp next to the car, soft light casting shadows on his features.

I almost ask him. The words come close to slipping out, but I stop them in time. It doesn't matter why he doesn't just quit if he hates it so much. He's not my friend.

It irritates me that I have to remind myself.

I put my phone on Do Not Disturb and lean it against the console so Alec can have the directions home. We drive in silence, which I'm so thankful for. Performing for all of those people while they stared and took photos was way more exhausting than I expected it to be.

When we're back at my father's house, Alec cuts off the car in the driveway.

"The thing with the old lady—that happens a lot?" he asks.

"All the time." I sigh. "I mean, not as much now. I don't really go anywhere. But when I was in school, or when I had to go grocery shopping, or when I needed to run errands. Yeah. It happened a lot."

"I'm sorry," he says. It catches me off guard. "That has to be—"

"No." My voice is sharp. "Don't."

Alec watches me, gaze searching. He looks so much like a regular person, like a boy I'd see at school or at an away game or in the back of a movie theater.

"Please," I add.

He doesn't make me say the rest—that I can't take any more pity, that the thought of him being nice to me because my mom is dead makes me so sick, I want to throw up my chicken-fried dinner.

"We still on for practice Friday, Horse Girl?" He smirks. The switch from concerned almost-friend back to aloof jerk is seamless.

"Of course. Unless you're backing out?"

"Me?" he says, eyebrows raised. "I never back down from a challenge."

My father's waiting on the couch when I come through the door.

He's doing a puzzle, the box propped up beside him so he can check his progress.

"The boy got you back on time. I'll give him that," he says without looking up from his puzzle.

I make a noncommittal noise, taking my shoes off and slipping them into one of the empty cubbies by the door. I head straight for the stairs, but my father speaks.

"Did you have a good time?" he asks.

"It was fine." I shrug. "The food was good," I lie.

He nods. I take a step backward toward the stairs, confused by this sudden interest in my eating habits.

"This boy—he's an actor?"

"Yeah," I say, startled. "Who told you that?"

"Cecelia. Small town. Gossip runs faster than a train around here."

I blush. "Right."

He clears his throat. "You're . . . You know what you're doing, Nora?"

Surely, he's not trying to be . . . paternal? He had all the time in the world for that—nearly eighteen years in fact. Instead of being there for my first date or staying up all night to make sure I got home from prom, he sent money. So why the hell does he seem intent on starting now?

"Yeah. I know what I'm doing."

He nods. "Okay."

Then he's back to his puzzle.

And I escape to the solitude of my room.

CHAPTER 7

Work is unbearable after our date.

Everyone watches me. Two of America's leading stars are wandering around the set and somehow, *I'm* the most interesting person here.

Sebastian asks me for directions to Addie's, telling me the food in all the photos of us looked outstanding. One of the wardrobe girls asks where I got the Rooney shirt, and it takes me a minute to realize she's referencing the one I wore on the date, the shirt that's plastered all over the internet. She shows me an Instagram thread with a hundred different girls asking for links and dupes of the crop top. I tell her it was from a concert my mom went to in 2006. Her disappointment is palpable.

It's like this for the next twenty-four hours. Even the stables aren't an escape. Amanda drills me for details, begging me to tell her about every second of the car ride, what my "parents" thought, if he liked white or brown gravy on his chicken-fried steak.

When Friday finally comes, I'm almost relieved at the prospect of getting off set for a couple of days—even if most of the time has to be spent with Alec.

Once filming wraps for the day, I walk to my car. Alec's there, leaning against his Mustang, a pair of aviators on. His auburn hair is like a beacon.

He throws a set of keys up in the air over and over again, watching them rise and fall.

When he sees me, he doesn't scowl.

I'll take that as a win. Maybe this won't be so bad after all.

"Alec."

His keys fly up, then clink back down into his hand. "Horse Girl."

Never mind. It is going to be hell.

"How are the horses getting there?" he asks, not looking at me.

"Amanda's dad brought them over to Shep Farm with his trailer an hour ago."

"Remind me why we can't just learn to ride here? Every crime podcast I've ever listened to warned against going to a second location."

I decide not to tell him that any kidnapper would send his annoying ass back in under an hour.

"Because last time, you froze up every time someone so much as glanced at you. No way you'd let your guard down enough to learn here with everyone watching."

"Fine," he sighs. "Can you air-drop me the address? I'll meet you there."

I laugh. "Service drops out ten miles outside of the ranch. Google can't guide you."

He finally looks at me. "Then how am I supposed to get there?"

"You can ride with me," I offer magnanimously.

"Yeah, right. There's no way I'm getting into that thing."

"Hey, that *thing* is a million times more reliable than this shiny piece of junk."

He looks like I've slapped him. "This is a hand-restored 1965 Mustang K-Code."

"Wow, I'm super impressed."

"I'm not getting in that truck."

The beginning of a headache starts to form around my temples. I do not want to give in, but the faster we get started, the faster I can stop spending time with Alec.

He must see the surrender on my face because he opens the passenger side door and bends at the waist, gesturing for me to make my way in. I roll my eyes as he slams the door behind me.

Alec starts the car, rolling the windows down before he shifts into gear. Pale Fire is playing, one of my favorite bands, but I don't say anything because I don't want him to look at me in that way again—the way that makes it clear that he thinks I'm uncultured and backwater, and that because I don't watch TV or movies, there's no way I could know any of the indie bands he loves.

He hands me his phone. I put in the address—it'll get him most of the way there. Once the service gives out, I'll tell him where to go.

"You worked all the way out on this ranch?" he asks after a few minutes of blissful peace.

"Yep. Lived there, too."

He raises his eyebrows. "And you were okay living like that? In the middle of nowhere?"

"I didn't mind." I shrug. "Everything I needed was on the ranch with me."

It's quiet for a minute. Then he says, so low I can barely make out the words, "Sounds kind of nice."

"It was." I hesitate for a second before I pull my phone out. I'm almost an adult, and my father isn't really my dad or anything. But I still feel like I should tell him when I won't be home for dinner. I send a quick text, letting him know that I'll be working out on the ranch until late.

He sends a thumbs-up emoji.

We make it less than a mile down the road before I have to take my flannel off.

Apparently old-ass Mustangs don't have AC. The hot leather clings to my shoulders when I lean back, the tank top I have on underneath not doing much to protect me from it. My thighs keep sticking to the seat, and I'm kicking myself for picking today to finally give in and wear shorts.

Absentmindedly, I pull the holders from the ends of my braids and run my fingers through them. Tendrils flow free and wild as we speed up, the wind twisting and turning through the car. The smell of raw peanuts and the promise of rain in the air sweeps into the space with us as we pass field after field. The way the wind whips in reminds me of what it's like to be on horseback, riding free through a field, going so fast no one can catch you. I haven't let myself ride with my hair down in years, too afraid of the tangles. I try to remember the last time I rode free and unrestrained. I was almost there today with Chestnut. But not quite. Some part of me was still holding back.

Alec turns the song up and "Satellites" pours from the speakers. The roar of the wind competes with the strumming of the guitar, and we wouldn't be able to hear each other if we shouted. I don't worry about him hearing me when I start singing along. Out of the corner of my eye, I see his mouth moving, doing the same. Every once in a while, I gesture for him to turn, guiding us closer and closer to Shep Farm.

For the breath of a car ride, I let myself forget about everything. No housing deposits, no photos, no Cecelia or my father.

Alec slows when he sees the first sign. He turns down the dirt road, and we both crank our windows halfway up to stop the dust from pouring in.

It takes us twenty more minutes to get close enough to the ranch to see it. Alec's car struggles on the bumpy, unpaved roads, and I worry at how heavy the smell of rain is in the air now. Alec doesn't seem to notice.

We pass the original barn first, the big one that used to hold the horses before Mrs. Shep had a new one built closer to the riding trails. Two miles later, the trees clear and the full ranch comes into view.

"Wow," he says, slipping off his aviators and sliding them on top of his head. He parks next to the front office and turns the car off. Then he stares. "You grew up here?"

Something in my stomach drops. Of course this must seem so quaint to him. He probably grew up somewhere like LA in a giant mansion and an Olympic-sized pool in the backyard.

"Moved in when I was seven."

"It's . . . stunning."

My heart flutters. I don't know why it means anything to me. He's made it clear he despises me, from the very first second I met him. It shouldn't make my heart thrill in my chest, shouldn't make my breath short to hear that he can see it. That he sees the beauty and the value here.

I look out the window, too, and I try to see it through his eyes. Georgia is all flat land and pine trees, and some people might not find that beautiful. But here, the land sprawls out so far you can

almost believe there's nothing else past the line of trees. Gorgeous
blue sky pours out one way and white, fluffy clouds stretch leisurely
across the vista.

When I get out of the car, I tie my flannel around my waist.

Alec follows next to me as I lead him to the stables. He's so close
I can smell him. It's different, somehow, than the way he smelled in
the trailer. Then, it was all rich department stores and tuxedos. This
is more like campfire and earth. It fits him better.

We make it to the stables, and honestly, it feels a little like coming home. Amanda's family stables are fine, but these are the ones
I learned to love horses in. One horse in particular. Ethel sticks her
head out over her gate and nickers. I walk right to her and slide my
hand down the side of her neck. She gently nudges me with her
nose, so I wrap my arm around her and lean in. After a moment, I
pull back and smile. She huffs, blowing my hair out. "Thanks for the
reminder," I say, laughing. I take one of the ponytail holders from
my wrist and fashion one long braid over my shoulder.

"Why do you do that?" Alec asks. When I turn, I find him
leaned against the empty stall door opposite Ethel and me, arms
crossed. He always stands like that near the horses, like he doesn't
know what to do with his hands in here. "With your hair?"

I shrug. "It's easier. When it's this long, it gets in the way if I
leave it down."

"Why don't you cut it?"

I look away, hoping he doesn't see how a simple question feels
like bleach on an open wound.

*"Look up a little," Mama had said, and I leaned my head back farther,
resting my temple on her knee. Once I got taller than her, our braiding*

sessions happened with me on the floor, crisscross applesauce in front of her while she sat on the couch. "That's better."

"French braid?" I had asked.

"Waterfall," she answered, her voice muffled by the ponytail holder clamped between her teeth.

"Glad I get to be your test subject. If I show up at school with lopsided braids again, Bree's going to make me skip first period so she can fix them."

"What in the world do you mean by again? Your braids are always impeccable."

"Okay, so we're forgetting the bubble-braid fiasco?"

She gently nudged the back of my head with her knee.

"I think you dreamt that. Or it's one of those false memories I read about the other day."

"Maybe. And maybe I also dreamt that I saw that old guy with the checkered blazer picking Mrs. Shep up for what looked suspiciously like a date yesterday."

She had gasped, tugging my hair a little too hard at the prospect of fresh gossip.

"Ow," I said through giggles.

"You saw this last night and you're telling me now? Spill it immediately, or I'm starting over, and you're getting bubble braids again."

I shake myself free of the memory.

There's no casual way to tell him that I grew my hair out because my mama loved it so much. That it makes me remember a time before the accident that took her away from me and stole my love of horses for too many months.

The silence after a simple question has gone on so long that I know he senses I've been thrown off-balance. I make myself answer.

"Don't really have time for things like going to the salon."

When I glance up, he's staring at me again, and my favorite look is there. The one that makes his face look like it's lit on the inside, powered by his curiosity. He has to know there's more, but he doesn't press. He just stares.

I look back a little longer than I should.

Ethel nudges the crown of my head with her nose, and I snap back to reality.

Quickly, I get her saddled and ready for Alec. When I'm done, I hand the reins to him.

"Lead her out to the paddock."

"Alone?" he asks, not taking the reins.

"You can handle leading her. It's like walking a dog."

"A really, really big dog," he says, taking the reins. He looks up at Ethel, unsure. She lowers her head and sniffs at the front pocket of his jeans. His eyes widen. I bite back a smile.

"He doesn't have any treats," I say, gently pulling her head away. She huffs. "Lead her out there," I say, pointing toward the wide, open paddock. "I'm right behind you."

He looks for a minute like he might argue, but eventually he gingerly leads Ethel down the stable aisle. She follows along, letting him lead. I trail after, just far enough to give them space to get to know one another.

At the paddock, he looks at me with such awkward desperation that I almost say something snarky, make him beg and say please like he would if the roles were reversed. Then I remind myself how much I need the money I'll earn by the end of the weekend. I hope we can figure this out in two days instead of three. I don't want to spend my birthday out here with him.

Before I can talk myself out of it, I move a step closer.

"How would you feel about a truce?" I ask.

He looks at me skeptically. "A truce?"

"Yes." I nod, businesslike. "For this weekend only, obviously. We'll pretend like you're just another person I'm teaching how to ride a horse, not the jerk who yelled at me in public the first time we met."

"I don't feel like that qualified as yelling," he says, narrowing his eyes.

"Semantics. Look, this will go so much faster if we can work together, no animosity. Clean slate?"

He looks down at his shoes, high-top Converse that are wholly inappropriate for horse riding. "I could use a day where I'm some-body else."

There's something lacing his words that I'm not sure he meant for me to hear. A stab of pity runs through me.

"It's settled, then. Truce." I stick out my hand. He hesitates, then he reaches out and clasps his fingers around mine.

"Truce."

His touch is soft and warm.

So quickly I almost don't see it, he uses his other hand to slide the extra ponytail holder on my wrist to his.

"Proof of our agreement." His eyes meet mine. I shudder, then tear my hand from his.

"Great. Let's get started. Go ahead and mount."

He raises an eyebrow.

I roll my eyes.

"Get on the horse, Alec."

He smiles a wicked grin but does as I tell him. I have him start her at a walk, and after watching them for a moment, I'm able to pinpoint ten different small mistakes.

To my surprise, Alec listens to everything I say. He concentrates and picks everything up so fast, I think we might actually have him passing for a horse rider by Monday.

Then, I ask him to work up to a trot.

His posture changes. He's too tense and reactive. Ethel can tell. She keeps pulling her head to the side, shaking it back and forth every few steps.

When they turn at the end of the paddock and come back my way, I wave for him to stop in front of me.

"You're too tense. You're riding like you're waiting for things to go wrong."

"Isn't it good to be prepared?"

"Sure, but you're sending signals to Ethel that something's wrong *now*. She reads your tension as a warning."

"She can get that all from the way I'm sitting?" he says with a raised eyebrow.

"I told you, they're perceptive. Straighten your back a little. Good. Now, relax your grip on her reins. You're putting too much pressure on her mouth. Okay, now, breathe."

"I am breathing."

"No you aren't. You're holding your breath when you get nervous. In through your nose, out through your mouth."

His lips thin, but he takes a deep breath.

"Try again."

Alec flicks Ethel's reins. For a minute, I think he's got it. Then they move to a trot and he leans forward, shoulders hunched. By the time they make it to the end of the paddock and start back my way, his hands are fists and his jaw is set so tight I wonder if his teeth are going to shatter.

They stop in front of me again and I chew the inside of my cheek, contemplating. Normally, I'd have plenty of time to work with a new rider. They'd be able to relax over the span of weeks, slowly growing used to the feel of a horse carrying them around. But Alec doesn't have that much time. I don't really care if he can't work in Hollywood ever again—but I highly doubt he's going to pay me if I don't successfully teach him how to ride.

We need to fix this.

Now.

I tap his foot. "Take this one out of the stirrup."

"You want me to get down?"

"No. I'm coming up."

I throw my foot into the stirrup and pull myself into the saddle, sitting in front of him.

There's even less room than I thought there was going to be. Alec tries to adjust, but there's nowhere for him to go.

"Is this really necessary?"

"You're not getting it."

"That time was better."

"For about ten seconds. Then you tensed right back up."

"We don't both fit up here."

"It'll work for now."

"There's no way this horse can carry both of us."

"On a full galloping ride? No. For a canter around the paddock? She'll be fine." I keep my eyes firmly locked ahead, refusing to let them travel down the length of his legs on either side of me.

I sigh. "Look, I hate this as much as you do." His hand brushes against my thigh, and my breath catches. I have to pause for a second, before continuing, "But it's the only thing that I can think of to help you get the feel of it fast enough. Act like I'm not here."

He laughs quietly, his warm breath tickling the back of my bare neck. I desperately hope he doesn't notice the way I shiver. I wish I would have put my flannel back on before I came up here, but it's still tied around my waist. Way too much of my skin is exposed.

My brain knows this thing with Alec is fake, but my traitorous body is having trouble remembering.

"How am I supposed to do that?" he asks.

"Try and sit like I told you. Pretend you're the experienced one and you're taking me out for a ride." He's silent and still for too long, so I turn awkwardly in the saddle to look at him. His face is close, and his eyes dart down to my lips. I snap the ponytail holder on his wrist.

"Truce, remember? I'm doing my job, and I'm good at it."

He nods. When I turn back around, he adjusts himself in the seat again.

"Good, that's better." It's so much easier to get a feel for what exactly he's doing wrong when I'm up here with him. Thankfully he's riding in a Western saddle so we have a bit more breathing room between the pommel and the cantle while still giving me a sense of his movements. "Straighten a little. That's it. Now, grab the reins."

He hesitates before reaching around me, and even though his body is warm and the sun is out in full force, I tremble when his arms slide around either side of me. He grabs the reins, but holds them out like he's afraid to come any closer. I grab his wrists, pulling him in toward my waist. Then I take his hands in mine and cradle them.

"Relax."

It takes a moment, but eventually, his fingers pull slightly away from his palms and his grip softens.

"Good. Now, tell her to walk."

He signals Ethel, and she starts forward slowly. We make it around the paddock once and he manages to keep his position and grip.

"Tell her to trot." He does. It takes about ten seconds before he leans in on me, shoulders hunched behind mine. His hands are fists in front of my stomach, and I can feel that his breathing has stopped completely.

Ethel reacts, her head pulling to one side.

I put my hands on top of his and squeeze once.

"Loosen." He does.

I press myself into him, the length of my back running along his chest. Our shoulders press together, front to back. I don't have to say anything this time, he takes my cue and I feel him straighten behind me, the small distance between us opening again.

Ethel notices, and she stops flicking her head to the side almost immediately. We complete four rounds of perfect trotting, and Alec only leans forward once. When I push back into him, he straightens immediately.

Once we're back where we started, he pulls Ethel to a stop. His chest rises and falls behind me, his breathing slightly elevated. He rests his arms lightly on my thighs, loosely holding Ethel's reins. I feel his chest rumble behind me when he laughs. I turn awkwardly in the saddle, trying to steal a glance at him.

"What?"

"That actually worked."

"I told you it would. Why is that funny?"

"I was imagining the face you'd make when I admitted you were right."

I smile. "And *you* were wrong. Not sure which one of those I like better."

"Yep. That's about what I expected."

His smile is brilliant this close. White teeth, perfect lips. I rip my gaze away when I realize I've been staring directly at his mouth. When I meet his eyes, they're dancing.

"Try it on your own now," I say, blushing in the heat of the Georgia sun. "Maybe we'll try a canter later."

I hop down, my back cold without the weight of him behind it.

We spend hours trying to get Ethel to canter.

I expect Alec to complain, to whine or fuss about the heat. He doesn't, though. He works hard, and listens to everything I say without backtalk.

Well, not much backtalk, anyway.

If I can only get him to freaking relax.

I knew it would be hard, but it's been hours and he can't stop seizing up right as Ethel breaks into anything above a trot. I consider getting in the saddle with him again, but then I think about how it felt when his breath ran along the back of my neck, and decide it might be better for me to stay down here.

I wave Alec over.

"What?" he snaps, the longer tendrils of his red hair plastered to his forehead with sweat.

He's getting more and more irritable.

I bite down my retort and instead glance at the sky, keeping an eye on the deep, dark clouds inching over from the west. The rain could miss us altogether, but if the storm blows this way, I want to get as much done as possible before we get rained out. We have all day tomorrow to practice, but the more we get done today, the better.

The thing is, I know *exactly* what to do. But I'm reluctant. It's going to open up old wounds. I don't want to pull those feelings up at all, much less in front of Alec.

But it's either that or ride in the saddle with him.

I don't mean to glance out to the right, to the spot where my world ended five months ago. But my gaze is pulled there, the force unstoppable.

I couldn't scream. The sound had been stuck inside of me, had torn the most tender parts of me to shreds.

"Move," I whispered as I ran. "Move. Move. Move."

But she did not move. She stayed still, like a broken doll, like a marionette without its strings. Jasper stood shaking a few steps away, the reins dangling on the ground, sweat lathered on his coat. His breathing was heavy, like mine. The jump he had landed on lay in splintered pieces around him. Around her.

"Call an ambulance," Mrs. Shep yelled to someone. "In my office, use the landline." I could hardly hear her over the pounding of blood in my head, over the thunder of my feet below me as I tried to get to her.

I wanted to be beside her.

I was terrified to be beside her.

I pull my eyes away from the patch of grass that still grew like nothing terrible had ever happened there and look at Alec.

"A few months ago, I was . . . I was afraid to ride—don't ask me why, we don't have time to get into it now," I add in a rush. "Every time I got near a horse—even Ethel, I got this real sick feeling in my stomach. Years of riding, and suddenly I couldn't do it anymore.

"Mrs. Shep tried a bunch of stuff. None of it worked. One day, she got frustrated with me and asked why I even wanted to get on a horse again if it made me that miserable. I don't think she really meant it, she was just heated. But it made me think. Why *did* I keep doing something that made me feel so sick? I took the night, figured it out." I pause before I say the words out loud to another person for the first time. What if he laughs?

"Living afraid isn't living."

He doesn't even crack a smile. There's no judgment. He just waits for me to go on.

"I said it to myself over and over again while I saddled Ethel, chanted it in my head while I put my feet in the stirrups. Made myself whisper it when I finally worked up the nerve to tell her to trot. It worked. Calmed me down enough to ride again. That's what you need."

"What, like a mantra?"

"Exactly."

He's quiet, and I can see the apprehension in his face. It sounds like something Charlotte would suggest—along with drinking water you left out when the moon is full—so I get why he's hesitant. But this had worked for me, and I know it could work for him, too.

"Do you want to figure out how to canter? Or do you want to go back and tell Ashton you can't do it and risk being blacklisted?"

He swallows once, hard, his Adam's apple bobbing. "I want to figure out how to canter."

"Why?"

"For a paycheck," he says, but the words are weak, like he knows neither of us is going to believe them. I don't say anything—I just stare up at him while he stares back down at me, refusing to be the one to break eye contact first. I see the little pieces of his mask coming back into place—eyes tightening, lips thinning—like he can't stand for someone to *see* him.

"Don't do that."

"Do what?"

"You can't be Alexander here. You have to be Alec. If you're going to find your mantra, you need to be real. With yourself, at least."

He studies me from atop the horse, eyes roving my face. Warmth from the sun runs along my skin at the place his gaze falls, a strange and uncomfortable coincidence.

"Why do you want to do this? Why won't you just give up and walk away?"

He glances down at the hair tie on his wrist before he speaks.

"Because I have to," he says, voice low but clear. "Because it isn't just about me, and this movie, and whatever the next one is. It's about them. I need to be enough for them."

It doesn't make sense to me, not completely. But it doesn't have to. The way he says it, his voice thickening a little around the words like they were hard to get out and a relief to speak at the same time, that tells me it means enough to him to push him to keep going.

I nod. "Then do it. Be enough for them."

Alec trots Ethel around the paddock, working her up to the canter. When she stops short the first couple of times instead of moving forward, my stomach drops, and I expect him to come riding back to tell me what a waste that whole exercise was. But he doesn't. He keeps trying. And then, like I'm seeing a miracle in real time, they make it around the paddock three times. He doesn't break form once.

He turns to me, exultant, and when his eyes find mine, I smile—genuine and bright.

They canter around and around until Alec finally rides over to where I'm watching, pride simmering in my chest.

"It's exhilarating."

I smile despite my exhaustion.

"It is. We can work on it more tomorrow. I think you've both worked hard enough today."

Alec glances out toward the fields. "Do you think I could take her out there? Just for a few minutes."

I look up at the sky, worried about the darkness headed our way. The wind is starting to pick up, and while that is so nice in the summer heat, it doesn't bode well.

I almost say no, almost tell Alec we need to get ahead of whatever storm is brewing. But then I look up at him, and I see it in his eyes. The need to be here a little longer—to be somewhere he doesn't have to worry about who's watching or a camera lurking around the corner.

I decide that I can give Alec this much. Another few minutes of peace.

"Chestnut probably wouldn't mind some exercise. He didn't get to ride at all, and I had Amanda's dad drag him all the way out here." I glance up at the sky again. "We've got a little time. I'll go get him saddled."

Alec beams. My chest warms.

I open the gate and he leads Ethel through. They wait while I quickly tack up Chestnut and get myself settled. I take a minute to undo my braid. Suddenly, I want nothing more than for my hair to flow behind me while I ride. I feel Alec's eyes on me as I shake it out. When I glance up, he gestures for me to lead the way.

We ride side by side, working our horses up from a walk to a trot to a canter. The rhythmic thud of the horses' hooves surrounds us, lulling my mind into the space I can only get to when I'm riding like this—free and unrestrained. Chestnut and I are nearing a gallop before I know it, and I crouch in the saddle, letting him work up to full speed. He carries me so fast the trees blur slightly in my peripheral vision. Every atom and cell inside my body responds to the feel of it, and unrestrained joy rushes through me. And even though I know it's reckless, I let go of the reins and I slowly bring my hands out on either side and let the wind rip through them, the breath of the world traveling through the space between my fingers. I close my eyes and tilt my head to the sky and, for a second, it feels like flying.

Then I remember I'm not alone. I look to my right and I see Alec behind me, Ethel cantering with surety.

And for the first time, I *see* him.

He's hovering above the saddle, his legs bent at the perfect angle in the stirrups. One hand holds the reins loosely, the other grips the horn. When our eyes meet, he smiles, and everything inside of me lights.

The smile I send back his way is as easy as breathing.

His eyes devour me.

I open my mouth to speak, even though I know he can't hear me. I don't know what I'm going to say—that I'm sorry we ever fought, that I want to know this side of him, that I like it so much better than the one that the rest of the world sees. Maybe I want to say that we can extend the truce, make it last a few days—hell, make it permanent. I pull on Chestnut's reins so I can get the words out, and Alec mirrors me.

The wind stops rushing around us, the adrenaline in my veins slows.

We stare at each other as he waits for me to speak.

I finally decide what I want to say, and I breathe in.

Then a clap of thunder explodes above us, and all hell breaks loose.

CHAPTER 8

We make it back to the stables in record time.

I ride behind Alec and Ethel, worried that the rain will make him nervous again, but he handles it well, his posture steady. He gives Ethel all the right cues, and they both stay calm on the ride back.

At the stable doors, we both dismount and lead the horses in, getting absolutely soaked in the process.

Thankfully the horses fare better than we do—they're only wet from the waist up and a little around their hooves. Alec watches me as I lead Chestnut into the stall, and then pulls Ethel into the one directly across. He mirrors my actions, removing her saddle after he watches me work on Chestnut's. I'm thankful he takes the initiative, because I'm uncomfortable in my wet clothes and I'm ready to leave, even if that means we have to run through the rain again to get to his car.

I hang Chestnut's saddle and tack, then walk across to Ethel's stall to help Alec finish. He steals glances at me as we work together, rain dripping from his hair that's more brown than auburn when it's soaked. His mouth keeps turning up at one end, and I'm dying to know what he's thinking—even if it is rude. But we finish our work in silence.

"Should we dry them off?" he asks once we're done, looking around the stall for something to pat Ethel down with. I shake my head.

"Chestnut came through at a full gallop and Ethel's been working all day. I'd never put them away like this, but there's nowhere to walk them down during a storm." Thunder booms overhead as if to prove my point.

"The water on their coats will do the same thing as a hose-down would—help them cool off."

Ethel gently pushes in between us and drops her head to the giant water bucket next to her stall door. She drinks deeply, and I gesture for Alec to follow me out.

We lock both stalls behind us so neither horse can wander out into the storm. Their water buckets are near overflowing, and there is plenty of hay to last them through the night. Amanda's dad had given them both several flakes when he dropped them off early this afternoon, and I'm glad he did, because there's no way anyone is making it down those dirt roads later tonight to feed them.

"We really need to go," I say, turning to Alec. He raises his eyebrows and looks out at the pouring rain. It really is torrential, the water falling so heavily that I can't even see the field where we were riding.

"Shouldn't we wait until this lets up? We're already drenched." He looks down at his Converse. "I don't think my shoes can take much more."

I shake my head. "If we wait much longer, we won't be able to get down the roads. They can turn almost impassable during this kind of rain."

"You're the boss, Horse G—" He cuts off, and smiles. "Sorry, forgot about the truce there for a second."

I roll my eyes. "Whatever, *Alexander*." His face falls a little, but he fixes it so quickly I almost think I imagined it.

"On my mark," he says, stretching one leg out behind him like he's getting ready to run the hundred-yard dash. I can't help but smile. "Ready. Set—" He grabs my hand at the last second, and drags me out into the rain with him. He lets out a raucous laugh.

"Go!" he shouts into the rain.

And then we run.

Alec keeps his hand wrapped around mine as we hit full speed, water pelting us from every side. I tell myself it's so we don't lose each other in the heavy rain.

It feels like it takes ten times longer to get to the car than it should. Once it comes into view, he finally drops my hand. We both fumble with the door handles, the wet making them hard to grip. Once the door is open, I slide in, and cry out in shock when I slip around on the leather, knocking my shoulder into Alec's arm over the middle console.

The doors slam shut, and for a moment, we both sit in silence, staring at the rivulets of water flying across the windshield. Then Alec moves his foot, and his shoe lets out the tiniest, wet squeak.

And then the car is full of our laughter.

There's a moment where I can't tell if it's the rain on the windshield blinding me, or the tears lining the rims of my eyes. I make myself take deep, grounding breaths—but a few short laughs slip through every time I look at Alec. It takes him less time to compose himself, and by the time I've got my hysterics under control, his arm is behind my headrest, his face dangerously close as he turns to watch through the rear window while he backs out.

"I hope you know where we're going," he says, laughter still lacing his voice. "I can barely see the end of the car."

The levity of our moment evaporates around us as we inch our way down the road, the rain slamming on the roof of the car drowning out all other sounds. Alec is leaned forward, trying to get a better look at the road in front of him. The windshield wipers swipe along at full speed, but it's nowhere near as fast as the rain.

We drive in silence for ten minutes, both of us watching the dirt road and hoping for the storm to let up.

It doesn't.

"Does this happen every time it rains?" Alec asks. We both grimace when the car dips down into a puddle that's way deeper than it looks.

I shake my head. "Just rain like this. The road doesn't have time to soak it all up when it falls this fast. We'll be fine as long as you don't—"

Alec hits a deep puddle, and the front bumper slams down into the road. I grit my teeth and push against the dashboard. Alec hits the brakes, and I swear I almost *feel* us sink down into the mud.

He lets out a slow breath. "As long as I don't what?"

"Stop."

He throws the car into first gear and slowly presses the gas pedal. The car lurches forward once, then the whir of wheels spinning adds to the noise of the rain. Mud flings up on either side of us, covering the windows in specks.

"Crap," Alec says.

I nod.

"I'll call Ashton, he'll send someone out to get us." He pulls out his phone from between the car door and his seat.

I shake my head. "There's no—"

"—service out here," he finishes, slamming his phone against the steering wheel the way only a rich person would.

After a second, he looks over at me. "Well, at least we've got somewhere dry to stay until the rain lets up."

I lean forward and, through the sheets of rain, see exactly what I was afraid of finding.

"We can't stay in here."

"It's not like I relish the idea of sleeping sitting up—"

"No," I interrupt. "We can't stay here because that tree is one good gust of wind from falling over right on top of your car. I don't really want to be underneath it when it does."

"Crap," he says again, running his hands over his face. He throws the car back into first and pushes the gas all the way to the floorboard. It accomplishes nothing other than sinking us another inch in the mud. He turns the ignition off and looks over at me, his expression pathetic.

"What do we do? Run back to the ranch?"

"Everything is locked up. We'd have to wait in the stables."

"That's better than waiting here, under the murder tree."

I shake my head.

He sighs. "You have a better idea?"

"Actually," I say, throwing my door open, "I do."

My shoes sink down into the mud immediately. They come out of the ground with a squelch as I turn and slam the door closed,

Alec's shocked face staring at me through the window. I gesture for him to get out.

We struggle through the mud, and I'm barely able to make him out through the rain, even though he's less than a foot away from me. When we get off of the road and onto the grass, it's easier to walk.

I run in what I hope is the right direction, because I can hardly get my bearings. After a full minute, I still don't see it, and I start to worry maybe we were farther out than I thought.

Finally, I glimpse the bright red face of the barn looming ahead of us.

Alec spots it, too, and we both sprint toward it. He grabs the giant handle once we're close enough and swings the door open. I rush inside and he follows. We both pull the door back in, shutting it and the storm behind us.

I slide down the door and sit. Alec slides down next to me, droplets from his hair hitting my shoulder with a soft patter.

"Well. At least we're safe?" He says it like a question, and the way his voice goes up at the end is so hilarious that I snort. His shoulders shake with quiet laughter next to me.

"At least we're safe," I agree.

He sighs. "You know, if this were one of my movies, we'd stumble on a magically unlocked door in the back of the barn. It would have everything we needed for a candlelight dinner: romantic MREs, a change of clothes that were curiously our size exactly, and a bottle of very expensive wine." He turns his head my way, and I can barely make out his face in the dim light from outside. "But wine sucks, so let's make it Mike's Hard Lemonade. You didn't happen to stash any in the rafters when you lived here, did you?"

"I didn't live *in* the barn, jerk." I push off the ground and walk to the back. "But there is a supply closet."

The muggy heat is heavy in the closet, the rain making the humidity in the air worse than normal. I fumble with the chain above me and pull it down once. Yellow light floods the long room, casting shadows on the dozens of random things scattered along the rows of shelves.

"Yes," I whisper when I find them.

"What?" Alec says, and I jump. When I turn, I find him in the doorframe, smirking.

"You're such a—"

"If the next word that comes out of your mouth is any form of *jerk*, then I totally get to call you Horse Girl." He shrugs. "Fair warning."

I roll my eyes and toss him one of the long pieces of fabric.

He looks at it skeptically. "What is this?"

"A horse rug."

"Which is?"

"Something that keeps the horses warm and dry. In other words, a godsend for us right now."

He puts it to his face and breathes in tentatively. His nose scrunches. "I'm assuming this isn't new."

"You'd assume right," I say, grabbing one of the rugs for myself and running the corner of it across the back of my neck. He watches me, face pinched.

"And this is your solution? To dry off with used horse towels?"

"You're welcome to grab a handful of that hay over in the corner," I say in my most hospitable voice. "It might smell a little better." I shrug. "Or it might not. Depends on which animals were in here last."

He rolls his eyes, but runs the rug along the length of one arm, grimacing slightly. I dry myself off, too, trying not to watch as he methodically wipes all of his exposed skin. When he drops the fabric and grabs the hem of his shirt to pull it over his head, my eyes dart down to my shoelaces, face burning.

Don't look don't look don't look don't look don't look.

Making quick work of untying the soaked flannel from my waist, I hang it on an empty hook for tacks near the door. Then I dry my arms and legs, and dry them again for good measure. When I look up again, Alec's hair is barely damp, and he's got the rug draped over his shoulders. My eyes trail over his chest without my permission, taking in the faint lines of muscle that cross over his abdomen. I linger on his stomach, then glance up to his bare chest. I pull my eyes upward, and it's so hard to make them listen, I feel like I'm fighting a horse for control of the reins.

I prepare myself for the look of satisfaction on his face, seeing as he caught me ogling him.

Instead, I watch as his gaze travels over the exposed parts of my legs, up to my hips. His pace is leisurely as he works his way over my stomach, and I'm painfully aware of how my tank top is like a second skin right now, wet with rain, hugging my curves. He drags his eyes to mine, and I'm so extraordinarily pleased with the way his face flushes.

Thunder booms above us and the storeroom light flickers. It snaps me back to reality.

I hang my damp rug next to my flannel, and grab a new one from the pile. I don't look at Alec as I pass by him, but he's still in the doorframe, so I have to turn sideways. My chest brushes against his, and my breath stills in my throat.

I spread the new rug in the barn, right outside of the light that spills through the storeroom doorway. Before I sit down, I take off my shoes and lay my sopping wet socks on the hay. Thankfully my shorts are barely damp, the material repelled most of the water.

Alec kicks off his Converse and socks, then stretches out beside me. We both lean back against the barn wall, listening to the rumble of the storm on the other side. My stomach growls, protesting at the lack of dinner.

Alec lets out a low chuckle. "This trip has not been at all what I expected."

I watch the river of water falling through the rafters on the other side of the barn. It's still storming, but it's slowing a little.

"What *did* you expect?" I ask.

Alec shrugs against my shoulder. "I don't know. Peace and quiet, honestly. Hanging out with Diya. Trying new food. Hopping on a horse and somehow magically knowing what to do."

We both laugh.

"I did *not* expect to find myself soaking wet, hiding from a murder tree in a half-dilapidated barn with the most—" He cuts off.

"The most irritating girl you've ever met," I finish for him.

"That's not at all what I was going to say." But he won't meet my eyes.

"Then what *were* you going to say?"

He doesn't answer.

"Isn't it enough that you're so famous, Alec? Do you really have to go out of your way to be mysterious all the time, too?"

"That's rich coming from you," he says.

My mouth falls open. "What? There's literally nothing mysterious about me."

"Right." He shakes his head. "I swear, every time we talk, I feel like you're only saying the tiniest possible part of whatever it is you're thinking. It's like a dance—I have to be so careful about how I try to drag things out of you. One wrong step and suddenly you're all clammed up again. And *no one* on set knows anything about you."

He's been asking people about me?

"Amanda does," I say. "We both grew up here."

He rolls his eyes. "Amanda can't get within ten feet of me without hyperventilating. She's not exactly helpful."

I pick at the blanket beneath us. "I don't clam up," I say defensively.

"You absolutely do. And over the strangest things." He shifts beside me. "Like earlier. All I did was ask you about your hair—why you tie it up. Then your face did that thing it does when you shut down, and I knew I wouldn't get a single word out of you after that."

I look up at him and find his curious eyes roaming my face. "Why *did* asking about your hair make you shut down?"

I look away, and he sighs. He shifts beside me, the blanket around his shoulders softly scratching against my arm. When he holds out his hand in front of me, I see my hair tie in it.

"Ending the truce so soon?" I ask, reaching out to take it. He pulls it back.

"No. I'm . . . extending its parameters. The bearer of the sacred hair tie gets to ask one question. The other person has to answer. No dodging."

"I answer this question, and then I get to ask you whatever I want?"

"Whatever you want," he says.

"Okay," I say hesitantly.

"Why did you freak out when I asked about cutting your hair?" he asks.

"I didn't freak," I snap.

"Fine, why did you shut down?"

Everything inside of me begs my eyes to pull down, to study the way the hay is scattered all over the floor, to watch the water dripping from the rooftop. But I make myself look at him instead.

His face is soft, brows raised slightly. I think about all the times he's watched me with deep-seated irritation, so clear and fierce that I would have sworn he would never do anything with more purpose than he did hating me. It's so different now, I almost feel like I'm talking to another person.

"My mom loved it long," I say, proud when my voice doesn't waver and my eyes don't drift away from his. "A couple of years before she died"—my voice struggles a little over the word, but I push on—"I cut it off. Right to my jaw. She hated it. Once she was gone, it felt . . . I don't know. I guess it felt wrong to cut it."

"What happened to her?" he asks, voice soft.

I shake my head, snatching the hair tie from his hand. "You already asked your question. It's my turn." But I hesitate, stretching the elastic band over my fingers.

This morning, Elizabeth had texted me again. She offers more money each time, like she thinks I'll finally crack if she hits the right number. But there's no amount that would make me feel right about selling someone's secrets for money. Not even Alec at his worst deserves that.

But I am desperate to know the truth. Not for her, even though I feel more sympathetic toward Elizabeth every time I google her name or check her TikTok page. Her life is falling apart worse than mine. I wonder if she wants to know who the girl was just to get some damn closure in her life.

On the other hand, Diya is *so* sure Alec is a good guy. And I find myself wanting to believe she's right.

"Did you cheat on Elizabeth?"

"I did not," he says, meeting my gaze without an ounce of shame.

I raise my eyebrows.

"I never cheated on Eliza."

We stare at each other for half a minute. I nod.

"You believe me?" he asks.

"I believe you." I'm surprised to find I mean it.

"Okay." He lets out a long breath and takes the hair tie when I hand it to him.

"Why don't you just tell her that?" I ask, thinking of how much peace that would bring Elizabeth. Maybe she'd even stop with the anti-Alec tirade online.

He shakes his head. "It's complicated. And you already asked your question." He toys with the hair tie, like he's afraid to voice the next question.

"What happened to your mom?" he finally says.

I don't answer.

"Did she . . . You said earlier you didn't ride for a long time. Was it because your mom fell?"

"She was thrown," I say. I shake my head gently, trying to rid myself of the image burned so deeply into my brain—the one of her horse crashing over the jump, her flying through the air. I still had nightmares about the way she lay there afterward, unmoving. "Didn't make it to the hospital. She was gone faster than I could run over to her."

The pounding of the rain is the only sound in the barn for the space of ten breaths.

"I'm sorry," he says.

I shrug. "I'm not the only person in the world to lose their mom."

"Still," Alec says.

"Still," I whisper.

I take the hair tie back. My turn.

"Did you really put kitty litter in George Clooney's food on set?"

His laughter booms through the barn. "Yeah. I wish you could have seen his face." He chuckles again and knocks his bare shoulder into mine. "You *did* google me. You never admitted it."

"Maybe I didn't google you. Maybe George told me himself."

"On a first-name basis with Clooney, are you?"

"What can I say?" I shrug. "I'm drowning in celebrities."

He smirks, but it wavers when I hand him the hair tie.

"What's the deal with your family?" he asks, somber. "The vibes were weird when I picked you up for our date."

I roll my eyes. "That one's easy. My father had an affair with my mother eighteen years ago while he was married to Cecelia. It resulted in me. Daddy dearest ran back to his wife. Mama raised me alone. Then she died. Even though they weren't together, she listed his name on the birth certificate. The state called and told him to be a parent or go to jail. Daddy got a daughter and Cecelia got the surprise of her life." I run my fingers along the blanket beneath us, rough and scratchy. "They pretend we've always been one happy family and that my mama never existed." My voice is thick, but it feels so good to say it out loud. "No one acknowledges anything remotely uncomfortable. I just know they're counting down to the moment I leave and everything goes back to the way it was before." I shrug. "But I can't blame them. I'm counting the seconds, too."

"Damn," Alec says.

I nod in agreement, and take the sacred tie of truth when he hands it back to me.

"Why did you want to be an actor?" I ask, hoping to bring up the mood a little.

He's studying the blanket now. "Do you know how this all started for me?"

"Not really. I saw a little bit online when I *didn't* google you, but it was mostly the stuff happening right now."

"My friends and I, we grew up in this trailer park in Arizona. Middle of nowhere. One year, my buddy Delilah gets a hand-me-down phone. We start messing around, making these videos we write and direct, and decided to upload them to YouTube. One day, this guy stumbles on them, posts one to Reddit, and it went uphill from there. Snapchat, Instagram, TikTok. It was insane. We had ten million followers.

"I have no idea why, but we became some kind of American darlings. Sean reached out to our parents. Delilah's said no; they had read horror stories, wanted her to have a normal life. They were already upset by the fame, angry at her for uploading them and at me for having any part in it. My mom, though—she saw a ticket out of the trailer park for her, my dad, and my uncle."

"You support your whole family?" His mantra makes sense now.

"My uncle isn't . . . He doesn't really come around anymore. My parents, though—I bought them a house a couple of years back. And I send money back to some of the families from the trailer park. I'm trying to take care of Delilah—it was her phone, her ideas. But she's so hardheaded. You remind me so much of her."

He takes the hair tie, and out of nowhere, he stops studying the blanket and looks me straight in the eyes. His gaze is so intense, I wonder if he can see right down into my soul.

"Did you know who I was that day? At the restaurant?"

"No." I stare back, willing the truth to beam out of my eyes and into his mind.

He watches me, searching my face for something. I think he must find it, because he seems to relax even more, the last vestiges of his mask disappearing. He hands me the hair tie.

"Why are you so weird about getting your picture taken? Didn't you realize what you were signing up for?"

He laughs once, hard and brittle. "I was thirteen. All I saw was an excuse to get out of school, and a way to help my mom. I had absolutely no idea what I was giving up."

"Okay, but you had to realize eventually it was a part of the job."

He pulls the blanket back over his shoulders, the ends of his now-dry hair brushing against it. "It didn't bother me so much, at first. I mean, yeah, it was weird to go home and try to get dinner with Delilah and see a crowd of people pushed up against the diner glass, trying to get a picture of me inhaling a hamburger. She hated it. Refused to go out with me.

"Still, I could have dealt with that. Then a few years ago, the *Seville* posted an entire ten-part segment on my childhood out of nowhere. My publicist didn't even know it was going to happen before it hit." He shakes his head. "They had everything. My christening, T-ball games, my junior high prom photo with Delilah. I cannot begin to describe to you how that felt. The very last part of me that no one had any claim to, the part of me that was still *mine*, up on the internet for the world to see."

"How did they get it?" I ask. I had felt laid bare after one photo. I couldn't imagine my whole childhood on display.

"My uncle."

"Why?" I whisper, horrified.

"Gambling. He had an addiction, hid it from all of us. I mean, he asked for money. A lot of it. And I had a hard time telling him no. But I guess he got in really deep, and he finally took someone up on it when they offered him more than he could refuse." He shakes his head. "I know I'm militant about it, that it bothers people who have to work on set with me. But I need some places where I can stop *worrying* all the time. There are so few places I get to feel safe."

The words are so open and honest it takes my breath away.

I think about Elizabeth, how she's so desperate for whatever he's hiding about the girl he was in the picture with. How, if it were anyone else but me, they may have taken her up on her offer.

I feel a rush of relief, suddenly so glad I didn't take her money. It would have felt gross before, when Alec was unbearable. But now, after whatever *this* is . . . I never would have been able to forgive myself if I sold him out.

He takes the ponytail holder. "Why are *you* here?"

"Hiding from the rain," I say, debating if I should tell him Elizabeth texted me. But it would be like kicking a horse with spurs the first time it lets you ride it. Our truce is too soft and new for me to tell him right now.

"I'm serious. Why aren't you heading off to some college town to drink cheap beer and cry over frat guys?"

"Because that sounds like a nightmare to me."

He laughs. "Yeah. I get that." There's a pause. "Diya told me someone mentioned you were going to Montana."

"For someone so concerned about privacy, you sure know a lot about me."

He flashes his secret just-Alec smile. "I like to know about the people I'm working with."

"Sure," I say, rolling my eyes. I hope he'll forget about the question and move on, but he doesn't.

"So? What's in Montana?"

"Mountains. Blue skies. Lots of snow, I think."

"That's super annoying, you know. You could answer a question straight."

"Fine," I say. "There's this really fantastic program out there. I mean, they say it's fantastic, anyway. I didn't know it even existed last week. But someone applied for me, and I got in."

"What's so fantastic about the program?"

"At first, it was the combination of being around horses and *not* being around my father and Cecelia. But then, I started thinking about how it felt when the ranch closed down. I had planned on working here my whole life, and when that wasn't an option anymore, I didn't know what the hell to do. I don't want to feel like that again." I shrug. "I don't want college, but I do want security. If I go to Montana, I'll have that."

"*If* you go to Montana?"

I grimace. "It's expensive. Really expensive. That's why I took this job—it pays so freaking well. It's why I agreed to go on the dates, have my picture taken. But every time I turn around, I need more money for it."

"How much do you need?"

"I think I have enough for the housing and the tuition. That's the immediate problem solved. But there's still the small matter of plane tickets. Food. Warm clothes. I don't know where to get that kind of money."

"There's no one you can ask?"

"No."

"What about your dad? I know things are weird, but doesn't he kind of owe you a little help?"

"If it was only him, maybe I'd ask. But his money is Cecelia's money. And I'm sure she thinks I've taken enough from her."

"Maybe—"

I shake my head. "I'm not going to ask them for it. I can get the money myself."

"And if you don't?"

I swallow.

"If I don't, well. At least I know the barn is cozy—because I'm not spending another second under their roof."

"You're so damn stubborn."

It's not a criticism. He looks at me like he wants to say more, but before he can, lights flash through the slats in the barn walls.

"Was that lightning?" Alec asks.

"I think they're headlights."

We both freeze, listening to the sound of tires splashing along the dirt road. The engine cuts off, the pattering of rain on the barn roof filling the silence until we hear a car door slam.

"Nora?"

I jump when I hear a man call my name from somewhere outside.

KATIE GILBERT

Alec stands first and offers me his hand, the blanket falling from his shoulders.

"NORA," the man shouts this time.

I run to the barn door and throw it open, expecting to find Amanda's dad here with his trailers to pick up the horses despite the bout of rain. But it's not him.

"Thomas?" I say, my voice weak with surprise.

I'm not supposed to call him that, I don't think, but in my surprise, I call my father by his real name. The rain is falling in sheets around him, his headlights illuminating his silhouette. Alec appears beside me.

"We're here!" I say, shouting this time. My father looks over, his shoulders dropping when he sees me. He jogs over to us, and I don't miss the way his eyes pass over Alec. I blush, and try to think of some non-awkward way to tell him he was only half naked because our clothes were soaking wet.

"What are you doing here?" I cringe inwardly at the way the words come out accusatory instead of appreciative. But I'm so confused.

"You said you'd be back right after dinner. It got later and later, and I started to wonder if y'all didn't get away before the roads got bad." He looks at Alec. "Where's your shirt, son?" he shouts over the rain.

"I—" Alec looks to me, eyes wide. I press my lips together to keep from laughing at the pure panic on his face. This situation is as far from funny as it gets. "It got wet," he says, words almost running together. "We had to hang some things up. I'll go grab them now."

"You go ahead and do that."

Alec wastes no time. My father watches him until he disappears through the barn door.

152

Then he looks at me again.

"You all right?"

"Wet and cold. But other than that, I'm fine."

He nods, and it's quiet while we wait for Alec to come back. A few seconds later, he returns, shirt on even though it's still soaked through. I take my damp flannel, shoes, and socks when he hands them to me. We run to the waiting truck and pile in, all of us shoved together in the front row.

"Thought we were going to have to sleep in that barn," Alec says, nervously glancing at my father.

"Don't get your hopes up," he says when he starts to back out. "Roads are real bad. May still end up in there if we're not careful."

He's right. Where we got stuck is nothing compared to the rest of the road, and I realize we never would have made it out in that Mustang—not in a million years. Thankfully we got stuck where we did, so close to the barn.

We ride in silence while my father navigates the roads, jostling up and down while we dip through the giant divots, water rushing up to hit the windows on both sides.

By the time we've made it out and hit the main highway, my head hurts from gritting my teeth together so hard. The rain hasn't let up at all out here, still slamming down on the windshield, making the wipers work for all they're worth.

My father speaks, breaking the tense silence.

"Where are you staying, son?"

"Alec," I say, and my father grunts. Alec may not realize it because he's not from around here, but it's not a nice thing when an older man calls you "son" in that tone of voice. "And he's staying out at the Stewart farm."

He grunts again. Apparently, that's his preferred method of communication tonight.

It takes half an hour longer than it should, but we make it out to the Stewart farm. The rain stops by the time we get there, and so have Alec's feeble attempts at making conversation with my father.

"Tough crowd," he says when we get out, headlights trained on us while we walk over to my truck. My father tried to get me to leave it overnight, but I didn't want to have to rely on him for a ride in the morning.

"It was honestly one of the more pleasant rides I've shared with him."

He laughs, resting against the outside of my truck, relaxed as ever. I keep waiting for him to switch back to the Alec I can't stand, the one that doesn't seem to have some kind of magnetic power that makes me lean against the truck next to him, not at all eager to end the night like I should be.

"You don't know any good towing companies, do you? Hate the idea of leaving Tessa out there alone all night."

"Tessa?" I ask.

"My car."

I roll my eyes. "Of course your car has a girl name."

"What's wrong with that?"

"I'm too exhausted to educate you on the long-reaching effects of the patriarchy, Alec."

"Really? Somewhere better to be?"

"Yeah. My steaming hot shower."

His gaze flicks down to my lips as the words leave my mouth. The air around us changes, grows heavier. I force myself to breathe.

"Good," he says, voice barely a whisper. "You reek."

"Such a way with words," I say. Then I stop breathing altogether when he reaches out, his fingertips brushing ever so slightly against my neck as he guides a strand of damp hair behind my ear.

My body leans forward without my permission.

Alec's breath caresses my lips.

A horn beeps behind us once, short and sharp.

Alec's laugh is slow and deep. "Guess that's my cue. Thanks for the ride, Horse Girl. Catch you in the morning."

He waves to my father, and I get in my truck.

The whole drive home I remind myself how much I'm supposed to hate that nickname.

My father pulls into the driveway right after me. After slamming my door shut, I look back to see he's just sitting there, staring at the windshield.

Instead of going straight inside, I walk over to his truck and open his door.

"Thanks for coming out. You didn't have to do that."

"Anytime." He snaps out of whatever funk he's in and looks over at me. "You know that, right? Anything you need."

I hesitate, gripping the door, and then nod, even though I don't know that at all. Why, now, is it *anytime*? Where was that security when I was growing up, when I actually needed a dad?

"Yeah, I know," I say. I'm too tired to have this fight right now.

His lips thin while he studies my face. Whatever he finds there must spur him to go on, because he turns his truck off and flicks his key ring around his finger.

"Can I . . . give you some advice?"

"I guess," I say hesitantly.

"This thing—whatever it is going on between you and that boy—I don't know if it's a good idea."

"I . . ." My face burns while I search for words. "There's nothing going on between me and Alec," I say, even though the words feel like a lie when I say them. I mean, *technically* nothing is going on between us. But the way he looked at my lips has me thinking something could be starting. My heart thrills. Then it calms right down when I see the look on my father's face.

"He's bad news, Nora. I did a google of him—"

"Googled him. You don't *do* a google."

He waves a hand in front of his face. "He's no good. Had another girl before he even broke it off with the last one. That's not right. And I don't want to see you hurt, especially not by that boy."

"Alec," I spit, every bit of the high I'd been on earlier evaporating. Did he *really* have to choose now to start butting in? "His name is Alec."

"I know the boy's name."

"Then stop calling him 'the boy.'"

A weird vein pops up in his forehead and I watch his jaw flex while he grits his teeth.

"This thing isn't right, the two of you. You have different lives. You live in different worlds. What's he even doing out here messing around with you? Doesn't he have enough women in Hollywood?"

My face heats. "Yeah, because who would choose to stick around and spend time with me, right?"

"That's not what I meant. You're twisting my words all around."

"What *did* you mean, then?"

"How could this possibly end well, Nora? What has he been telling you, that he's gonna whisk you off to Hollywood afterward?

He won't. All that boy will do is toy with you and then break your heart when he's had his fun."

"You mean like you did with Mama?"

The silence in the truck is like the moment after glass shatters. We're both frozen in place, afraid to move and cut ourselves on a shard.

He finally speaks.

"That's not fair."

The way hurt laces his voice should soften me. It should make me choose my next words more carefully, should make me apologize. Instead, it pisses me off. What right does he have to be hurt?

"Yeah, well. Life isn't fair. Sometimes your daughter says mean things, sometimes your dad abandons you for seventeen years."

"Abandons you?" he says in a breathless voice, like he's had the wind knocked out of him.

"It's a small town. My mama shows up ten years after y'all break up with a nine-and-a-half-year-old in tow. I know you heard about it. I know everyone in this stupid, miserable town was talking about it. Gossip runs faster than the train, remember? What, you can't do math?" My hand is white on the door handle. I'm gripping it so hard it's liable to snap in half. "You don't get to give me fatherly advice now. You had plenty of time to put two and two together and be a dad. But you weren't interested."

"It's more complicated than that, Nora."

"That's the thing, *Dad*. It's really not."

I slam his door before he can respond.

Once I'm inside, I don't even bother showering. I rush into my bedroom and lock the door behind me. I put my AirPods in, ignoring a text from Elizabeth.

Pale Fire blasts into my ears so loud I think I might burst an eardrum, but I don't care. If I can't hear them knocking, then I don't have to open the door. If I can't hear my father calling my name, I don't have to respond.

And if I can't hear my soft sobs, then my heart isn't really broken over a family that doesn't want me, a family that—no matter how hard we all pretend—can't ever replace the one I lost.

CHAPTER 9

I plan on sneaking out of the house before anyone else is up, desperate to avoid both my father and Cecelia—but someone knocks on my door right as I'm putting my boots on. It's Saturday morning, so you'd think they'd be sleeping in, but I can't remember ever waking up before either of them.

There's a minute where I think it might be worth the possibility of a sprained ankle from jumping out of the window, but I can't afford even a small injury right now. I crack open the door an inch, expecting to see my father. But instead, I find Bree.

Something catches in my throat at the sight of her. I throw open my door and wrap her in a hug so tight, it might be considered attempted murder.

"Okay, Ro. I missed you, too, but can you not break my ribs?"

I loosen my hold.

"Awesome. Now they'll just be lightly bruised."

"You're home," I say, trying to keep my voice down. But I'm so excited to see her it's difficult. "When did you get back? What was the best part? How did you get in the house?"

"Which one of those do you want me to answer first?" she asks, laughing. Bree comes in and plops down on my bed. The Bantu knots she wore while she was in Italy are gone, and her hair rests around her face like a lightly curled halo.

"I'm limited on time, so let's start with how you got in."

"Cecelia was out in the garden, told me you were up here."

Jumping out of the window wouldn't have worked after all.

I sit on the bed next to her and start lacing up my boots. If I had any way to get ahold of Alec, I'd call and cancel right this second. But I really do need the money, and while he won't be taking on a second job as a jockey anytime soon, he's almost ready to ride on camera. I have to go.

"As for when I got back: yesterday. I'm all kinds of messed up—fell asleep at four p.m., woke up at four a.m. Couldn't wait another second to see my favorite friend." She pokes my leg with her foot. "Don't tell Char, but I brought you something home from Italy. A birthday gift."

I hold out my hands. "This is totally a valid reason to show up this early on a Saturday. Let me see it."

"You can't have it now," she says, laughing. "Tomorrow, it's yours."

"You're going to make me wait until my actual birthday?" I whine.

"Totally waiting until your birthday, and my mind is made up, so don't waste your energy begging. Where do you have to be this early on a Saturday, by the way?" She sits up and pinches my arm. "Do you and Char have plans? If you think y'all are going to the farmers' market to see the hottie who makes the boiled peanuts without me, you're wrong."

"Ow," I say, laughing and rubbing my arm. "No, we're not going to the farmers' market. And you're the only one who thinks he's cute. Char thinks he's boring, and mullets don't really do it for me."

"Me either," she says, shrugging. "But I can see the potential underneath the mullet, Ro. You have to visualize him with a man bun or undercut."

"Okay, well, I'm not going to see Mullet Man Bun. I have riding lessons this morning."

"With *Alexander*?" she says in this weird falsetto, fluttering her eyes. "Girl, I've seen more of you online in the past few days than I have in all the years I've known you. What's going on? Because last time we talked, you told me this was fake. But it doesn't look fake online."

I sigh, wishing I had pushed harder for her to tell me about Italy. I really, *really* don't want to talk about this. It's weird and confusing and made all the worse by the fact that last night, I'm pretty sure I *wanted* Alec to lean over a few more inches and kiss me, whether my dad was watching or not. This morning, with a clear head and no ridiculously handsome guy in a wet shirt in front of me, I'm glad he didn't. Our situation is complicated enough.

"It's a couple of dates to make some fast money. He needs a few pictures with a plain, boring all-American girl, and I need the cash. It's as simple as that."

"So, we still hate him?"

"Yeah," I say, biting the inside of my lip. "We still hate him."

"I find it hard to believe he's as bad as you say," Bree says, slipping on a pair of earrings she finds on my bedside table. "He's so nice in every interview."

"Well," I say, grabbing her hand and pulling her off the bed. "Why don't you come see for yourself?"

Bree helps me get Chestnut and Ethel fed and saddled.

The more I think about seeing Alec today, the more nervous I am. Did *I* imagine the way he leaned in? Did *he* fall asleep thinking of what would have happened with five more seconds and the absence of space between us?

Tires crunch on the gravel outside of the stable. Alec's car wasn't on the road when we drove in, though I could still see where he had gotten stuck. I don't know how he got it towed away so quickly, but when you have more money than you know what to do with, I guess things sort of happen for you.

"Do you think that's him?" Bree asks, hands stalling on the horse brush. Chestnut swings his head to look at her and huffs.

She drops the brush altogether and pulls lip gloss from her front pocket.

"Is there a mirror in here?"

"In the stables?" I ask, laughing. "No. What's up with you?"

She looks at me, eyebrows raised. "The hottest movie star in America is currently getting out of his vehicle and walking my way." A car door slams, punctuating her point. "Do you know how many times I watched *Love and Love Lost* with my mom?" She shrugs. "Anyway—why do you care? You said this was all fake. Right?" She looks at me with a raised eyebrow.

"Right," I say, not sure why my stomach is in knots. "If you're into pretentious jerks, have at it."

"Can't keep me off your mind, can you, Horse Girl?" Alec asks from the entrance to the stables.

"Not everything is about you," I say.

"True. But when the word *pretentious* or *jerk* comes from your general vicinity, it's safe to assume I'm on your mind."

"You're never on my mind," I say as he stops in front of me.

He smirks and takes a step closer. "Really?"

I swallow, my mouth suddenly dry as hay.

"Really," I say. He smirks and my face warms.

"Good. Then we're on the same page."

"The same paragraph."

"Fantastic." His eyes dart down to my lips.

"Awesome," I say, staring at the golden spot in his green eyes.

Bree clears her throat from the stall beside us.

"Um, hi," she says. I jump, and Alec takes a step back.

Right. Bree's here.

"Alec," I say, rubbing my hands on the front of my jeans. "This is Bree. One of my best friends. Be nice to her."

Alec rolls his eyes. "Hey, Bree. Nice to meet you." He runs a hand through his hair. "I'm Alexander."

To her credit, she doesn't react anything like Amanda did. But she's still got this look on her face that makes it clear she's as enamored with Alec as everyone else is.

"Nice to meet you," she says in a soft voice, her eyes roaming all over his face, taking everything in.

"You ride horses, too?" he asks, kindly ignoring how starstruck she is.

"I think it's impossible to be friends with Nora and not end up on a horse eventually."

They both laugh, and I realize right then how good they'd look together. Bree is beauty personified. Something roils inside of me, but I can't put a name to what I'm feeling. All I know is it sucks.

I glance at Alec, wondering if he's thinking the same thing—noticing how different she is from me; soft and graceful instead of hard and rough around the edges. But it's me he's looking at.

"True. Kind of like . . . watching her love them so much makes you love them a little, too."

It's my turn to say something. That's evident by the way both Bree and Alec are staring at me now. But I can't find any words, because what Alec said to me was wholly and completely *nice*. No underlying quip, no hidden sharp jab.

"You okay, Horse Girl?"

That knocks me out of my stupor.

"I'm waiting for the backhanded part of the compliment."

He smirks and holds up his wrist. "Truce, remember? I mean, I get to call you Horse Girl because you called me jerk *and* pretentious. But a deal is a deal. Right?"

I hesitate for a breath. "Right." I can feel Bree's eyes on my face, but I can't look at her right now. "Let's get Ethel out to the paddock."

"Bring Chestnut, too," Alec says. "Diya's waiting outside with Amanda's dad. She wanted some time with the horses, and I couldn't remember how to get out here without GPS, so Mr. Stewart offered us a ride."

"Fine."

We finish saddling both horses and walk them out, Bree ahead of us with Chestnut. Alec's leading Ethel, and I decide to walk right beside him in case he needs help with her.

"So," he says after a few moments of silence. "You thought we needed a chaperone?"

"What?" I ask, confused.

"Bree." He nods her way. "Afraid to be alone with me after last night?"

"What's that supposed to mean?"

"You totally almost kissed me."

I jerk to a stop. Alec does, too, Ethel sniffing at the pocket of his jeans.

"I did *not*," I hiss. "If anything, *you're* the one who almost kissed *me*."

He shrugs. "Maybe. Maybe not. But I didn't see you moving to stop me."

"That . . . You . . ." I sputter, too shocked to finish a thought.

Alec smirks, and I want to knock it right off his face. "Come on, Ethel," he says, turning and leaving me red in the face and fuming behind him.

I make myself take three deep breaths before I decide to give Alec a wide berth. There's no way I'm following him into the enclosed field now, though I do watch warily as he closes the gate behind them. He's talking to Ethel, but I'm too far away to hear what he's saying.

Diya and Bree are doting on Chestnut just outside of the paddock fence.

"Nora," Diya calls, all bright skies and sunny disposition. "Can Chestnut have a peppermint?"

"Sure," I say, walking over. "They're his favorite."

"Nice," she says, grinning up at us and unwrapping the candy. Chestnut eats it out of her hand and she giggles at the feel of his lips on her palm. "Weird."

"It takes some getting used to," I say. Diya's calmness is catching.

"Do you have another?" Bree asks, looking at Diya the same way she studied Alec. She's good at keeping her cool—I don't think anyone other than her best friend would be able to tell she's starstruck.

"I brought half a dozen," Diya says, looking at her guiltily. "I want to make sure he remembers me when we're done." She pulls another from her pocket and hands it to Bree.

She turns and looks up at me, her face open and kind. "I've been meaning to come and see you, Nora. I hate that we haven't been able to spend more time together."

Amanda had been the one to match Diya with a horse. She had talked about it for hours afterward. I hadn't minded missing it—she was just another celebrity I didn't know, after all. But there's something about her, something in the way she's looking at me like we're just two friends catching up, and not someone more famous than Lady Gaga talking to a barista.

"Yeah, I'm sorry I've missed seeing you on set," I say.

"We'll have to remedy that. Alec is always hogging you," she says. I blush, glancing toward him. He's already in the saddle, gently leading Ethel around the paddock. "You girls up to anything fun tonight?" Diya asks.

I snort, and Chestnut turns to nuzzle my forehead, his breath minty and fresh. "Kind of hard to have big plans in a small town."

"Actually," Bree says, "I was going to beg Nora to come with me to Pearson tonight."

"Pearson?" Diya asks with a furrowed brow.

I groan. "It's the next town over," I tell Diya. Then I look at Bree. "You're not serious, right?"

"Let me remind you that I've been gone, sequestered away with my parents for weeks. I need some kind of interaction with people who don't go to bed at ten-thirty every night."

"You've been in Italy, not a retirement home."

"Still." She shrugs. "Italy with my *parents*." She folds her hands like she's saying a prayer. "Please, Ro. I already messaged Charlotte about it. She's ditching her sister for the weekend and driving down."

"I thought we were finally done with that town once we graduated," I whine.

"What's going on?" Diya asks, amused confusion on her face.

I sigh. "Bree and Charlotte used to drag me out to these stupid parties in Pearson every Saturday for the entirety of our high school career." I gently nudge Chestnut's nose away from my face so I can see Diya clearly. "It's a bunch of people sitting in a barn, drinking bad beer. It's going to be miserable."

Bree squeals. "That's totally a yes."

"It wasn't a yes," I say, even though we both know I'm going to go with her.

"Well, it wasn't a *no*. That's basically a yes. You're legally bound to come now. It's my last wish before I leave for college." She turns to Diya, working on her now that she knew she had me locked in. "You should totally join. It's way more fun than Nora's making it sound."

Diya laughs. "Usually I'd jump at the chance to get off set, but I have a standing Saturday FaceTime date that I can't miss. But I know someone who would love to join you. Right, Alec?"

Chestnut nickers and reaches his nose over the paddock fence to gently touch Ethel as she and Alec finish a rotation and stop beside us.

"What am I joining?" Alec asks, watching Ethel's ears intently. He really is learning.

"Nora and Bree are going to a party tonight."

"It's not really a party," I say, suddenly desperate for him to come with us and *not* come with us at the same time.

"Will there be people there?" Alec asks.

"Yeah," I say. "That's usually what a party entails."

"People with cell phones that can take pictures of us together?"

"I don't know anyone with a nineties flip phone, so, yeah."

"Great." He smiles. "Sounds like the perfect place for our second date."

"Fine," I say. I don't want to go, but this means I'm one date closer to Montana—one date closer to having freedom *and* security. "Get back out there. If we're going to a party, we don't have time to waste."

Diya swings into Chestnut's saddle with ease and steers him into the paddock. Alec takes Ethel around the enclosure again, staying at a walk for now. I watch intently, looking for any signs of hesitation or tension.

Bree's shoulder brushes mine as we lean against the railing. I keep trying to remind myself to watch Diya, too, but my eyes always wander back to Ethel.

Alec's back is straight while he rides, but not tense. His broad shoulders are squared, and they don't hunch forward the way they did on his first few rides, even when Ethel begins to trot.

He's not a professional. Nowhere near it. But he'll be fine on Monday.

Bree gently elbows me.

"Hm," I say, finally looking away when she nudges me again, this time with her hip.

"You know what you're doing, Ro?" she asks.

"Of course. I've taught hundreds of people how to ride. You included."

She shakes her head. "You know that's not what I mean."

"What do you mean, then?"

"You want me to come out and say it?" Bree looks at me with raised eyebrows. When I don't respond, she goes on. "This doesn't look fake," she says, nodding her head toward Alec.

I look down, desperately interested in a spot that needs to be buffed out of my boot.

"It *is* fake."

Bree laughs. "You haven't blinked since he sat down on that horse. Took me saying your name three times before you even acknowledged I was here beside you."

"I'm doing my job," I say, heat rushing to my cheeks. "He's worth a trillion bucks. No way I'm letting him get hurt while I'm in charge."

There's a beat of silence.

"I'm doing my job," I say again.

Bree shrugs. "Okay, Ro. If you say so."

"I do," I tell her, looking back out to find Alec's managed to work himself up to a canter.

"Now, describe every single Italian dish you ate—in detail."

My entire truck smells like Alec.

It didn't take much convincing to get him to ride with me. His car is still in a local detailing shop, getting scrubbed clean, so really, there was no other option unless he wanted to hitchhike.

He apparently learned his lesson after our last date. A total one-eighty from his slacks and button up, he's now in ripped jeans (not the kind that get torn after a billion wears because your mom can't afford new ones, but the kind that look like someone distressed each section intentionally), a Manchester United T-shirt, and a pair of

Vans. You'd think dressing down would make him less attractive, but it doesn't. He's wearing these brown woven leather bracelets that keep pulling my attention to his arms. The way his veins pop and his muscles peek out from under his sleeves has me gripping the steering wheel so tight my knuckles are white.

Thankfully, he's got the window down and is watching the pine trees and peanut fields pass by, so I don't think he notices me glancing over every twenty-three seconds.

We turn off of the highway and onto a dirt road. Madison's barn, and the three dozen cars parked haphazardly around it, come into view after a few minutes.

"You seriously have your parties in a barn here?"

When the engine cuts off, the sound of subpar guitar playing fills the air. The band is up and going, which is a good sign. We've timed it perfectly.

"It's more of a *spot* than a barn. Madison's parents converted their farm into one of those specialty yoga places. Now people drive from all over to have goats bleat around them while they're in downward dog. Then they drink overpriced matcha before heading back to the city. Nights and weekends, it reverts back to just us locals. And the goats."

"This town is so weird," he says, opening his door.

"Tell me about it." We get out of the truck and stand awkwardly at the hood, staring at the barn. "Everyone's gonna be wasted on the Coors Lights they stole from their parents' garage fridge. They'll have no inhibitions to keep them from taking a picture and posting it online."

"Fine," he sighs. "But one of these days, I'm taking you somewhere I have to wear a tie, and you have to wear something that couldn't also double as farmhand attire."

He doesn't give me time to process what he's said—the *one day* he drops so casually, implying that he's thought about the kind of dates we'd go on if they weren't for show. Alec grabs my hand, entwining his fingers with mine. When I glance down at our hands and back up at him, he raises his eyebrows and says, "For the pictures."

Madison's brother's band is in a corner of the renovated barn. They're playing some classic-rock throwback covers. The vibe is hard to take seriously with the overflowing wicker baskets of miniature stuffed goats surrounding them.

No one notices us at first. There's almost fifty people in here (none of which are Charlotte or Bree) and they're all in various stages of drunk or high. I think maybe we'll have to do something more than walk in through the doors to make an impression, but then Alec squeezes my hand and leans down to whisper something in my ear.

"They always think they're being so sneaky." I shiver at the feel of his breath on the shell of my ear. "But I always notice."

I glance up, goosebumps still spreading from my neck down my arms, and see a group of girls piled on a sofa, a card game, and empty White Claws on the table in front of them. Every single one of them has a phone pointed our way. I vaguely recognize them all but I don't *know* any of them. When I lock eyes with the brunette that I'm pretty sure always sat at the table next to Charlotte, Bree, and I at lunch, she looks away and pretends to take a selfie instead.

Alec lets go of my hand and slides his arm around my lower back, guiding me over to the table of various drinks. He grabs a red Solo cup and pours a healthy measure of cheap vodka, then cracks open a Diet Coke and dumps half of it in.

"Diet?"

"Still filming," he explains. "Have that shirtless scene coming up soon. Don't worry, I'm sure you can find an excuse to come watch."

"I've already seen you shirtless." I shrug. "It's not worth the walk over from the stables." His laugh is booming.

"Want some?" He offers me his cup, like he wouldn't mind me drinking right out of it.

I shake my head. "I'm your ride, remember?"

"Right, no Uber. Maybe we could call a horse and buggy to get us back home."

"The surcharges on those are outrageous."

"Should I not be drinking?" he asks. "If you aren't, I mean?"

"No, go for it." I fill a cup with RC Cola.

"Good. Elizabeth put out another TikTok today, so. I could use it."

"A bad one?" Maybe she's giving up, moving onto something else. Her texts come less and less often lately.

He shrugs and takes a long drink. "She's rehashing the whole thing over again, reminding people why they're supposed to hate me. I'm a cheater, I forgot what it's like to be a real person, blah blah blah. She's grasping at straws, and I think some people are starting to see that." He looks down at me, green eyes bright and soft. "Thanks to you."

"Nora," someone suddenly says, threading her arm through mine. It's Madison's older sister, Janna. We never talked, not a single time, until everything came out about who my father was.

She called my mom a whore at lunch one day. Not to my face, but close enough that she knew I'd hear it. Before I could do anything, Charlotte had *accidentally* spilled her green juice all over Janna's top.

"So good to see you out and about!" She looks over at Alec. "This one doesn't really like to show her face. Thinks everyone's always talking about her. Don't worry, Nora. Your drama is old news." Her laugh is high, and it turns my stomach. Alec looks at me in confusion, raising his eyebrows.

"Who's your friend?" Janna asks, looking over at Alec, pretending she doesn't recognize him.

It's not until this very moment that I understand fully why Alec acts the way he does. The angry outburst at the restaurant, how he never seems to fully open up, his immediate distrust of everyone. People would do anything to get close to him.

It must be such a lonely way to live.

"This is my friend Alexander," I say, refusing to give her his nickname. Hearing her say it in her syrupy-sweet voice might make me vomit.

"Alexander," she says, finally letting go of my arm. She reaches out and shakes his hand.

"Nice to meet you," Alec says, smile tight.

"Same." She smiles like a beauty queen, her hand lingering in his.

Pinpricks rush down the back of my neck and shoulders. I bite the inside of my lip.

Alec is not your boyfriend. You don't get to care that she's touching him.

I try to talk myself down.

It's not working very well.

"Listen, Alexander. I don't know what your plans are tonight but my friends and I have an empty seat." She gestures over her shoulder with her free hand, still holding onto his with her other. I don't miss the way she says "seat" instead of "seats," clearly not inviting me. "We're playing Cards Against Humanity and we've got room for one more."

I wonder if anyone has a spare green juice lying around. Though my RC Cola might stain the pretty little dress she's wearing.

Alec drops her hand and slides it back around me in one smooth gesture, hooking around my waist. He pulls me in and I watch Janna track our every movement, taking in how close we stand now.

"I think my girlfriend and I will opt out. We have plans. But thank you so much for your generous offer." She looks like she's going to say something else, one last-ditch effort at getting him to join her for the night. But Alec, apparently wanting to really drive the point home, turns and looks at me. He's such a damn good actor, I almost believe the adoration in his eyes. He raises his eyebrows infinitesimally, giving me a chance to object. I hold his gaze.

He leans down and brushes his lips against the corner of mine, brief and gentle.

It's not a kiss. Not really. But it sends chills down my body all the same.

Janna finally gets the hint and, with a weak wave, turns and leaves us in peace. I expect Alec to disengage, to take a step away and put as much distance between us as he can while still keeping up the show.

Instead, he slowly drags his hand from the base of my back to my shoulders, and drapes his arm around me, guiding me back over to the refreshment table.

"I need a refill after that," he says, pouring another vodka and Diet Coke.

Before he can take a drink, someone speaks.

"Are you going to throw that drink on Janna, or do I need to start pouring?"

"Finally," I sigh. "Thought you'd never get here."

Charlotte smiles from across the card table full of drinks. Bree is behind her, talking with a group of girls.

"You look gorgeous," Charlotte says. Before I can reply, her eyes flit to Alec's face.

He's taking a sip, watching her over the rim of the cup. I wait for that moment, the one where her eyes glaze over and her face flushes and she goes all gooey in her bones—but that is *not* what's happening. Not in the slightest.

Staring daggers at him, she spits, "Did you tell Janna to screw off, or are you completely devoid of balls?"

Alec chokes on his drink.

"Well?" she asks when he finishes his coughing fit.

"I wouldn't say I told her to screw off, but I don't think she'll bother us again tonight." He glances over at me. I raise my hands, letting him know he's on his own.

Charlotte stares him down. "I'm not a fan of this." She gestures between us. "Don't hurt my friend."

Alec, to his credit, doesn't cower. He looks right back and says, "Wasn't planning on it."

She nods once. "Good. I'm Charlotte."

"Alec," he says. I don't miss that she's the only one he's introduced himself as Alec to.

"All right, Alec." She hands him her empty Solo cup from the other side of the table. "Let's see how weak your vodka soda is."

U

"You can't see the stars in LA."

Alec has been watching the sky for the past twenty minutes. Somehow, in between the endless stream of people hitting on Alexander, fawning over Alexander, taking pictures of Alexander, pretending to talk to me to get to Alexander, we ended up outside in the bed of my truck. Alec had no problem taking cushions from the lawn furniture and carrying them over so we didn't have to lay directly on the metal truck bed.

"I don't think they have different stars in LA." I pause. "Well, I mean they do have different *stars* in LA. But I think the ones in the sky are the same."

He laughs. That's one thing I've learned about Alec tonight; he loves to laugh when he's been drinking. Drunk Alec finds me hilarious. Even though I'm sober, his laugh makes me feel warm all the way through, just like whiskey.

"It's too bright there to see them," he says, sliding a hand beneath his head. "So many lights all the time. No matter what. That's part of the view you pay for. Even at night everything is lit up. It's vibrant, fun. But sometimes, I think about how Delilah and I used to climb the tree next to her trailer and lay on the roof for hours in the dark. We were wearing the same clothes we'd worn the summer before, our parents were so poor. But I miss it."

He turns away from the sky and looks at me, his face mere inches from mine. "Is that stupid? Missing it, I mean?"

"No." My voice is a whisper. "That's not stupid at all." We're quiet for a while before I decide it's okay to give him another little piece of me, out here in the quiet night, the moon watching us. "I'm in that big house now, with my father. Have my own room and everything. Mama and I shared one the entire time we lived at Shep Farm. But I miss it all the same. I'd give anything to be fighting over counter space in the bathroom again."

The chatter from the barn comes over in soft waves, bits and pieces of conversation floating on the wind. Alec moves beside me, slipping the hair tie off his wrist and holding it up.

"What was the best thing about her?" Alec asks.

The question makes my heart skip. No one asks about my mama. They're so afraid of my grief they avoid even the barest mention of her. Everyone has erased her so thoroughly I feel like I'm crazy sometimes, like I'm the only one who even remembers she was real.

"She was so happy," I say in a whisper. The tears are already at the corners of my eyes as I think about how she already had permanent smile lines, even though she was far too young for them. "Mama never fought a laugh. They bubbled up like she might burst if she didn't let a dozen loose every hour. God, she was happy." I swallow against a lump in my throat. "I'm so scared I'll forget what it sounded like."

He doesn't say anything. His hand brushes gently against mine, a soft comfort. Alec doesn't try to lessen my grief so it's more comfortable for him. He doesn't lie to me and tell me I'll never forget and the memories won't fade. He sits here beside me in my sadness.

When I've had my fill, I take the hair tie from his hand.

"Why don't you go on TikTok or *Good Morning America* or something and tell the world Elizabeth's wrong? Why this whole elaborate charade instead of defending yourself?"

"Diya asked me the same thing yesterday. She doesn't like what we're doing, you and I. Like Charlotte."

You and I.

"Really? I thought Diya liked me. She's always so nice."

"Oh, Diya *loves* you. Won't shut up about you. Diya doesn't love our . . . agreement, though. She thinks it's a recipe for disaster. She was even more upset when I told her it was Sean's idea. She loathes Sean."

"Your agent?" I ask.

"Yeah. But she doesn't get it. Her fame has always been so easy and secure, and her parents are rich as hell. Sean has to fight for my career, tooth and nail. If this all disappeared for her tomorrow, she'd be fine. Her family would be fine." He takes a deep breath of the night air, thick with humidity and secrets.

"There *are* things he's asked me to do that make my skin crawl." He pauses again, and I wonder how much of his candor is alcohol induced. "When he told me to take you out, he didn't mean this way—with you knowing it was fake. He didn't care if you were aware of being used or if you got anything out of it. He saw you as a solution to a problem. He'd sacrifice anything, or anyone, for me. That's a good thing, having someone like that in your corner. Sometimes, it's just hard to think about just how far he'd be willing to go for me."

"Apart from Diya, you're kind of surrounded by crappy people."

He sighs. "Yeah. I kind of am. And that's why I can't go on Tik-Tok or Drew Barrymore's show or whatever and tell everyone who I was with. I can't reveal that I've never cheated on anyone in my life, that it goes against the core of who I am. And I sure as hell can't tell everyone that it wasn't some A-list celebrity in that photo. Because defending myself would hurt one of the only non-crappy people I have left." He looks up for what feels like ages. I make myself wait quietly, resisting the urge to fill his silence.

"Delilah's mom called me a few weeks ago." My breath catches when he says her name. His childhood best friend, the girl he'd gone to prom with. The one person he'd do anything for. "Told me she needed me. So I went. Even though Elizabeth's parents' divorce had hit the news. Even though they were everywhere all of a sudden, riding her coattails. Eliza was mortified. Begged me to stay, to help her figure out how to deal with all of it. Strategize how to get ahead of it. But Delilah needed me. And I just couldn't risk explaining that to Elizabeth."

His voice is so earnest. I get why he's reluctant, I really do. But if he talked to Elizabeth the way he's talking to me now, there's no way she wouldn't understand.

"I mean, it makes sense," he says. "Her parents have zero regard for her image. They're both making idiots of themselves online, trying to stay relevant. Dating the TikTok celebrity of the month so they can have a further reach. Of course she'd think I was doing the same. Of course her first thought would be that I was looking for the next stepping stone into more fame."

My voice shakes when I finally speak. I hope Alec is too drunk to notice. "Is Delilah . . ." I trip over her name. "Is she okay?"

He sobers for a brief moment, all traces of the Alec who has been so quick to laugh tonight are gone. "No. She's not."

I don't press. I give him the same grace he gave me—a quiet, soft space to feel whatever it is he's feeling.

Eventually, he continues. "She has cancer. Thyroid." He takes a breath, steadying himself. "Right before she found out, I was ready to walk. Sean was ramping up his intensity daily, pressuring me to do more and be more and make more. It wasn't fun. It hadn't been for a long time. But Delilah's mom called me. Made me fly out. Delilah took me to the roof of the house they live in now." He doesn't say it, but I know it's a house he bought them. "She told me. Said things were really bad. I promised her that I'd pay for everything. Make sure her parents didn't even have to work so someone was always there. Treatments are expensive and, depending on how aggressive the cancer is, it may be a long course. I can't stop now. Not when I could use the money or the connections. Not when it could mean losing her."

It's painful—so very painful how wrong I've been about him. He's looking up, green eyes bright with unshed tears, and I'm studying his face, wondering when exactly I stopped hating him.

Eventually, I *have* to ask.

"If you just told Elizabeth, would that really . . . be so bad? You don't have to tell the world, or make some big announcement. But wouldn't telling her get rid of the issue?" With the added benefit of giving Elizabeth some closure.

"No," Alec says, deep finality in the word. "Maybe I could trust her. Maybe she wouldn't tell anyone. But I'm not risking Delilah's peace and comfort on a maybe."

"But—"

"No," he says again.

I swallow the rest of my words down.

He waits a beat. "It's not like this with Elizabeth," he says, gesturing between us. "She . . . doesn't want me to be *Alec*. She wants *Alexander* all the time; always *on*, ready to perform. Even for her."

He stops staring at the sky and turns to face me, our noses inches apart. Alec's breath tickles my lips when he speaks.

"I'm so tired of performing. Of pretending."

He's so close that I wouldn't have to move more than an inch to feel his lips on mine—but this time, it wouldn't be a chaste almost-kiss designed to get rid of Janna. It would be real. The lines between us might be blurring, but this one is crystal clear. A kiss in the quiet of my truck bed, no one watching, would mean neither of us could pretend anymore.

"Stop performing, then," I say, my voice a whisper.

"Easier said than done." Alec sighs, turning back to the moon, leaving the lines between us firm and clear. "Out here, it doesn't seem impossible to just be Alec forever. But the second I'm surrounded by those people again, people like Elizabeth, it's an inevitability." He laughs, but there's no humor in it. "I have this movie premiere next week. Right back in the lion's den."

"You can't skip it?" I ask, my stomach tensing at the thought that he'll be gone, even for a day. For the first time, I wonder what my life will be like when Alec's out of it forever—gone for good, not just for a day.

"One of my favorite directors sent an invite. Means they're starting to accept me again. I can't risk not going, so I'm leaving after filming wraps on Thursday and I'll be back Saturday morning for some scheduled scenes with Diya." He clears his throat and fumbles with the collar of his shirt. "Do you . . . do you want to come with me?"

I look at him, stunned into silence.

"I'd take care of everything. The dress, the flight, the food."

"You want me to come with you. To a premiere. In LA."

He smiles. Drunk, happy Alec is back.

"I was going to bring my mom; she loves the director."

"I'm not taking your mom's invite."

What if he sobers up and regrets asking me?

"I can get as many tickets as I want. Super famous, remember? My mom will still be there."

I shoot up to a sitting position. "I'm meeting your *mother*?"

He sits up next to me, laughing. "Don't worry, she'll love you."

"I don't care if—I'm not worried about your mom liking me."

"Sure." He grabs my phone from the cushion we've been laying on. "I'll text myself from your phone. That way I'll have your number and I can send over the details." His fingers are lightning fast for someone so drunk. When he hands my phone back, there's a new message thread with an unsaved number, a singular horse emoji in the chat.

I want to find a reason to refuse, but I can't. Despite myself, the idea is growing on me second by second. Time away from my father and Cecelia? A flight? New clothes? It almost sounds . . . fun.

"Fine," I say, jumping off the truck bed. "But it's your problem if I piss off someone important."

"I hope you do." He gets out of the truck bed much less gracefully than I did, the vodka making it hard for him to walk straight as we take the cushions back to the lawn furniture.

He slams the tailgate shut once we're back at the truck and it makes a crunching noise.

"Hey, careful with my baby."

"Careful? What's your baby worth? Fifty bucks?"

"This priceless antique is about to carry you home safely, so be nice."

He gets in the truck with overstated care, making a show of it.

Bree left with a group of girls headed to the Waffle House an hour ago, and last I saw, Charlotte was super busy with her ex on the fainting couch in the corner of the barn, so we leave without saying goodbye.

Alec is asleep in the seat next to me before we're on paved roads again.

I think and think and think while I drive.

Things aren't great at home, but at least I have an escape. At least the entire world isn't watching when my father, Cecelia, and I sit down to an awkward supper and avoid the subject of my mama. Elizabeth doesn't have that luxury. How much pain would it ease for her to know the truth?

And for Alec to be cast as the villain in all of this—it's not right. Sure, the tide is starting to turn, people are slowly coming over to Alec's side. But how much faster would this all blow over if Elizabeth just called off her attacks?

"Rise and shine," I say once we're back at the Stewart farm.

Alec stirs. It doesn't take me long to realize he's not going to make it to his trailer on his own. I sigh and get out of the truck. When I open his door, he folds and I barely manage to steady him before he face-plants.

"Such a gentlewoman."

"Come on. I'll walk you to your trailer."

"I'm not that drunk."

"Sure you're not."

Security waves us through. It's not Sebastian—he tripped over a giant wire earlier today, and last I heard was getting a cast for a broken ankle.

"Where are your keys?" I ask once we're at his trailer. He ignores me and closes one eye while punching a code into the electronic lock on his door. It doesn't work. He tries again, but it still doesn't unlock.

He leans against the door and steps on the backs of his shoes, working to get his feet out of them. When the last one comes off, he loses his balance. I catch him by the arm, and he pulls me toward him, righting himself by balancing his hands on my shoulders.

"Okay. Maybe I'm drunk."

"You hide it well."

When I look up, Alec's face is close.

"It's irritating how beautiful you are. Has anyone ever told you that?"

My breath catches.

"They usually don't mention the irritating bit."

"Really?" he whispers. "I find that to be the most intriguing part."

His eyes roam over my face. His hand has left my shoulder and his thumb is now gently tracing the outline of my jaw. I shiver. He leans forward an inch. I rest my palm on his chest.

"Alec."

A small noise escapes him. "I loathe the way you say my name." His fingers are trailing softly along my ear. He leans forward and his breath follows the same path when he whispers, "Say it again."

Another shiver runs through me.

"Alec." It's involuntary. His lips brush against my ear. He pulls back, eyes locked on mine.

I want desperately for him to lean forward, to graze his mouth against mine, to make me whisper his name as we break for air.

He leans forward.

I press gently against his chest.

"Not like this," I whisper, my voice thick with desire and regret.

He looks down at my lips once more before he nods and takes a step backward.

Then he trips over his shoe and falls directly onto the door.

The sound is so loud I expect the entire set to wake up. Instead, one light turns on in the trailer behind him.

"What the hell?" Alec says. "Who's inside my trailer?"

The doorknob turns, and Alec gently guides me safely behind him. I peek over his shoulder and watch as Diya opens the door, gorgeous even at this time of night.

"Alec?" she says, clearly confused.

"Didi. Well, that explains why the code didn't work."

She smiles at me over his shoulder. "Hello, Nora. Vodka?"

"How'd you know?"

"He only calls me Didi when he's drunk."

"If the two of you are done talking about me like I'm not here," Alec says, leaning down to pick up his shoes, "I'll be going." He almost topples in through Diya's door when he bends over.

"You're not going anywhere," she says. "I don't think you'd make the walk next door. Come in, you'll sleep on my couch." She looks up at me smiling. "Thanks, Nora. I'll take it from here."

"Night, Horse Girl."

"Alexander," Diya chides. "Sorry. I'm sure he'll apologize tomorrow. If he remembers any of this." She says the last part in a stage whisper. I tell her good night and walk back to my truck.

The whole drive home, I hope she's wrong.

I hope he remembers leaning in to kiss me.

I hope he remembers the way my voice broke around his name.

Most of all, I hope—when he's sober and clear eyed and wholly himself—he tries again.

CHAPTER 10

I wake up to several text messages.

One is from Elizabeth's unsaved number.

> Updates?

I haven't eaten breakfast yet, but seeing our message thread nauseates me.

I hate how badly I feel for her. But after last night, it's clear it's not my responsibility to ease her pain. That's between her and Alec.

I thank my lucky stars that she didn't happen to text last night when Alec had my phone. How the hell would I have explained that? Soon. I'll explain it all to him soon.

Another unsaved number is next.

Under a horse emoji is a new message.

> Diya says I need to say thanks, and I'm sorry.
> So. There. I've said them both.

He doesn't remember. Another wave of nausea.

> Didn't think you'd be out of bed yet. Figured you'd be
> sleeping it off.

I hit Send before I can talk myself out of it.

Even though his text was sent over an hour ago, he responds immediately.

> Diya woke me before dawn as retaliation for showing up on her doorstep late last night.

> Joke's on her. This headache would have woken me sooner or later anyway.

Now I'm even happier I didn't join him in drinking last night. Who wants a hangover on their birthday?

> Send me your email address. I'll book your plane ticket.

Fancy.

I don't respond right away, adjusting to the fact that I'm going to be on a flight to LA in a few days. He must worry at my delayed response, because he messages me again.

> As long as we're still on, I mean?

> We're still on.

> Good. I already told Sean he's taking my mom. He's a little too excited tbh.

> Don't want to disappoint Sean. I'm still down.

> Good.

The last unread messages are from Charlotte and Bree, wishing me a happy birthday.

I should be happy. I'm eighteen today.

Their text messages are blurry now, too hard to read through the lining of tears.

"So, I'll definitely get to try champagne?"

"Totally," Mama said, her long blonde hair tied back in an intricate braid. Little strands still flew free from the tight plaits, the wind rushing in through the car window pulling them free.

"Even though I'll only be eighteen?"

"My mom gave me my first glass of champagne at sixteen. I'm much more responsible than her, though, so we'll wait until eighteen." She looked over at me and smiled, the setting sun lighting her face. "You'll hate it, though."

"No way," I protested.

"Yes way. You should be more excited about the lottery tickets. We'll buy a hundred and scratch them all off at midnight. Then we'll take the winnings and buy a giant mansion and have three dozen stables and fill them all with our own horses."

I smiled. "Just one would be nice. A horse all our own."

She winked at me, turning to look back at the road ahead of us. "Yeah. Just one would be nice, too."

I wipe the tears from my face and press a kiss against my fingers. When I stand, I touch them against the picture on my bedside table.

The smell of actual bacon meets me outside of the kitchen.

"Hey, kiddo," my father says, taking off his reading glasses and putting down the latest James Patterson when I come into the dining room. "Happy birthday."

I'm a little surprised he remembers.

"Thanks," I say, determined not to start a fight.

"Good morning to the world's newest eighteen-year-old," Cecelia says, putting a plate of whole-wheat pancakes and a giant pile of bacon in front of me. "Thought you might enjoy a celebratory breakfast."

"I'm starving. Thanks."

"Of course," she says, sitting next to my father across the table from me. I don't particularly want to eat with them both staring at me like I'm an animal in the zoo, but the bacon smells too good to resist, so I give in and take a bite. They watch me chew.

We *really* need to get a TV.

"Any plans for your birthday?" my father asks.

"Bree and Charlotte are taking me out for karaoke."

"That'll be fun," Cecelia says. She's way more excited than a night of karaoke calls for.

"Yeah, I think so." I take a sip of water, debating my next words. "By the way, I'm going to go to LA next week. For work. I just found out."

It's quiet for so long I have to look up from my food and actually meet their eyes. "If that's okay, I mean."

I hate myself for saying it.

"For how long?" my father asks.

"Two days."

He and Cecelia glance at each other, communicating silently.

"They need a horse wrangler in LA?" he asks skeptically.

"Not exactly." I fidget in my seat. "I mean, I guess it's less for work and more of a date."

Heat rises from my neck to my forehead. "Alec's taking me to some premiere he was invited to."

A muscle in his jaw twitches.

"Well," he says after a long pause. "You're eighteen now. Can make your own decisions. If you think it's a good idea . . ." He trails off. "Be careful, all right?"

"Yeah. I will."

They watch me take another bite of bacon.

"Thomas," Cecelia says, clearly as sick of the awkward silence as I am. "Why don't you tell Nora about the, *you know*." She elbows him theatrically.

"Hmph," he sounds. "Right. Well, eighteen is a big birthday. And every time you start up that truck, I'm afraid it'll finally combust. Not safe to be driving around in." He scratches his ear.

"Thought we'd get you something brand new. More reliable. Get rid of that old piece of junk."

My fork clatters against the plate.

"Junk?" I repeat.

"I'm surprised they still allow it on the road," Cecelia jokes "Must be some kind of hazard."

They both laugh.

Junk.

Mama had dropped me off for my first day of middle school in that truck. Had picked me up for my last day of sophomore year, Alice Cooper blaring. Sometimes, when I open the door, I swear I smell her. Just for a second, I think I might see her sitting in the driver's seat, patting the spot next to her.

And they want it gone. Out of their driveway.

Gone, just like her.

Just like I'll be.

I don't remember standing.

"Thanks, but I did okay without your birthday gifts for seventeen years. I think I'll be okay this year, too."

"What?" my father says, jaw slack. "I just thought—"

"I know what you thought," I say.

"Wait a minute," Cecelia says, rising from her seat. "Let's talk about this. There's some kind of miscommunication happening here and we need to settle it. Now."

"My stomach hurts," I lie.

"Nora," my father starts.

"We can talk about it later," I lie again. "Thanks for breakfast."

I'm up the stairs before they can say another word. I grab my keys from the bedside table and get dressed at light speed. Then, because I have to have *some* sort of birthday luck, I decide today is the day to brave the jump from the second story onto the covered porch below. I don't give myself time to think about it—I open my window and hop down onto the eave of the porch. When I make it without spraining an ankle, I shuffle to the edge of the porch roof. I'm barely six feet off the ground from here, and I make myself jump again without thinking. Then I'm on the grass and both ankles are still intact.

They have to hear the truck start up, but I don't wait to see if they come outside. I start the drive to Charlotte's, hoping she doesn't mind me showing up way too early for our night out.

There are pictures all over the internet of my best friends and I singing karaoke.

Even days after my birthday, we're still everywhere online.

We all look great, and I mean, I *guess* that's a win. I'm wearing an adorable top Bree brought back from Italy for my birthday. But I didn't even notice people taking the photos and it creeps me out to the fullest extent to realize we were being watched so closely without Alec around.

People recognize *me*.

I check my messages again, just in case Alec landed early. He left earlier today, some kind of publicity thing he has to handle while in LA. But he still hasn't messaged.

I put my phone down and try to concentrate on packing for tomorrow. Thankfully, my father and Cecelia haven't brought our fight up again. Bree and Charlotte had listened as I rehashed the whole thing, and even though they didn't say it, I could tell they thought I overreacted. And the more time I had to think about it, the more I wondered if they were right.

My mama had always been my compass. I feel so lost without her. Everything stings and I don't know how to tell if what I'm feeling is real, or if it's the pain of losing her bleeding into every moment, every breath, every blink.

There's a knock at my bedroom door.

"Nora?"

It's Cecelia.

"Hey," I answer, guilt surging through me when I see her.

She comes in tentatively, looking around. "You know, we could head to Target next week if you want. It's only a forty-five-minute drive. I'd be happy to take a day off of work. We could make a morning of it. Get some posters for your walls. I guess I didn't realize everything was still so bare in here."

"That's nice of you," I say. "I won't be done with filming yet, though." *And then I'll be in Montana.*

"Another time, then." She's quiet for a moment. "Listen," she says, sitting on the bed beside my suitcase. "I want to talk about your birthday."

"We don't have to," I say quickly.

She smiles, but it's sad. Tired. "I think we do, doll. In fact, I think we've needed to talk for a while. Your daddy, well, the man can't dance to save his life, unless it's dancing around a topic of conversation. That he's fantastic at. You're both too willing to clam up until things just burst out. It's not healthy."

I pick at my fingernail. "I don't think there's really much to say."

"Well, it doesn't have to be a long, drawn-out conversation. I guess, well. I was just thinking. About that truck."

I tense.

"To us, that thing out there, it's just a way to get from point A to point B. And we thought we'd be doing right by you to get something more reliable. Then, I thought about that old, ratty Atlanta Braves hat I wore every day of my eighth-grade year."

I look up at her, confused. She's got this look on her face, like she's here, but her mind is somewhere else.

"I wore that hat rain or shine. Lord, I even wore it to Sunday services." She laughs once, soft. "Loved that old thing. Who knows how long I would have kept at it—had it not been for my mama sneaking it out of my bedroom one night and throwing it in the wash. In her defense, it was disgusting. It needed to be incinerated. But it couldn't handle the wash cycle. Came out in tatters."

She runs her fingers along the seams of my bedding. "My papa gave me that hat. When he died, and I couldn't hold his hand anymore, couldn't sit in the stands next to him with a hot dog and popcorn, I still had that hat."

She seems sincere. She's trying. So I decide maybe I'll try a little, too.

"Did you ever forgive your mom?" I ask.

"Eventually. Though I gave her hell for it." She stops toying with the bedding and tentatively slides her hand over on top of mine. "I understand, Nora. I get why you gave us hell about the truck. We'll do better. Just promise you'll stop clamming up on us, all right? I know we're not her, darling. But we're trying."

Tears prick at my eyes.

I wonder, then—if Cecelia and I had gotten to know each other under less terrible circumstances, would we have been close? If she and my father had been in my life from the start, what would our relationship have been like?

Cecelia pulls something from the pocket of her cardigan.

"I wanted you to have this."

She gives me one of the reusable Ziploc bags she usually puts her lunch in. I open it. There's fifty dollars, a Starbucks gift card, and a slip of paper with her name and a handful of numbers by it.

I try to give it back to her. She immediately puts her hand up to block it.

"No. You're taking it."

"I can't take money from you. I don't know when I'd be able to pay it back."

There's a second where she looks like I've slapped her. "You don't need to pay me back, Nora. We're family."

I fold the paper open and closed a few times in the awkward silence.

"My mama used to do that," Cecelia says. I look up at her and she nods at the paper.

"Would write down everyone's numbers, anyone she could think of that I might need to call if there was an emergency. I know things are different now; everyone has a cell phone and internet at the tips of their fingers all the time. But I thought . . ." She pauses. "I always thought, when I had a daughter, I'd do the same for her. Always dreamed about sending her off to camp with her neon pink sleeping bag and an index card full of numbers. I missed all the campouts with you."

I swallow. "Oh." I don't look up until my vision clears. "Thanks."

"Of course." She awkwardly pats me on the leg before she gets up and looks around again. "And if you change your mind about the Target run?"

"I'll let you know."

She closes the door behind her.

I slip the Ziploc bag into the front pocket of my suitcase.

All I can imagine is Cecelia in line at Walmart with a Starbucks gift card. I picture her sitting at her desk at work, writing all her numbers down on that paper. I think about my father showing up outside of the barn that day. I remember him saying *It's not that simple* when I asked why he wasn't there once he knew about me.

I finish packing, and my sleep is restless.

My alarm goes off at 3:45 a.m. I go downstairs with my bag to find my father drinking coffee and reading a book about WWII. We make awkward conversation, neither of us bringing up his offer to buy me a car, or the fit I threw afterward. He pretends it's normal for him to be up this early, and that it has nothing to do with me flying across the country.

When a very expensive Mercedes comes to pick me up, my father walks me out, insisting on carrying my luggage.

The ride is silent and gives me way too much time to think.

When the stewardess in first class offers me a drink, I don't take it. I also don't tell her it's my first time on a plane, or that I definitely don't belong up here with people who bought their own very expensive ticket.

Instead, I spend the time agonizing over a million things. Number one—is this an *actual* date? I don't know when I stopped hating Alec. I don't think he hates me anymore, either. But does he *like* me? Or is this all still just business to him?

After a constant influx of hot towels and free snacks and ample leg room, I'm almost disappointed when the flight lands. I'm grabbing my bag from the overhead compartment, tiny thanks to the fact that Alec promised to arrange my clothes for the night, when I realize I don't know how I'm getting from the airport to wherever I'm supposed to go next.

When I pull out my phone to call him in a panic, I see his text. He'd sent it while I was in the air.

"Your driver will be here." There's a screenshot of the layout of LAX, a circle around the place he wants me to go. "He'll have your name. Safe flight."

I follow the flow of people from the plane. It takes me a few tries, and I get lost once, but eventually, I make it to the part of the airport Alec circled for me. I scan the crowd of people waiting near the door, spotting a group of drivers with names on signs.

The flash of red hair peeking out from under a baseball cap catches my eye before the sign does.

There's a second where I'm weirdly happy it's him.

Then I look down at the sign and scowl.

Horse Girl.

His eyes are shining, waiting for the reaction he seems to love pulling from me.

"Hilarious," I say as I approach.

"Ah, so you can read. I wasn't sure."

"Did you really take the time out of your morning to drive over here and torture me?"

"Torture?" he says, walking up to me and closing the distance, the noise around us growing as loved ones hug and reunited friends laugh and talk. "Is it really all that bad? I suppose I could have sent in the driver instead, if I knew it would be torturous to have to find me here."

"His breath would probably be more tolerable."

It's a lie and we both know it. Alec always smells incredible.

He laughs. "I'll make sure to bring gum next time."

Something inside me, wild and unrestrained like the horses I'd had to break, pushes me to take one more step forward—to see if he tastes as good as he smells.

"Are you glad to be back in LA, surrounded by your team of butt-kissers?"

"No, actually. Not a single person told me what a prick I was last night when I used chopsticks to eat a bag of Takis. Made me miss you."

We both realize what he said at the same time. I give him the space of four breaths to take it back.

He doesn't.

"Well. Don't worry. I'm here now to tell you that the jeans you're wearing are at least a size too small."

"Ah, there's that smart mouth I adore so much." His eyes flick down to my lips, and I hear the double meaning in his words. "I spent the night thinking," he says, eyes still trained on my lips. I have to remind myself to breathe.

"About my mouth?" I'm surprised by my daring.

Alec is, too. His smirk widens.

"About ways to keep you quiet for once."

"Come up with anything good?"

I wonder if this is what acting is supposed to feel like. Does Alec's heart race every time he pretends to fall in love with someone? Does his skin prickle, does every cell inside of him beg for his hand to reach out and touch the person standing in front of him, pretending to be his?

As his eyes study my face and he brings himself one step closer to me, I wonder if this isn't acting at all.

I wonder if this is what it feels like for a little piece of you to belong to Alexander Mathis.

"There were a few things I thought I'd try, if I found it necessary." His hand brushes along my back.

I swallow. "Shut me up, then. Before I tell you how hideous those shoes are."

Alec leans in.

My heart stops beating altogether.

His lips graze against mine in a way that sends shivers all the way to my fingertips. I press my hand against his chest, reveling in the soft, luxurious cotton. He's tentative at first, questioning. I lean in, pressing my mouth firmly against his, and he reacts instantly, gently cupping the back of my neck and pulling me even closer.

No one in the world is *this* good of an actor.

One second, I'm lost in a world that holds only Alec and me. The next, he's being ripped away, and I come crashing back to reality.

There's a hand on his arm, a girl close enough to him to insert herself right where I was two seconds ago.

"I KNEW it was you! Leanne, I told you it was him! Alexander Mathis, I can't believe it!"

Alec steps back, turning slightly sideways to put himself fully between myself and the girl currently trying to squeeze all signs of life out of his arm.

"I mean, I told my friend over there—Leanne!" She turns and gestures to a girl watching from a group of seats. Her eyes are wide. She fumbles with her phone. "That's Leanne," she says, turning back to Alec. "She's your biggest fan—I mean, beside me of course. I LOVE you, Alexander!"

Attention turns our way. Moments before, we were two people in an airport. Now we're Alexander Mathis and Friend.

"Aways happy to meet a fan," Alec says. His voice is calm and low—but I hear the trace of panic in it. It reminds me of how nervous he was riding Ethel the first time. "Sorry, though, we're in a hurry today." He gestures at me, and she holds her phone out.

"Yeah, totally. One picture—you don't mind, do you?" she asks without looking at me.

"Actually—"

She shoves her phone into my hand. Hers is still in a vise grip around Alec's arm and she turns him toward me.

I figure taking the photo is the fastest way to get out of this super uncomfortable situation.

"Smile," I say, trying to shake the spell our kiss placed me under and plant my feet firmly back in reality. There's no time to question what that meant, or if it will ever happen again. I take half a dozen photos. When I try to give her the phone back, she shakes her head.

"Landscape now."

I turn the phone and take her photos. Then I hand it back and slide my hand up Alec's arm, placing it directly underneath hers. She seems to finally get the picture.

"Thanks. I still can't believe it's *you*."

Alec's looking her right in the eyes, doing that thing he did to Amanda where he makes every fan feel special. It's sweet. But while he's looking at her, I'm looking around us. My stomach churns.

"Um, Alec?" I murmur, watching as word spreads. Heads turn toward us. This isn't like at home, where a restaurant full of people look on in wonder. This is a big, big airport with so many people I can't even begin to guess the number. And they're all looking our way.

"Here," the girl says, thrusting a pen she dragged out of the belt bag she's wearing. "Sign my shirt." She turns around and pulls her hair over her shoulder, waiting.

"Are you okay?" Alec murmurs, watching me out of the corner of his eye as he signs.

"No," I say, embarrassed by how out of breath I sound. But my panic builds as people stop staring and start walking over, phones out. Heat rushes to my face.

Alec signs quickly and then turns to follow my gaze. "I thought the hat would help."

"It didn't."

"Nice to meet you," Alec says. He grabs my hand and guides me toward a giant wall of doors. People are watching us there, too. I don't know how we're going to get out.

"Take a deep breath," Alec says, pulling his phone from his pocket while we walk.

"I can't."

He runs his thumb along the outside of my hand and guides me closer to the doors.

"No one's going to hurt you. They only want a picture of us."

"Of you."

"Of *us*. You're everywhere. Everyone loves you, including my agent. He was right, you're great for my image." His voice is light and joking, but I can feel the anxiety radiating off of him. He puts the phone to his ear, and I focus on breathing.

There, in the middle of all the chaos, those words echo around in my mind.

Great for his image. Is that *all* I am?

There are dozens of people yelling "Alexander!" now, but what's freaking me out more is the occasional "Nora" that gets shouted our way.

I sold my name to the world for fifteen hundred dollars.

The crowd pushes in. Where there was a bubble before, a line no one seemed willing to cross, now there's not even a breath of space. First, it's one or two people. Then a dozen. Then, so many I can no longer see the doors.

Panic rises inside of me. I can't breathe.

Alec's hand is my only lifeline. When his fingers slip from mine, I start to spiral.

People are pushing in so hard I'm terrified I might fall.

"Alec," I cry out—but everyone around me is doing the same.

I have to get out of here, I have to get to the doors, I have to—

"MOVE," Alec shouts. A small hole opens up in the wave of people, then closes again. "I said MOVE. NOW." Then the hole opens again and Alec forces his way through it.

A girl next to me loses her mind when she sees him coming toward us, not realizing it's me she's standing beside, it's me he's coming for. In an attempt to get his attention, she waves her arms wildly, and elbows me straight in the face.

"Ouch," I hiss, doubling over at the pain. Something else slams into me, almost knocking me over. Terror rises at the thought of being on the ground, but someone saves me right before I lose my balance completely.

"Nora," he says my name, right next to my ear.

My name. He's saying my name.

"Nora," he says again, pleading.

"I'm fine," I breathe. "Fine. Please get me out of here." I can hear the tinge of hysteria in my voice.

"Out of the way," a deep, booming voice shouts over the clamor of the crowd.

"Finally," Alec says. A giant mammoth of a man cuts through the people like a warm knife through butter. He falls in step with Alec, staring down anyone who dares to get within ten feet of us. We're out of the airport in less than a minute.

There's a car idling next to a **DO NOT PARK** sign and we're whisked into it so fast I'm not even sure there's a full five seconds between when we exit the airport and are in the back seat next to each other. The giant man gets in the front seat—apparently, he doubles as driver and bouncer.

Alec's hand is on my chin before the car is even out of park.

"You're hurt," he breathes.

"I'm fine," I lie.

"Nora," he says, reprimanding and pleading.

Now that he's said my name, the floodgates have opened. I want to beg the same way he begged me. I want him to say it a million more times.

His fingers gently brush against a tender spot on my lip. I wince, and his brow furrows with concern.

"Is it bleeding?" I ask in a whisper.

"No. Just red. It might bruise a little."

His thumb gently runs under my lip again.

"Making my red-carpet debut with a busted lip. Fabulous. I understand if you want to take one of the many girls waiting for your call."

"It's you or no one on that carpet with me," he says, his eyes still roaming my face for injuries.

"How'd the hat work out for you?" the giant man in the driver's seat asks. Apparently, he's unaware of my entire world turning on its axis in the back seat. *It's you or no one.*

"Don't start, Eric," Alec mumbles. He finally drops his hand and leans back.

"I asked a simple question," Eric says.

"Your tone implies otherwise."

"This is my normal tone."

"This is your judgmental tone. It's the same one you used when I wanted to go shopping," Alec says.

"When you wanted to go shopping. By yourself. In broad daylight."

"Buying underwear alone. What an insane concept."

"You were swarmed within the first ten minutes of leaving the car."

"It was at least fifteen minutes."

"No, it was nine. I remember. Maybe if you had a hat, things would have gone as well as they did today."

Alec sighs. "Can we not talk about this?"

Eric watches him from the rearview mirror as we inch into the most atrocious line of traffic I've ever seen. "Sure. Let's not talk about how you could have gotten so buried in people in an instant that I never would have made it to you before someone ripped your clothes off to make a shrine or sell on the internet or whatever it is they do with your overpriced T-shirts. Let's not talk about how you not only refuse to have more security, but you won't even let me do my job the right way."

"Glad we're not talking about it." Alec says.

Eric's eyes flick to me in the mirror. "Let's definitely not talk about how your pretty friend was almost a casualty because you wanted to pretend a hat could hide who you are, when you going out in public causes a scene akin to the Backstreet Boys walking into a high school."

Alec's face is sober when he looks at me. There's a brief silence in the car while he seems to ponder Eric's words. "Fine. The hat didn't work."

"I know," Eric says.

"But neither did your analogy," Alec says, taking his hat off and running his fingers through his auburn hair. "If the Backstreet Boys walked into a high school, the students would think they were substitute teachers. Your references are as outdated as ever. Also, I'm an actor. Not a singer."

Eric scrunches up his face while he drives. "Leonardo DiCaprio?"

"Worse," Alec says.

"What do you think?" Eric asks, smiling at me in the mirror.

"You're asking the wrong person," I manage to say. My voice still sounds strained. The airport is far behind us, and we're safe in the car with windows so dark you'd need night-vision goggles to see through them, but there's still a trace of panic underneath my skin.

"Harry Styles," Alec answers. His arm presses against mine, warm and solid, even though there's plenty of space in the roomy back seat. My heart calms a little at his touch, and, too rattled to be embarrassed, I lean into him.

"He's a singer," Eric says.

"Harry does it all."

"Harry Styles is an icon. You think you're Harry Styles level?"

"You're the one who started this," Alec says, miffed. I almost feel like laughing.

Eric just shrugs, finally dropping the subject.

Eventually, we pull off the freeway and into the parking lot of the nicest hotel I've ever seen in my life.

Charlotte was obsessed with the Biltmore for a few years, constantly making us look at pictures and virtual walk-throughs. This hotel screamed old money and prestige, the same way the Biltmore always did to me.

"You stay in the car this time, Mr. Styles. I'll get the room keys."

Eric's gone before Alec can respond. I'm finally calm enough to laugh.

"I'm glad you're enjoying this." His words are sharp but his eyes are soft. I know he's still reeling from the airport scene, too.

"I like Eric."

"Of course you do." Alec rolls his eyes. There's a beat of silence.

"Nora," he says my name again. "I'm so sorry. I don't know what I was thinking. If anything worse would have happened to you . . ."

"It wasn't your fault."

"It was. It absolutely was my fault." He looks away, hand rubbing across the little bit of red stubble that's covering his jaw. "I'm amazed at how fast I forgot."

"Forgot what?"

"Who I am. What real life is." He rubs his eyes. "Eric told me not to go in there alone. He already hates that he's the only security detail I have around most of the time. I point-blank refused when he wanted to come to set with me, mainly because I never really planned on leaving my trailer. But I got used to being out and being looked at, but not bothered. It was so refreshing.

"It's different here, with the crowds. All it takes is one person to start the avalanche. Then, everyone else thinks it must be okay." He turns and looks at me, his green eyes soft and sad. "I wanted to hold onto that feeling a little longer. I know that must sound ridiculous."

"It doesn't."

His smile is sad.

There's a gentle quiet in the car. I have a startling realization that it's not at all awkward to sit in silence with him. With Char and Bree, when there's nothing to say, we exist in the same space comfortably. It's the same with Alec.

I think back on the day I met him in the restaurant. I had hated him. Working together without killing each other had seemed impossible. But now, here we are, confiding in each other.

Sitting in comfortable silence.

When did Alec become my friend?

I blush as I remember the way he had begged me to say his name again outside of his trailer, the way he had leaned in like he wanted to kiss me. The way neither of us could resist kissing in the airport, all eyes on us.

When did I start wanting Alec to be *more* than my friend?

Eric opens the front door and gets in, passing a card back to each of us. "Top floor. Penthouse."

Alec nods.

"Um. We're in the same room?"

"Technically, yes. But no, not really. It's the whole top floor. Multiple rooms. Multiple bedrooms."

Eric opens Alec's door, then mine.

The staring once we're in the hotel is different.

Here, there are deft looks and quiet clearing of throats. Employees glance our way and *perceive* us, but otherwise, we're left alone.

When the elevator opens, I stand aside to let the man inside exit. But the man standing in the elevator doesn't move. Alec and Eric walk in, and there's a second where I think they're being rude. Then I realize this hotel is so fancy that someone spends their day riding up and down the elevator pressing buttons for people too lazy to do it themselves.

I don't look at Alec while I get in, but I can still feel his smirk.

"Shut up," I whisper.

"I didn't say a word." he says.

"You wanted to."

He laughs quietly, and his hand brushes gently against mine as the elevator doors close.

And even though there are no cameras to see him do it, he curls his pinkie finger around mine.

"You're right. Sorry."

"You aren't forgiven."

He runs his thumb over the palm of my hand.

He's totally forgiven.

When the elevator doors open, there's no hallway. Instead, there's a giant living room with a fully windowed wall.

"Holy crap," I say, walking in without waiting for Alec to go first.

I'm across the room before anyone else has even left the elevator. LA is sprawled out in front of me, a strange mix of buildings and trees and roads and land. I don't know what I expected, but it wasn't something this beautiful.

"It's nice," Alec says from beside me.

"Nice? This is unbelievable. It's . . ."

"Smoggy? Pretentious? Crowded?"

"Gorgeous," I breathe.

"I guess," Alec says, leaving the window. "It gets old after a while."

"Does having someone drive you around, open your doors, and press elevator buttons for you get old, too?"

Eric laughs, and Alec shoots him a look. A phone beside the couch rings and Eric jogs over to answer it.

"Hello? Yes. Sure—send them up." He hangs up the phone. "Hair and makeup are on the way."

"Already?" I ask, grabbing a croissant from the granite counter in the full kitchen and taking a bite. I groan. "What is this magical pastry?"

"Magnolia Bakery," Alec says. "Best in LA. And yes, hair and makeup are already here. We have to be at the premiere in five hours."

"It takes you five hours to get ready?" I say, mouth full.

"Bet it takes Harry Styles longer," Eric says.

"Is there something going on between you and Harry I should know about?" Alec asks.

"I wish," Eric says, helping himself to one of the croissants. "Wonder if he's looking for new security detail."

I snort.

I lock eyes with Alec. He's smiling and looking at me in a way that causes my cheeks to tingle. I want to hide from his gaze and bask in it, all at the same time. What do I have to say to get him to make good on his promise and shut me up again?

The elevator dings. Half a dozen people pile out, giant bags slung over their shoulders. Alec makes introductions, and everyone is nice enough to pretend I'm someone worth knowing.

Unfortunately, it does take almost five full hours.

People file in and out of the suite all afternoon. An aesthetician comes in and gives me a five-step facial. My nails are given better treatment than they've ever seen, and I can't stop wiggling my new pearly-pink sparkling toes. My hair isn't just styled, it's treated, given a mask, blown out, *then* styled to perfection. It's up in a way that I never would have been able to achieve, leaving my neck bare. My makeup is applied layer on layer. It's so perfect I'm afraid to scratch the itch I've had above my eyebrow for the past ten minutes.

Once they're done turning me into the richer, more stylish version of myself, I'm left alone in my room to get dressed. There's a hanging bag inside the closet, right next to my very beaten-up Vera Bradley tote bag my mom bought me on my twelfth birthday. It reminds me how much I don't belong here.

I slowly unzip the bag and run my fingers along the silky fabric. It's a gorgeous sea blue, like the water in Destin where Mama and I used to go every summer. She'd rent a little Airbnb we couldn't afford and we'd sit out on the beach in lawn chairs eating ham sandwiches and drinking RC Cola. The water was so pure and blue it almost seemed like a dream.

So does this dress. It's like the deeper parts of the ocean, where you can't really see your feet anymore. I pull it out of the bag and watch it shimmer in awe.

I slip it on. It takes some maneuvering, but I'm able to zip it up halfway. I walk to the bathroom mirror and I'm shocked when I see my reflection. The person staring back is still me. I'm not looking at a stranger. Just a version of myself I didn't know existed. One that has money and time and knows the perfect place to highlight her cheekbones.

There's no matching purse, and I don't think the belt bag I packed is really appropriate. I dump out everything and try to decide what I can't live without for the night.

Eventually I manage to fit my driver's license, fifty dollars, and the slip of paper Cecelia had given me in a tiny, translucent card holder that used to hold my school ID.

Cecelia has only explicitly asked one thing of me since I moved in, and it was to keep this card on me at all times while I was gone. So I slide the tiny pouch inside my bra, which, thankfully, has removable straps. Unfortunately, it can't also hold my phone. Looks like I'll be tech free tonight. Cecelia would be proud.

There's a knock at my bedroom door. I force myself to stop admiring my own reflection like the Evil Queen in Snow White and open it.

My breath hitches.

Alec in a suit is deadly.

It's tailored to fit every inch of him to perfection. His hair is styled in that purposefully messy way men have that makes you want to run your fingers through it. Even the way he stands, like he's never been unsure of anything in his life, is so attractive I think I might catch fire right on the spot. His collar is open and one button is undone, no tie, and I can see the barest hint of his collarbone. I blush.

"Adequate." The word falls from his mouth in a whisper, as if it's torn from the depths of his chest.

"Zip me up?" I ask, turning my back to him, so he doesn't see how his one singular word has affected me.

Even though I'm expecting it, his touch on my shoulder sends a shiver through me. The zipping of my dress takes much longer than necessary, but I do not complain. He steps closer, and his fingers run gently along the nape of my neck. I shiver and lean back into his touch. I'm flush against him when I feel something cool against my chest.

"I saw this yesterday, by chance." He takes a small step back and his fingers are on my skin again as he clasps the necklace closed. "Eric and I were out; it caught my eye." He turns me toward the mirror, moving with me. The image of us reflected back steals my breath. Alec's cheekbones are tinged the slightest shade of red. "It has nothing to do with the dozens of posts I saw of you and your friends out for your birthday."

Silver gleams at my neck.

"It's beautiful," I whisper.

"Stunning," he says from behind me, staring at my reflection in the glass. "Happy eighteenth."

I take a step closer to the mirror, and the light hits the necklace the right way. It's an outline of a horse, but done in such a way that I'm not sure anyone else would be able to tell without looking purposefully, intent on understanding the shape. My throat tightens as I imagine how long Alec had to look to find something so perfect. Something he knew I'd love.

I look over my shoulder to thank him.

His lips are on mine before I can say a word.

The elevator dings in the living room.

"Soup's on," Eric yells.

Alec slowly, gingerly ends our kiss.

I follow him into the living room, holding tight to the memory of moment that belongs only to the two of us. The kiss we didn't have to share with the world.

"You're a lifesaver," Alec says, walking over to grab two cups from Eric. He hands me one. "The food at the premiere will be ritzy and terrible. Drink your milkshake or you'll starve until the after-party."

Eric whistles. "Blue's really your color, eh, Nora?"

I smile. "Thanks."

"And I see you got the necklace. Had to drive his highness to eight stores yesterday to find the perfect one."

Alec gently kicks Eric's ankle.

"Ouch—hey. That only works if we're sitting at a table where no one can see our legs."

"I'd say it worked fine. You shut up, didn't you?"

They bicker all the way down to the first floor, where Eric leads us to the same black-windowed car he picked us up from the airport in. I finish my milkshake on the drive, my mind alternating three thoughts on a loop: Alec in a store, looking for a necklace that fit me perfectly. Cecelia, writing all of her numbers down on an index card. My father, having coffee at the dining room table at four a.m. so he could tell me to be safe on my flight.

It would have been so easy for me to betray Alec. To break his trust and tell Elizabeth what was really happening, so she would know the truth. So easy to go to Montana and leave Cecelia and my father behind without a word. I would have hurt them because I was so sure they were temporary situations, temporary people in my life. That I didn't love them and they could never love me.

I grimace, eternally grateful that I had not given any information to Elizabeth.

The stuff with my father and Cecelia—I can fix that before I leave. I can extend an olive branch.

But Alec . . . I have to tell him I talked to Elizabeth. Explain everything to him. I think he'll be able to understand. I haven't said anything to her that gave Delilah up—I've just allowed her to use our message thread as a therapy session.

I resolve to tell him tonight, after the premiere. When we're back in the hotel, in our pajamas, eating ice cream and laughing about the terrible food here. I'll tell him everything.

The venue is less than a five-minute drive, and most of that is traffic.

We join a line of vehicles, all with blacked-out windows. I'm sure each carries its own set of very important people—people I probably won't recognize. A few cars ahead, there's a red carpet, lined on either side with hundreds of people.

Someone slams against our car window and I gasp, flinching away. Alec makes an irritated noise and puts an arm around me, pulling me into him. We watch through the tinted glass as a man in a suit drags a pair of screeching girls away from our car.

"It's fine, no one can get in. It's bulletproof."

"That doesn't make me feel better," I choke out. "Why do you need bulletproof glass?"

"Styles has it, so I figured I should, too. Got to keep up with the Joneses."

I can't make myself laugh.

"We don't have to do this," he says.

I swallow. "Trying to get out of paying me?"

"Oh, I'm not paying you for this," he says.

I look at him, confused.

"I picked the dress, the shoes, and the venue. This is a date, Nora. You still owe me a fake one when we're back. But this?" His eyes bore into mine. "This is real."

I'm speechless.

He smirks. "Once we get out, we'll walk the carpet. You'll hear a million people calling your name—"

"You mean your name?"

"No. I mean your name, Nora." I shiver. I'll never get enough of my name on his lips. "Speaking of, my publicist says a piece is dropping on you in the *Seville*. They talked to some girl—Cami, Camellia—"

"Cambrie?"

"Yeah, that's it."

"We were on the soccer team together one year when Brianna forced me to go to tryouts with her. I didn't even make it through the whole season."

"Yeah, well. Welcome to the world of fame. Anyone you've ever looked at will sell any piece of you they have for a quick buck or, more likely, a moment of fame."

"It sucks here."

"Now imagine never being able to leave it." Our car pulls forward. It's our turn to get out.

Alec's face transforms a split second before the door opens. Cameras click, voices call out—but I still hear Alec's soft sigh before his foot hits the ground.

My stomach churns.

What am I doing here? There's a red carpet in front of me. There are celebrities here, directors, writers, really, *really* rich people. I can't do this. I can't get out of this car. I can't move. I can't—

Alec turns away from the cameras. He extends his hand out to me. The grin he gives me is so familiar, so irritatingly attractive, everything else falls away. I reach out, take his hand, and step foot onto my first red carpet.

His hand on my back is the only thing that gets me through. People scream our names—both of them. He turns me the right way, angles us toward the right cameras. He whispers for me to smile without moving his lips. We shake hands and he signs whatever people push his way.

Once we're done with the most terrifying walk I've ever been on, we're led into a building that is so lavishly decorated I cannot fathom how much even the carpets cost. It's quiet and there are no screaming fans, but cameras are everywhere. It's not the same as outside, with the frantically flashing lights and desperate calls for our attention. But there are soft clicks that remind me it isn't anywhere near time to relax.

We're led into a room that's full of quiet conversation. A waiter walks by with a tray of cat vomit on crackers. I shake my head politely when he offers me some and Alec does the same.

"Told you the milkshake was a good idea."

"It was an okay idea," I say, looking around the room.

"Would it kill you to say I'm right?"

"Probably."

"Xander!" someone calls from across the room. Alec stiffens beside me.

"Great." We both turn to watch the person making his way toward us from the crowd. "Um, Xander?"

"Don't ask," Alec says through his teeth, forcing a smile.

"Okay. But do *I* get to call you Xander?"

"Absolutely not."

"I'll take that as a yes."

"Thin ice, Horse Girl."

"Whatever you say, Xandie."

Alec's jaw ticks, but he manages to hold his smile as his friend—or not-friend, I can't really tell—walks up and shakes his hand.

"Aw, come on. A handshake? Bring it in, Xander!"

They do that thing guys do when they hug, pulling each other in and slapping their hands on the other's back way too aggressively to really be comfortable.

Once they're done with whatever weird pissing contest that hug was, they take a step back and Alec's friend-not-friend leans against the table next to us.

"How's it going my little YouTube sensation? I've heard times are rough."

"Times are fantastic, actually. Couldn't be better."

"Really?" The prick who hasn't bothered to acknowledge me raises his eyebrows. "That's not what I'm hearing."

"And what exactly are you hearing?"

He shrugs. "That you're not quite the darling you were this time last year. But maybe I heard wrong. You can't believe everything you read."

"You should know that already, Seb. Especially after that whole piece about you and the hamsters. Or was it gerbils?"

"Once you reach my level of fame, people will say anything for an excuse to use your name in an article. Don't worry though, pal," he says, winking at Alec. "You'll get there one day."

The guy glances at me, and my skin crawls when he takes his time looking me up and down. Twice.

"Ah, and you must be the one I've been seeing all over TikTok and Instagram. Noreen, right?"

"Nora," Alec snaps.

"Nora. So sorry." He pushes away from the table and takes my hand without asking for it. "Nice to meet you, Nora."

I pull my hand from his, sliding it through Alec's arm. "Nice to meet you, too. Sorry, I didn't catch your name."

He laughs.

When I don't join in, he looks at Alec, then back at me again.

"I'm Sebastian. Sebastian Garfield." He raises his eyebrows.

"Oh. Like the cat?" I ask.

"The—the what?"

"The cat. You know, 'I hate Fridays.' 'Lasagna.'"

Sebastian's mouth hangs slightly ajar as he looks between Alec and me again, waiting for one of us to laugh. He finally realizes I'm serious.

"I—sure. Like the cat, I guess. Listen, I see Sarah Porter over there and she owes me a drink, so I'll leave you to enjoy the night."

He gives me one last confused look before walking off to patronize someone else.

"*Like the cat?*" Alec says while we watch him disappear into the crowd of people mingling. "Seriously?"

"In my defense, Garfield is a very popular cat. You can't blame my mind for going straight there."

"I would pay so much money to have that face he made memorialized. I wonder the last time someone over the age of five didn't immediately recognize him."

"*Noreen*," I say, mimicking the weird faux-British-touched accent he did. Why didn't anyone tell him how embarrassing that was?

"I thought your girl was from Georgia, not England," a voice says from behind me.

Alec's eyes flip right over my head.

"Sean," he says, looking wary.

I turn around and find a man exactly my height, balding and red-cheeked.

"Glad you made it okay. Saw your mom a few minutes ago, looks lovely as ever. Guess who else I ran into?"

Alec looks sick, like he already knows what Sean's going to say.

Sean nods. "Elizabeth's here. Could get ugly, so my advice is: avoid, avoid, avoid. A public confrontation only works in her favor and makes you look like the villain, no matter what's actually said. It's good you're here, Nora. But the optics of you with a small-town girl on your arm aren't going to be enough after tomorrow. We need to brainstorm something good, and now."

Man, Sean really gets straight to business.

Alec sighs. "Why?"

"Because Mischa Carter has come forward as the woman you were with in the infamous photo."

"What?" Alec says. "I've never even been in the same room as Mischa Carter."

"Doesn't matter if it's really her or not, she's claiming it is. She's also claiming you were sliding into her Instagram DMs well before you and Elizabeth ever broke up. Says you two had an illicit affair spanning weeks. It's not good, Alexander."

"But, it's not true. Shouldn't that matter?" I ask.

"Truth is irrelevant. All that matters is if she's convincing enough. We're getting your image back on track. This hits tomorrow, and not only did you cheat on TikTok's sweetheart, you did it with reality TV's biggest villain in years." He raises his eyebrows. "You know the easiest solution."

"Not happening," Alec says.

"If you just tell me—"

"Damn it, Sean. Drop it."

"Language, dear."

A beautiful redheaded woman in her late forties walks up and slides her arm through Alec's. "You're not too old to have your mouth washed out with soap. I did it once, and I'll do it again."

"Still can't look at a bar of Dial the same way." Alec's face softens and he embraces the woman next to him. "Hello, Mom."

She looks at me after their hug, her smile warm and inviting. "Hello, dear. You must be Nora. I'm Joanne."

She lets go of Alec and I freeze when she wraps her arms around me, pulling me into her.

Everything about the gesture comes so naturally from her, but I can't remember the last time someone besides Bree or Char or Mrs. Shep hugged me. Before I can decide if I like it or not, the hug is over.

"I've heard so much about you."

"You have?" I ask, dumbfounded.

"Of course. I knew something was up the moment our phone calls went from a diatribe of how he'd never set foot in Georgia again to, 'Oh, it's not that bad, Mom.' Didn't take him long after that to casually drop your name."

"Mother, please." Alec is blushing again. His hair almost matches his face. I feel my own cheeks grow warm.

"What? It's true," she says, not a drop of shame in sight. "A mother always knows."

"I thought this was a, you know, an *understanding*," Sean says, gesturing at us with his drink—which is in a crystal cup that probably cost more than a purebred horse.

"The two of you in the same room might kill me." Alec keeps fidgeting with the collar of his shirt. I decide to put him out of his misery.

"We're all on the same page here, don't worry," I say.

Alec stares at me, finally dropping his hand from his collar. "Great. Same page. Are there drinks here?" He mumbles the last part, and leaves me alone with his mom and Sean.

"Alexander," I hiss, using his full name. He turns back and mouths, *Good luck*. I want to mouth back *Screw you*, but I can feel his mom's eyes on me, so I smile.

"So, Nora," Sean says. "You're everywhere these days. We could capitalize on this, you know. Maybe put your name out there for a few commercials—horse food brand deals, contracts with riding schools. Anything you want, the possibilities are endless."

"Um," I say, wishing desperately that Alec would teleport back and save me from this conversation. "I don't think—"

"Ah, just a minute," Sean says, attention on his phone now. "Simone's having a breakdown, give me five to text her out of a spiral."

He takes a few steps back, fingers flying over his screen. Joanne rolls her eyes, turning her back on Sean.

"Alec tells me you're heading to Montana?"

"Yes, ma'am." I'm shocked she knows about my plans to move across the country—how much did Alec tell her about me?

"Do not call me that. I appreciate the southern charm, dear. But the 'ma'am' is an offense out here where everyone wants to look eternally twenty. And you don't need to look so stunned." She laughs. "Alec and I talk once a day. I'm used to hearing about three things from him: work, Diya, and Delilah. It's been hard for him lately. It's good he has you."

"How is she?" I ask, choosing to focus on Delilah instead of wondering how much Alec has been talking about me.

Joanne sighs. "She has good days and bad ones. The chemo is terrible. She's always been a thin little thing, but now . . ." She throws her hands up, like she doesn't have the words. "Well, you saw her in that terrible photo, the one all over the place. But we're optimistic. Thankfully she had Alec's hoodie and didn't have to deal with public scrutiny on top of starting treatment. He takes good care of her."

"She's lucky to have a friend like Alec."

Joanne nods sadly. "My heart just breaks for him. A lot of people would have buckled under the pressure. It's horrific how he's been accused of cheating and has no way of clearing his name without giving Delilah up. But my Alec would never do that—I raised him better than that. He cares more about her than he ever cared about his career. Guess that's what he has Sean for," Joanne says with a grimace.

"My job to do the dirty work," Sean says, joining us again, his phone nowhere in sight. He grabs two glasses of champagne off of a plate when a waiter walks by, and hands one to Joanne.

"So, Nora. About that horse food deal—"

"Could one of you point me to the restroom?" I interrupt. Alec still isn't back, and I need a breather.

"Just that way, dear," Joanne says, pointing to a back corner through a giant crowd of well-dressed celebrities.

"Thanks," I say, smiling softly when I meet her concerned gaze. I don't want her to try to follow to make sure I'm okay. "I'll be back in a minute."

The interior of the bathroom is so normal I almost laugh. It looks like a cleaner version of the girls' room at school.

Celebrities pee in beige mundanity like the rest of us.

I take an extra-long time washing my hands, hoping that by the time I'm out, Alec will have surfaced again.

The door swings open right as I turn the water off.

I look up, wondering if maybe Joanne got sick of Sean and followed me in. But it's not Alec's mom. It's a gorgeous blonde, more stunningly beautiful in person than she was in any of the TikToks I stalked. She's looking down on me from five-inch heels, and I really wish that I wasn't meeting Alec's ex for the first time with dripping wet hands.

Elizabeth tosses me an embroidered hand towel from a stack by the door. Okay, maybe it's not *exactly* like my high school bathroom.

"You're so good at ignoring text messages. Thought I'd try to catch you in person, where you can't dodge me."

"I haven't been dodging you," I say, a slight tremor in my voice. "There's just nothing to tell."

She rolls her eyes. There are dark circles under them that concealer doesn't quite cover. One of her almost-perfect nails looks like it's been chewed on one too many times. She's exhausted. And young. Too young to be this famous. Too young to be looking out for herself.

"You must know *something*," she says, desperation tinging her words. "Just a name, or a lead. Anything."

"You should talk to Alec," I blurt. "Go find him."

I walk past her and out of the bathroom before I say something I can't take back.

Unfortunately, she follows.

She grabs my arm. "Nora." Her voice is desperate and louder than it should be in this quiet, refined room. I feel the wave of eyes as they look for the disturbance. If I felt out of place before, it's nothing compared to now. At least we're in a corner, too tucked away to be seen by most of the people here.

When I turn to face Elizabeth, there's a split second where she's still that vulnerable girl. Then she looks over my head at the crowd behind us and her back straightens. She lets go of my arm. "Whatever. Forget it."

I want to tell her I'm sorry, that I wish I could help ease her pain, but she's already turned to scowl at a waiter with a plate of appetizers in one hand and a phone pointed at us in the other.

"Seriously?" she says, giving him a look that would set a forest on fire. He looks at her like a deer in headlights.

I take the opportunity to escape and search for Alec, not wanting to give her time to turn that anger my way.

I see him, walking back from the bar, and I know it has to be now. No more waiting until we're in pajamas eating ice cream. I have to tell him about Elizabeth—about the bathroom showdown, the text messages, all of it.

My hand finds his the second I'm close enough to grab it.

"I need to talk to you."

The lights flash twice above us.

Alec looks up, then back at me. "Can it wait? That's our cue to find our seats, and we're sitting behind the director. I promise we'll make a beeline for the exit the second the credits roll."

Before I can protest, Joanne is on his other side, and he's escorting us both into a smaller room, one full of chairs and a large, gilded screen surrounded by red curtains.

"Where the hell is Sean?" Alec asks.

"Said he had to make a phone call," Joanne says with a shrug.

"Alec—" The lights go down and a woman walks up in front of the screen, a spotlight following her. It's the director. She gives a speech, but I don't hear a word.

The second she's done, she sits directly in front of us. The screen lights up and the movie starts.

My leg bounces for the first hour, until Alec finally puts his hand on my knee.

The movie is almost over when Sean finally shows up at the end of our row and slides his way past us.

"Where the hell have you been?" Alec asks.

"Phone calls. Couldn't wait." Then he presses his finger to his lips and points at the back of the director's head, like Alec doesn't realize she's sitting right there.

The movie finally ends, and the director bows as everyone applauds. Alec stands and shakes her hand, gushing about the editorial vision. I bite the inside of my cheek as I wait, determined to grab him the second he's done talking. But before I can, Sean puts his hand on Alec's back and guides him out of the row of seats.

"We need to get you in front of the press junket."

"Why the rush?" Alec asks, grabbing my hand as they pass by, dragging me with him.

"I want you out of here before there's any more contact with Elizabeth."

"More contact?" Alec asks.

I flush.

"Nora had a run-in with her outside of the bathroom. Pictures are already circulating."

The damn waiter.

Alec looks at me, sympathy in his face. "That's what you wanted to talk to me about."

"Kind of," I say, rushing to keep up with the pace Sean is setting for us. He's still got his hand on Alec's back. I can't even see Joanne anymore. "But if we could just take a second before you—"

"It's going to have to wait." Sean glances at me as we walk. "I really am sorry, but it's my job to make sure Alec does *his* job. Five minutes and you'll be out of here, I promise."

We're led through the crowd of people to a hallway that leads to an open ballroom.

There's no music or dancing, though, just a room full of cameras and people holding microphones. They almost turn rabid at the sight of Alec, and I can see them all getting ready to converge on him. But Sean leads him straight toward a woman with jet-black hair.

"What's going on?" Alec asks. "Shouldn't we make the rounds?"

"*Seville* is going live in thirty seconds. They want first dibs. I agreed."

"We're doing one interview?" Alec asks, confused.

"Just the one."

"And then we can go?"

"Then you're free," Sean confirms.

Alec slides his hand along my back. "One quick snippet about how much I loved the movie and it's over," he says against my ear.

"Alexander?" the reporter says. "Are you ready? We're live in ten."

"Of course." He shoots her his million-dollar smile. "Stand off camera here." He walks me over. "You can watch me work my magic and we'll head out for tacos. I'm starving." Then he presses his lips gently against my temple.

Sean comes to stand next to me.

Someone next to the reporter counts down from five, going silent and using his fingers for three, two, one.

Alec's megawatt smile, the one that charmed millions of people into watching his skits on YouTube and millions more to fall in love with him on the big screen, lights up for the onlooking public. He doesn't seem at all rattled by the idea that thousands—tens of thousands?—of people could be watching him in real time right now.

"We're here with Alexander Mathis at the premiere of Mavis Schell's latest movie, predicted to be another blockbuster hit. Alexander, what were your thoughts?"

"It's a gorgeous film. Not only is it visually stunning—what an eye Mavis has for framing shots, right?—but contentwise, dialogue, casting. All of it was done so well it almost knocks you over. I can't wait for the public to see it."

"We saw you walk the carpet with your new darling. She looked gorgeous tonight."

"Didn't she?" Alec says. I force myself to breathe.

"What did she think of the film?"

"Nora adored it as well, though we haven't had much time to discuss. We're actually heading over to grab some dinner now—" Alec tries to end the interview. I think he's done it, that I was wrong and all my worries were for nothing. But the reporter interrupts him.

"After a very public breakup, I'm sure you're glad to have someone by your side who keeps you grounded."

Alec's smile falters for the first time, but it's so slight there's a possibility only I noticed it.

"Nora's great," he says, completely ignoring the part about his public breakup. It's obvious he's thrown by the track this interview is taking, but they're live.

"Elizabeth Max turned the public against you there for a while, insinuating that not only were you cheating on her during her parents' divorce, but that it was with an unnamed A-list starlet you were dating for 'clout.'" She uses her fingers to make air quotes, holding the microphone precariously. Alec doesn't respond. I can see his mind working for a way out of this. "How does it feel, after so many weeks of vitriol and hate, to be vindicated?" She thrusts the microphone in Alec's face.

"I'm sorry, Katelyn," he says. "I have no idea what you mean." His eyes flick to the camera and back to the reporter.

"No," I whisper. Alarm bells are going off inside of me, warning that something bad is coming. I step forward, not sure how to stop the interview—but I have to *try*. Sean places an arm on my shoulder.

"Can't do anything now, Nora." He looks at me, half apologetic, half determined.

I know, right then, what he's done. What he overheard when Joanne and I were talking, after Alec was so careful to keep it from him and everyone else.

"She doesn't deserve this," I tell him.

"Of course not. And I'm sorry for whatever pain this causes her. But it's my job to protect Alec. Not Delilah."

The reporter keeps talking, and I watch in horror as she undoes weeks of Alec's efforts to protect his friend.

"*Seville* broke the story twenty minutes ago. An anonymous source tipped us off about the person in the photo with you. Childhood friend, Delilah Jones. A mere two days after starting chemo, you were pictured out with her. You dealt with the backlash of an entire nation to shield her. That makes you a hero in the eyes of our viewers and readers. The story has already been viewed over ten million times. Elizabeth's account has been deactivated on TikTok. We have footage of her leaving halfway through the premiere. You've won, Alexander. So, I'll ask again. How does it feel?"

CHAPTER 11

I don't know how Alec finishes the interview. All I can hear is the blood pumping through my head. The loud *thwack-thwack-thwack* continues as he walks over to me, puts an arm around my waist, and leads me directly through a door.

We're in an alleyway. There are empty trucks with their trunks open, ready to load up all the tables and chairs when the party is finally over. Which it is. For us, anyway.

Alec doesn't say anything. He's pacing right outside the door, running his fingers in his hair in a way that worries me, like he's going to pull it all out by the root. I keep waiting for Sean to come out; to apologize or fix things or grovel, I don't know. But he doesn't.

"How?" he says, pacing back and forth in front of the door. "How?"

"Alec, maybe we should—"

"One of the doctors? They have student loans. They could be bought off. Someone on the staff?"

"Alec—"

"Another patient? But no, they'd have to know our connection." He stops and rubs his hands over his face. "I was so careful. She wouldn't even let me visit in the hospital. So careful, for nothing. This is my fault, all my fault."

"You didn't do this," I say. But he doesn't hear me.

"I have to call her." He's so rattled he can barely get his hand into his pocket. "She has to hear it from me. If she was watching . . . I—" He stops mid-sentence, looking away from his phone and turning to stare at me.

"Elizabeth."

He's so frantic I can barely follow his train of thought.

"She's gone. They said she left during the premiere. You don't have to worry, she—"

"Why were you and Elizabeth talking?" he interrupts.

"What?" I ask, confused. He turns his phone to me, a photo of Elizabeth and I in a text message from Diya, the words What's going on? Is Nora okay? underneath.

"Sean said it earlier and I brushed it off, assumed that's why you were acting so jumpy through the whole movie. But it doesn't make sense. I'm gone for five minutes to get a drink, and you happen to run into her?"

"She cornered me."

"What did she want?"

My face goes cold. This is not the time. I wanted to tell him before, I had planned on telling him before—but not like this. There's too much happening too fast. It all looks so bad now.

"I went to the bathroom, Alec. I was upset because you left me alone with Sean and—"

"So this is my fault," he says. I can see the panic in his eyes, see clearly how he's just looking for something to be mad at, some other pain to hold onto than the pain of hurting Delilah.

"I didn't say that. Maybe . . . maybe you should take a breath. We could go back in and find your mom."

Maybe if we found her, she'd know what to do, what to say to make him see sense. He could calm down long enough to see the whole picture.

"I don't want to go back in there. What I want is for you to tell me what you and Elizabeth talked about."

My breaths are short, and I have to force myself to fill my lungs all the way just once. Alec will calm down. There's no way he could think I did this, not after the barn or the night at the party or our kiss. Not after everything I've shared with him and everything he told me. He *knows* me.

"She asked me some questions," I say, not wanting to tell him exactly what she asked about, though he has to know. "She—Alec, she looked terrible. She's miserable. I could tell from her text messages that she's been having a hard time, but seeing it in person was different. I think she deserves to know, but I didn't, would never—"

"What do you mean, 'her text messages'?" he says, voice cutting through my words like a knife, severing them completely, stopping me in my tracks.

I realize my mistake too late.

"Alec—"

"What text messages?" he asks again.

There's none of the tenderness that he's shown the past week, none of the kindness and closeness that I'd started to see every time he looked at me.

There is nothing but pure hatred. Like the first time he looked at me in that restaurant.

No.

This is so much worse.

"Let me explain," I whisper. He's supposed to be mad at Sean. Not me. It's obvious, so clear. This was *Sean*.

But I know. I know by the look in his eyes that there is *nothing* I can say now. It's too much—the news, the photo of me and Elizabeth, the stupid, idiotic slip about her messages to me.

Alec looks at me, and I think my heart breaks when I see the tears lining his eyes.

"Maybe I should give you Sean's number. You'd make a phenomenal actress." He tries to laugh, but it's a strangled, broken sound.

"Alec, please—"

"You know, I didn't understand at first. Why you couldn't figure things out with your dad. The man came out to find you in a rainstorm and even that wasn't enough for you." Alec swallows, eyes locked with mine. "I get it now, though. You're stubborn. So damn stubborn, Nora."

"That has nothing to do with us," I say, my voice thick with tears. He's hurt, I know he is, but I can feel him walking on a razor thin line and I'm terrified he's going to say something we can't come back from.

"It has everything to do with us," he says, voice breaking. "You told her about Delilah. You decided, no matter who it would hurt, that Elizabeth needed to know. It wasn't enough that I told you at the party I didn't want to tell her. No, Nora knew what was best and now you've not only hurt me, you've hurt Delilah."

He swallows once, hard, his tear-filled eyes locked with mine.

"You hurt people, Nora. I'm just glad that this is over before you could do more damage than you already have."

There's an absence of sound.

Alec's face is stricken. But he doesn't take it back.

I was right. Alec does know me. He knows me so well, he can find the perfect thing to say to break my heart.

Slowly, so slowly, the world beyond Alec and me and those horrible, terrible words comes back into focus. I hear the sound of cars rushing by. A glass bottle breaking somewhere in the distance. A string of muttered curses. The creak of a door.

The last one finally pulls my eyes away from Alec. We see the camera at the same time, peeking through the exit door, trained right on us. I don't know how much it caught, don't know when they followed us out. Did they hear the whole thing? Or just the end, when my heart was shattered?

"I can't be here," he says, almost to himself. He looks at me. "Eric's waiting out front. Take the car back to the hotel. Stay in the penthouse. I'll find somewhere else to sleep."

Then he turns his back on me.

He walks down the alleyway.

He turns a corner.

And I'm alone.

CHAPTER 12

The door clicking shut pulls my gaze away from where Alec disappears. It finally spurs me into motion.

Alec doesn't get to walk away from me without even listening.

But when I run to the end of the alleyway, he's nowhere in sight.

Fine, I'll call him. He can ignore my first hundred calls if he wants, but I'll keep calling. He doesn't get to do this.

But my phone is in the penthouse. I don't have pockets or a purse.

The panic shifts then.

I walk back to the door that the jerk with the camera was spying on us through, but it's locked.

My chest tightens.

Think. Think.

I turn a corner out of the alleyway and see the line of people and cameras still camping out at the front entrance.

Eric isn't there. He's so tall, I'm sure I'd see him over the crowd of people if he was. All the cars look the same.

How am I supposed to find him—knock on each window until I finally find the right one?

Bile rises in my throat.

So many people are still lined up along the red carpet, waiting for the celebrities to leave.

I can't go that way. I can't get back in.

I make myself put one foot in front of the other.

This isn't as bad. Not as bad. Not even close. I keep reminding myself, keep repeating it over and over. Because it was true. This was bad. But I had been through worse.

Where do I go?

The hotel.

I start to walk even though I don't know exactly where it is. The windows in the car were so black and I was so distracted by how Alec looked in his suit I could barely take my eyes off him. That was less than three hours ago. Less than three hours ago, my life was perfect.

Now it's ruined.

No, I tell myself. *You can't freak out.*

It takes me twenty minutes of wandering in what I think is the right direction before I see the hotel on a crossroad.

My steps are hurried. It's not really dark here, because there are lights everywhere, but it's got to be after nine at this point and something about being out here at night, alone, is terrifying to me.

I'm in the lobby when I realize I don't have a key.

The lady at the front desk smiles blandly as I walk up to her.

"Hi," I say. "I can't find my key." My voice shakes on the last word.

"Of course. What room number?"

"Um. The penthouse."

Her bland smile falters.

"And what was your name?"

"Nora Green."

"Sorry, that's not the name listed on the room."

I lower my voice. "I'm staying with Alexander Mathis."

"And . . . is Mr. Mathis with you, by any chance?"

"No," I say, trying to smile, but I can feel how wrong it is. "We got separated."

"I'm sorry. We aren't allowed to issue extra keys for our penthouse suite without the person on the account present."

"Look . . ." I can hear the desperation in my voice. "If you could take me up there—"

"I'm not authorized to do that," she says. Then her eyes flit over my shoulder. I turn, hoping it's Alec she's spotted in the lobby. But it isn't. It's a security guard.

The last thing I want is to be thrown out on the streets of LA after dark. I need to get it together now or my night's going to get much worse.

My purse is in that room. Either Alec really isn't coming back, he's already up there getting his things, or he's going to use the hidden garage entrance we used before. Which means I won't see him.

Panic ripples through me. I realize, right there, in front of the receptionist, how utterly screwed I am.

I am alone in a city I don't know.

I cannot fix this.

I have nothing but a dress and shoes that don't even belong to me.

She raises her eyebrows. "Maybe you could wait in the bar?"

"No, I don't want to wait in the—" I make myself stop and think. Waiting in the bar is better than being kicked out. Waiting in the bar is better than being on the streets of LA, alone.

"Fine," I say, swallowing down my tears. "I'll wait in the bar."

She smiles, relieved to be free of me, and gestures to a large open room behind us.

I walk as fast as I can without drawing attention to myself. Almost all of the tables are full, but I manage to find an empty one next to a woman on a laptop. She's so concentrated on the screen she doesn't even glance up when I walk past.

Think. Think.

I run my fingers along the groove in the tabletop, trying to ground myself.

Alec said he wasn't coming back, that he'd find another place to stay. I know no one else here, no one else in the state. The closest person is Mrs. Shep, and she's in Nevada.

Don't panic, I tell myself. But I can't help it. My breaths are coming faster and I can no longer see the tabletop in front of me.

"Are you all right?" a voice asks from beside me. I look up to find the woman has closed her laptop, and she's studying me now instead.

"I'm fine," I say reflexively. The words come out snappy and strained, and I immediately regret them.

"Okay," she says, tilting her head. "But you don't really look fine."

I make myself look up at the ceiling and blink, refusing to let the tears fall.

"Nice dress," she says. "Bad date?"

You hurt people, Nora.

"Something like that," I say, swallowing hard.

She nods, her lips pursed in that same way Cecelia does when she's got something she wants to say, but she's trying to keep it in.

Cecelia.

I clasp my hand to the top of my dress and let out a soft "*Oh.*"

I look up at her, meeting her kind brown eyes. "Can I borrow your phone?"

She pulls a phone out of her purse, unlocks it, and hands it over.

"Thanks," I say. Then I fish the paper out of my bra, right in front of her, because I'm not sure I have a single drop of pride left.

My hands are so shaky that the first time I try to dial Cecelia's number, I mess it up and have to end the call and try again.

The phone rings. And rings. And rings.

Cecelia's voice comes on the line. "Hi. I can't come to the phone right now, please leave—"

I hang up. If it's nine here, then it's midnight at home. What if she silenced her phone?

Stop spiraling.

I take a breath and dial her number again.

Please. Please. Please.

It rings once. Twice. Three times. I'm almost ready to hang up when a sleepy voice answers.

"Hello?"

My throat is tight. I can't speak.

"Hello?"

"Who is it?" I hear my father say in the background.

I swallow twice.

"Cecelia?"

"Nora?" she says.

"What's wrong?" My father's voice is closer now, more urgent.

"I don't know," she says, her mouth away from the receiver. "Nora? Is everything all right?"

The concern in her voice finally gets me. One single tear breaks past the dam I've built up.

"No," I whisper, afraid that if I talk too loudly an entire flood of tears will break through. "Alec and I had a fight."

"What kind of fight, honey?"

"They had a fight?" my dad repeats in the background. Cecelia shushes him.

"A bad one. I tried to come back to the hotel but I can't get in and they won't give me a key."

"He left you there? In the middle of LA?" I've never once heard Cecelia mad. Not a single time. I mean, she's a principal. It makes sense that she's patient to a fault. Apparently, this is her limit.

"We were arguing outside of the theater." I skip over the details of exactly what we were fighting about because I have no idea how to get into that. "He thought I had a ride home, but I couldn't find the car. And I don't have a room key. I don't know what to do." The last part is a whisper.

"Where are you?"

I tell her the name of the hotel.

"Do you have your ID?"

"Yeah, and some money. But that's it. Everything else is in the room."

"Don't worry about that," Cecelia says. "We can replace all of it. My priority now is getting you home safe."

Home. The word sticks inside of my brain like a burr. I didn't think I *had* a home. But now, stuck two thousand miles away, I want nothing more than to be in my room, in my pajamas, watching *Gilmore Girls* on DVD. I want nothing more than to know my father and Cecelia are sleeping soundly in the room down the hall.

Is that home?

"There's an Uber on the way," Cecelia says, bringing me back to the present. "You sit in that lobby and don't move. If anyone says a word, give them my number. I'll buy you a room if I have to, but I don't want you wandering the streets of LA."

"An Uber to where?"

"The airport."

"I don't have a ticket," I say. "Al—" I stumble over his name. "He took care of all of that."

"I'm online now getting you the soonest flight out."

There's no telling how expensive that's going to be. "I'll pay you back."

Obviously, my arrangement with Alec is over. I won't have the money for a housing deposit, so I won't need to pay the rest of my tuition with the money from the movie.

There's a long pause.

"Nora," Cecelia says. "You're my daughter. My daughter isn't paying me back, not one red cent. Get on the airplane and come home safe."

I have to swallow twice before I can speak.

"Okay," I whisper softly.

"Your dad is on his way out the door now, he'll be there by the time you land."

"He'll . . . what? It's midnight. He can't drive that far this late. I can sleep in the airport, or take a bus."

"Nora." Her voice is firm. "Let him love you, okay? Just this once."

You're so stubborn.

I was so sure keeping my father at arm's length was the best thing for both of us.

I want to be so mad at Alec. I *am* so mad at him.

But what if he was a little bit right in the very worst way?

"Your dad will be there when you land."

When Dante wrote about the circles of hell, he missed the one where I went through airport security and an almost five-hour flight in a ball gown.

People look at me first because of the gown. Then, they look at me because they realize it's the same gown the girl was wearing with Alec in the now-viral clip of us fighting. I heard it dozens of times in the airport, playing on repeat from different phones and laptops and tablets.

So many pictures are taken. Eventually, I hide in a bathroom stall until the flight number on the ticket the front desk lady printed me is called. To be safe, I wait until they do that one that's like, *Get to the gate now or we're leaving you.* But that's another mistake, because then everyone watches me walk down the aisle. In a ball gown. At least my makeup still looks great.

Silver lining of not being able to cry more than that one singular tear I shed talking to Cecelia.

After we land, I find my father waiting right outside our arrival gate.

I stop, and people flow around me as we stare at each other. Eventually, my legs work again.

"How did you get past security?" I ask.

He holds up a crumpled and bent ticket. He's been twisting it over and over again.

"Bought a ticket."

Something pricks at the backs of my eyes.

"You bought a ticket?"

"Didn't want to miss you. It's a big airport. You don't have a phone."

He says it like it's nothing.

You're my daughter. Cecelia's words echo in my head, followed by my father's.

It's more complicated than that, Nora.

"Thanks," I say.

He nods and holds up a bag with the airport logo on it. "Saw the pictures. Figured you could use a change of clothes."

He gently hands the bag over to me. I can't see it. My eyes are so blurred there's no world around me anymore. It's me and this bag and my father who I can't see through the tears, but I can smell. It's coffee and the candle Cecelia always has burning and the soil that's permanently etched into his hands from the flower beds. I realize that it smells like home. Not in the way Mama did. In a new way, that would never be the same as the old one that was all horses and Aqua Net and Creme Savers.

But still.

"You bought me clothes?"

"You needed them," is all he says.

I change into the matching ATL airport sweatpants and shirt in a bathroom stall and hang the dress on the hook of the door. Maybe someone would take it, maybe they'd throw it out. I don't care. The right thing to do would be to give it back to Alec somehow. But I don't think I'll ever see Alexander Mathis again.

My heart skips a beat.

There's a slew of paparazzi outside the airport, and while I can't say they're camped out here looking for me with 100 percent surety, I'm still glad for the change of clothes and the hat. If I was still in that gown, I would have been done for.

We make it to my father's truck without incident. I settle in for the long ride, trying to decide between saying thank you again and asking why he did it. But before I can decide which to go with, he pulls off the freeway and into the parking lot of a Waffle House.

"Come on," he says. "You need something to eat."

Steam rises steadily from the cup of coffee in front of my father.

My waffle sits mostly untouched. I am starving, but in that way where you can't really feel it. You know you're hungry, you know you need to eat, but you can't quite figure out how exactly to make your mouth work right, to make your hand pick up the food and get it in there. Somehow all of a sudden, I've forgotten how to be a human being.

Every time I think I might be about to figure out how to get one more bite in my mouth and down my throat, I think of the way Alec looked at me in that alley.

"Your mama was an easy woman to love."

I freeze. It takes me a minute to even look up at him. When I do, I find him stirring his coffee, studying it hard.

"I know," I say.

He nods. "So free-spirited. Blew in and turned my whole world upside down. I loved her. Should have told you that a long time ago. Didn't know how to say it."

The information is so sudden and blunt I don't have time to decide how I feel about it. Is that a good thing? Do I feel better, knowing he loved my mama? Or is it worse, knowing he loved her, but not enough to be my dad?

"Cecelia and I, we weren't even having troubles. I just saw your mama and I felt something spark inside of me I hadn't felt in a long time. I think I was being stupid, like old men who don't feel old yet sometimes are. I liked the way I felt when I was with her. The whole thing, it was selfish. And wrong. Hurt a lot of people to make myself feel good.

"One day, she came to my work. Showed up and waltzed into my office. Told me I had to decide right then and there—her, or Cecelia. I hesitated. Just for a few seconds. Didn't know what to say. But your mama, she had whatever she was looking for. Saw it on my face, I guess. I didn't see her after that. Not until ten years later."

"When we moved back."

He nods.

"Walked into Danny's. Was doing a pickup for pizza night, a rare occasion in our house, as you know."

He laughs a little, but I'm too enveloped in the story to do the same.

"Saw her sitting in the back. Couldn't breathe. She was still so beautiful. Maybe a few more lines on her face, but honestly, she was the prettier for it. I walked over without even thinking. Realized all of a sudden that I was halfway to her table. She looked up, locked eyes with me. Her face fell. I can still see it. Plays like a movie." He sighs. "She shook her head, once. Then she looked at the young girl sitting in front of her."

"Me," I whisper.

"You," he says.

It's quiet for a minute. He fiddles with the Splenda package and little crystals cascade down onto the table one by one.

"She met me out in the parking lot. Must have known I'd wait for her. We didn't talk long. Long enough for her to tell me what I already knew, from the minute I saw you sitting there with her. That I was a dad. Had been for years and had no idea. Then she told me to leave the two of you alone. That you had been living without me for all this time and y'all could do it for longer. Said y'all didn't need me."

This is a whole new kind of mourning. She knew how much I wanted to know him, and kept him from me anyway.

I breathe. I breathe and breathe and breathe and try to get rid of the burning deep anger.

Because I don't know how to be mad at a dead person. How do you get that kind of mad out?

"I needed you."

It's all I can say.

He looks up at the ceiling blinking rapidly. "I tried for years, but she told me the same thing every time. Told me I couldn't be a part-time dad, pop in and then go back to my real family. When I told her I wanted more than to pop in, she said that it would throw your life into chaos to have to spend time here and there and uproot you from a loving home. Eventually, I believed her. You seemed happy. Maybe you didn't want me. Maybe it was better if I wasn't around. Better to leave y'all be. So, I did, mostly. But I couldn't help myself. Came to your games when you played soccer for half a season. Watched every performance when you were in *Footloose*. Bought all the yearbooks. They're in the back of my closet."

"You were at my soccer games?" I say.

"I was."

I push my waffles around in the syrup. They're cold now.

"You should have tried harder," I whisper. It's not a fair thing to say, I know it before the words are even out of my mouth.

"I know," he says. "But I was scared. Too scared to fight your mom and uproot your life. Too scared to tell Cecelia and uproot hers. No matter what I did, I was ruining someone's life."

"I'm sorry."

He looks at me, brows furrowed. "Sorry for what?"

"Because I ruined your lives anyway."

"No." His voice is sharp. He stares at me. "Don't you ever say that again. You have never been anything but wanted. Some nights, I wanted to see you so badly it physically hurt. So don't you ever say that again."

I drink in the words. I let them seep down into the darkest parts of me, the ones that ache.

I let them run over me like a balm.

"I know you can't forgive me. Not this fast. But I hope—" His voice catches and he swallows, his Adam's apple bobbing. "I hope you can let me try. To be your dad, I mean."

I can't stop the tears. They've started and there's no avoiding them. But I still manage to speak.

"Yeah," I say, even though every part of me wants to say no, to run and curl up into myself, where I can't get hurt. But a bigger part of me is tired of working so hard to stay mad. "I'd like to try, too."

Charlotte and Brianna are at my dining room table when we make it home.

Cecelia is on me so fast I don't even have time to get all the way through the door. She wraps her arms around me, hugging so tight I'm genuinely afraid I might never breathe again. But I lean into it. I push away the thoughts that tell me I'm betraying my mom by letting her love me, that there's no way for a woman to *not* hate me when I ruined her marriage. The way she holds on makes me feel put together. The pieces that have been threatening to fall apart are held in place until I can get them back where they belong.

I lean into Cecelia.

"Oh, sweetheart."

Then Brianna and Charlotte are there, wrapping their arms around the two of us.

My father leans against the wall. Cecelia leaves me in the care of my friends and pulls out the hot cocoa mix. Organic.

"I'm DEFCON level five pissed," Charlotte says once we're at the table.

"That's the low one," Brianna says. "You're DEFCON one pissed."

"Uh, five is higher than one."

"Yeah, that's not the way it works."

Charlotte shakes her head. "Whatever. The point is, I'm pissed, Nora."

"Lay off, Char. Give the girl a minute to breathe," Brianna says, holding my hand under the table.

"No. Giving her space got us into this in the first place. We should have asked more questions because it never made sense." She looks at me. "None of it does. So, welcome home, hope you slept on the flight. Cause you're not leaving this table until I know exactly what happened and why Alexander Mathis called me from your phone six hours ago in a panic asking where you were."

"He called you?" I say, my stomach dropping.

"Both of us," Brianna says. "The first time he was a mess. Didn't even sound like himself. Then he called another time to let us know you'd been spotted at the airport. Said you were safe, and that he was only calling to let us know he'd be leaving your phone and bag with security on set. So. What's going on? Are you guys *actually* dating? And why would he leave your phone with security instead of bringing it to you?"

I am fully aware of Cecelia and my father behind me, puttering around in the kitchen.

There's a part of me that wants to lie. Wants to tell the bare minimum and cover the rest up and figure it out myself.

But figuring things out myself has not gone well for me so far. Not when I tried to find the money for Montana myself. Not when I kept the text messages from Alec and tried to fix it all on my own.

I tell them everything. I start with the housing deposit and the deadline that was so tight I thought I'd never find the money. I tell them how badly I wanted to go, how I thought I would have done anything for it. How I wanted it so bad, I agreed to fake date a guy I couldn't stand to even look at.

Then I tell them about how I stopped hating him. How we almost kissed, and then really kissed. About how well he got to know me, and how, despite that, he could still believe I told Elizabeth anything.

The room is silent, except for the sound of Cecelia placing the mugs in front of each of us one by one.

"So," Charlotte finally says. "You fell in love. With Alexander Mathis."

"Yeah," I say. "I guess I did."

"And you're not going to Montana?" Brianna asks.

"No. I can't take Alec's money. I won't. And even if the production pays me, that money was for tuition, and it wouldn't come in time for the housing deposit anyway."

"So, in all, your life went to crap. And you didn't think to tell your best friends the whole story."

"Yeah," I say, face heating.

Alec threw it in my face to hurt me, just like he was hurting. But he had been right. How quickly he had seen to the true root of my problem. I decide what's best and I do it, regardless of how it makes anyone else feel. I'm like a damn horse with blinders on, can't see anything but what's right in front of me.

I only think about what letting people in might do to *me*. How it could hurt *me*.

I never think about how shutting everyone out might be hurting *them*.

"You can't keep pushing us away."

"I think she feels bad enough about it, Charlotte. Lay off."

"Fine. I'm done. For now." She shoots me a look and even though her words are tight, there is fierce love in her eyes. I know I'm forgiven. But I'll still work to earn it. "Instead, we can talk about how you're going to go to that movie set and make Alexander listen to you."

"It won't do any good," I say, my heart shattering as I realize how right I am. He'd never give me a chance to explain. I saw the utter betrayal in his face. He thinks I chose Elizabeth's happiness over Delilah's safety. He thinks I hurt his best friend, the person he'd do anything for. There's no coming back from that.

"But you love him," Charlotte says.

"I don't think that matters," I say, avoiding the question.

"Even if it doesn't," she says, trying another angle, "you have to tell him it was Sean. At least so he knows what a snake the guy is."

"Tomorrow," Cecelia says. She's been silent the entire time I told my story. Hasn't said a word. Neither has my father. I'd almost forgotten they were here. "Nora had a hell of a twenty-four hours. It's time for her to take a shower and get some sleep."

As much as I love having Charlotte and Brianna here, Cecelia's right. And I'm thankful that she said it, because everything is crashing down on me at once and I think I might not make it through a shower without passing out.

"The two of you can come with me to Belk in the morning. We need to get Nora some new clothes to replace the ones she left in LA."

"It was some pajamas and a change of clothes for the flight."

"Don't deprive me of an opportunity to shop, dear," she says, gently pulling me up from the chair and leading me to the stairs. "Shower, then rest."

"Okay," I say. My foot is on the first step, but I stop and turn back around, looking her in the face fully. Her eyes are so kind. I'm not sure how I didn't notice it before. "Thank you," I say. "For everything."

Her lip quivers and she leans in for another crushingly tight hug. "Anytime, dear."

Charlotte and Brianna drive me to set the next day. I want to say I would have made it myself. That I wouldn't have chickened out when the paved road turned to dirt, or when I saw the white top of the tent for the first time in the distance. But with Brianna at the wheel and Charlotte in the seat between us, the windows of my truck down so our hair twists and tangles together, I'm arriving on set whether I want to or not.

Brianna parks in the lot.

"This is way less cool than I expected," she says.

"It's like finding out Santa isn't real," Charlotte says. "Where's the magic?"

I stare at Sebastian's makeshift office.

"Ripping a Band-Aid off slowly makes it worse, you know?" Bree says.

I grip the door handle, forcing myself to push it open after I count to three in my head.

Twice.

"We'll be here waiting," Charlotte yells through the open window.

Sebastian sees me halfway through my walk over. His sweet, amenable face falls a little, and my stomach drops. Not good.

"Nora," he says once I'm a few steps away. "How are you?" His smile is tense.

"Could be better."

He nods sympathetically. "I bet. The internet can be a brutal place."

Waves of nausea hit me. I haven't even been near a screen. What was the internet saying about me?

He leans back in his chair and I catch a glimpse of neon green.

"How's the ankle?" I ask, nodding toward his cast.

"Doc says six weeks and I'll be good as new."

"I'm glad you're okay."

Sebastian looks me up and down. "How about you? You all right?"

"No," I say, deciding to keep with my new goal of honesty.

"May take a little longer than six weeks." He shrugs, leaning back in his chair. "You'll get there."

"I hope so."

He leans forward awkwardly, his cast keeping his leg at an uncomfortable angle. When he sits up straight again, he's got my bag in his lap, a manila folder on top of it. My name is handwritten on the front.

Sebastian hands them over with a grimace.

"This was left for you."

I drop my bag in the dirt and open the envelope right there in front of him. My phone slides out first. Then a check. I flip it over to see it's my promised salary, made out to me from the production company. "I haven't finished my work," I say. "Filming hasn't wrapped yet."

"The production no longer needs your services," he says simply.

I have to bite my tongue. This isn't Sebastian's fault. This is mine.

Does that mean I don't get to say goodbye to Ethel?

I sigh and start to put everything back in the envelope, but I feel something else inside.

When I flip it over, a stack of hundreds falls out with a note.

What I owe. I've doubled it to cover the cost of the flight home, since you ran off without even explaining yourself.

I actually see red.

Since *I* ran off without *explaining myself*? Is he serious?

There's something brewing inside of me, slowly inching into all the spots that had been filled with sadness and remorse and heartbreak. I had been so focused on the guilt for my part in this, for what I had done, that I had forgotten about how Alec had left me in LA, how he didn't hesitate to believe it was me who had sold him out. And now, with his stupid, self-righteous note in my hand, I'm finding that there's a lot of room for anger inside of me, too. And it was about to make me do something I'd probably regret.

"Sebastian," I say, my voice low and controlled. Much more controlled than the tempest raging inside of me. "Do you have a pair of crutches?"

"No," he says, brow furrowed.

"There's no golf cart hidden behind the office?"

"No."

"Scooter?"

He seems to catch on then.

"Nora—"

"It's nothing personal," I say, shoving my phone and the check in my back pocket and grabbing the stack of money that was enough to cover my housing and more. "I'll be back in five."

"Now, Nora, you can't—"

But I don't hear the rest. I'm already past his little office and run-walking toward the crowd of white tents, fueled by nothing but anger and adrenaline.

Heads turn my way when I walk through craft services. Forks clatter and voices rise but I don't catch any of the words. I'm too focused on trying to find a singular glimpse of red hair.

A flap blows open in the breeze and I see him, then. By luck, I happen to catch sight of him sitting in his makeup chair, the one they have reserved for him. That I see him at all is a miracle with the crowd of women around him, messing with his hair and dotting concealer on his face.

I don't let myself see how dark the circles underneath his eyes are, don't let myself focus on the way his mouth turns downward, or ruminate on how I'd kill to watch his frown turn into that irritable, annoying smirk of his.

"Ran off without even explaining myself?" I say, bursting into the tent. Every head turns my way. Alec's eyes widen, and I hate the way my heart flutters at seeing him again, despise how one look from him causes desperation to claw at my insides. I want his lips on my forehead, his hands on my waist. "That's what you think happened?"

"That's exactly what happened," Alec says. His voice is cold. He's furious. That does nothing but fan the flames of my anger.

"You're an idiot, you know that?"

His eyes flash. "Did you really trespass onto set to tell me that?"

"Should we call security?" one of the girls whispers.

"*You* abandoned *me* in an alleyway, Alec."

He stands up, ripping off the barber cape and throwing it in his seat. "I took a walk around the block. I left Eric for you. Imagine my surprise when I come back and find him still waiting for me, you nowhere in sight. Eric spent hours driving around looking for you. I searched the entire building. I called your friends. Despite everything, I searched for you nonstop until I saw a picture of you in LAX. Making an executive decision without consulting anyone, running away from your problems—what a surprise."

I want to scream. "You left me alone without a phone. You told me you weren't coming back. *You* told *me* to go. Eric was nowhere in sight. I had to walk back to the hotel at night. They wouldn't let me in the room. I was alone in a city I didn't know with nowhere to stay and no idea if, or when, you were coming back. Do you have any idea how terrifying that was for me?"

He falters. "I didn't think—"

"No, you didn't think. I was scared. You were gone. So I found a way home. You don't get to call me a coward for that. You don't get to judge me for that." The anger is starting to fade. I can feel everyone in the tent staring at me, can hear the silence outside that lets me know others are listening. I'm mortified when I feel the tears at the corners of my eyes. "I know you were mad. And hurt. That what you found out must have—" I stop, a sob choking me.

Alec watches me, pain and anger and betrayal in his eyes.

I swallow down the tears. "I'm sorry I didn't tell you about Elizabeth's messages, I really am. But you and I could barely tolerate each other when she first started texting me. You couldn't even bring yourself to say my *name*. She offered me money to find out who you were with, and even though I couldn't stand you I all but told her to go to hell. I should have blocked her, should have told her to get a therapist and leave me out of it. Then I should have told you she messaged. I'm sorry I didn't."

I gulp down my tears. "I didn't sell you out, Alec. Not to her, not to anyone. I have made my share of mistakes. But so have you."

I throw the money on the floor in front of him, but he doesn't even glance at it.

"That's your money," he says. His voice isn't angry anymore, but it isn't sorrowful, either. He's torn, and I hate it—hate that he still doubts me. "You did a job. Take it."

I laugh once, soft. "My job was to *pretend* to fall in love with you, Alec. I completely and utterly failed."

He stares at me with that unfathomable expression in his eyes.

An assistant comes into the tent, headset on and clipboard clutched to her chest.

"Security is on the way."

"Don't bother," I say. "I'm leaving." I turn to go, but before I'm out of the tent, I look back at Alec. "You should fire your agent, by the way."

His face falls, and I know he understands immediately.

Then, before anyone can stop me, I run out of the tent.

I run past my coworkers. Past Amanda, who's looking on while biting her nails to the quick. Past Diya, who I desperately wish I could explain myself to. I run to the stables, because I can live without explaining myself to Diya. I can live with never seeing anyone on this stupid set ever again. But there's someone I can't leave without saying goodbye to.

She nickers softly when she sees me.

I'm in her stall when the tears start to fall in earnest. She nudges the top of my head with her nose, and then, like she can feel how much I need her, she dips her head down and rests it softly on my chest.

A deep sob rips through me.

Ethel doesn't move.

I run my fingers through her mane.

"I made such a mess," I say, hiccupping on the last word. "Such a mess." She breathes softly against my chest.

This isn't the first time Ethel has held me steady while I cried. But I think it might be the last.

I can't catch my breath after that thought.

She stands there, warm and steady, until I finally collect myself. When someone clears their throat at the end of the stables, Ethel looks up and breathes softly on my cheek.

"Nora," Sebastian says. "I'm sorry. But you need to follow me out now."

I run my hand across her muzzle.

"I love you so much," I tell her. "I'll miss you, sweet girl." She touches my cheek gently with her nose. Then I whisper goodbye.

Sebastian escorts me back to the parking lot, hobbling along.

Alec does not catch me as I leave. He does not run after me to apologize, or to ask me to explain.

Bree and Charlotte don't say a word when I get in the truck. I think they can tell just how bad it was by looking at me.

Char puts her arm around me, and Bree drives us safely home.

CHAPTER 13

I spend days cleaning out my messages.

People from high school, media outlets, countless invites to interviews. Though I don't know exactly how they got my number, I suspect it was Elizabeth who leaked it. I want to be mad. But at least I have Charlotte and Bree. I have my dad. I have Cecelia. Who does Elizabeth have in her corner?

Eventually, Cecelia takes me to have my number changed. It's not worth the hassle of trying to block everyone who reaches out.

I'm sending an apology text to Mrs. Shep (whose messages had gotten progressively more irritated over the last week as she asked me over and over again why she was seeing new pictures of me on the internet every day) when an email comes through. The subject line catches my eye.

Room Assignment

I open it before the notification can disappear.

Dear Ms. Green,

Below you will find your roommate, with their contact information and links to any social media sites they have shared with us.

We recommend reaching out before move-in day so you have sufficient time to become acquainted with one another. Along with your roommate assignment, you will find a list of both recommended and required items for your first semester. Please contact Lynn Stanton with any questions. We look forward to welcoming you in Billings soon.

Each day I give myself an allotted twenty minutes to feel really, really crappy about not being able to go to Montana. After that, I'm not allowed to think about it anymore. I made my decision when I threw the money at Alec's feet, which, in retrospect, was maybe a *bit* dramatic. Looks like I'm going to have my twenty minutes of pity-partying right now.

Sighing, I press the hyperlink and hold my breath as the line starts ringing. I hope I get her voicemail so I don't have to talk to an actual human being. My luck is still garbage, apparently, because a cheery voice answers after the fifth ring.

"Lynn Stanton's office."

"Um, hi. Can I talk to Ms. Stanton?"

"Hold, please."

I don't even have enough time to hate the hold music before another, less peppy, voice answers.

"Lynn Stanton."

"Hi, I'm calling to clear up a mistake regarding the housing emails sent out today."

"Name?"

"Nora Green. I need to—"

"Roomed with Chessie Morales. Is the issue with your roommate herself?"

"No, it's not the roommate, I'm sure she's great."

"The room assignment, then? Sorry, bottom floor is spoken for. We're looking into putting in an elevator, but the building's old." She clicks her keyboard. "You're only on the second floor, though. You're fine."

"Stairs are fine, that's not my problem."

"Okay," she says, sighing. "Let's hear it, then."

"Well, there's the small matter of me not having *paid* for the housing. Which I'd be happy to do, second floor or not—but I can't." My voice is steady, and I'm proud, because I really don't want to cry on the phone to this poor woman. She doesn't need to hear about my very public breakup with a very public figure, or about *why* exactly I couldn't pay for my housing.

"Assignments don't go out for students who aren't paid in full. It's a whole system. Doesn't fail."

"Well, it failed, because I am definitely not paid in full." My bank account is healthier than it has ever been, thanks to the production check. It is a lot of money, but not enough.

Never had been.

There's a cascade of clicking, and I can almost picture her acrylics on the clacky keyboard.

Lynn sighs, and I expect her to start apologizing, to tell me there was in fact an error.

"Wire transfer came through yesterday. Tuition for two years, housing for two years, an additional allowance for supplies, saddles, uniforms, etcetera. You're paid in full. Anything else I can help you with?"

The impatience drips off of her voice, but I ignore it. "Um, you need to look at that again. The money was applied to the wrong student's account."

"Not assigned to the wrong account, Ms. Green. Noted under the payment is a detailed account of each phone call. One to ask the payment amount, one to inform us it was coming, and one today, ensuring it was applied." She laughs. "I don't think I've ever had anyone argue so hard that their payment *wasn't* made. The opposite, sure."

"Who?"

"Excuse me?"

"Who made the payment?"

She says a name.

I make her repeat it twice.

Then I tell her thanks.

I hang up the phone.

And I burst into tears.

Well. So much for keeping it together.

The thing about me is I can't cook.

Mama couldn't, either. We did not eat well, not unless Mrs. Shep made us dinner. Every single Sunday we were at her table with whoever else on the ranch was lucky enough to get invited that week. But we didn't get random invites—we had a standing one. Every Sunday. No excuses.

Now, when Cecelia and my father come home, there's a lot of food on the table. But I did not cook a single lick of it. Cleo Gaskins at the farm-to-table restaurant in town did. Cost a pretty penny, but that's all right, because I'm flush now.

"Smells mighty good in here," my father says. I feel a little blush creep up even though I wasn't the one who did the cooking.

"What's the occasion?" Cecelia asks.

"For fun," I say. "Come on. Have a seat." They give each other a look, but they do what I say. We dig in, and I listen while they talk about their day. When they finally ask how mine went, I decide it's time.

"I had a weird phone call today, actually."

"Really?" Cecelia says, brow furrowed.

"Really. From that equine program. The one I told Charlotte and Brianna about the other day." I look at my dad, but at the mention of the program, he suddenly starts to find his dinner plate very interesting. "You two were in the kitchen then. I forgot, because you were so quiet. But then I remembered the hot cocoa you made, Cecelia."

Cecelia's cheeks are pink, and she's trying to catch my father's eye, but he's determined to look hard enough to discern the atomic makeup of the sweet potatoes.

"I got an email, and called to inform them I did not, in fact, pay for my housing. Or the other half of my tuition, for that matter. But they told me I was paid in full. Interesting, right?"

My father finally looks up, and it breaks my heart a little to see how worried he is. He thinks I'm about to yell at him or storm out of the room because he made my dreams come true.

"Probably should have asked first."

"Maybe," I say, smiling so he knows I'm not mad. "Lynn in the bursar's office might have had a less stressful day if you had."

"Do you remember that stack of college applications I left on your dresser?" Cecelia asks.

I nod.

"Well. Oh, why don't you tell her, Thomas."

My father nods. "When I learned about—" He stops and looks at Cecelia out of the corner of his eye, but she gestures for him to go on. "When I found out about you, I wanted a lot of things. But couldn't make much of it happen." He shifts in his seat. "I went to that quiz bowl of yours, the one in the old theater building downtown. You were smart as a whip. Should have won that, but that boy dragged your team down."

"Nathan," I say in a whisper. He had missed every single question.

My father nods. "Realized then, you were going to be something big. And I knew, if I couldn't do everything I wanted, I could do *something*. I could save up some money, for when you went to college. So, I started putting a little bit away, here and there. Then a little bit became a lot."

I don't know what to say.

"You look as shocked as I was," Cecelia says, and I marvel at how she takes all of this in stride.

It's quiet for a minute. They're good about that, I realize. Letting me think for a minute.

I'm the one to break the silence.

"You went to my quiz bowl."

He nods.

"And you saved money for my college."

He nods again.

"I don't think—" I start, but I have to clear my throat and blink away the tears before I try again. "I don't think that's the kind of thing you do for a kid you regret having."

A single tear falls down his cheek and disappears behind his beard. "No, Nora. You sure don't."

I don't know which one of us stands first. Were his arms around me before mine were around him? But it doesn't matter, really, who started it.

What matters is, I'm in our kitchen. In our home. In the arms of my dad who does not hate me. Who does not regret me or my existence or my presence. A dad who could have done better, could have done more. But a dad who was here now, hugging me in a way I've always dreamed about.

It takes me a minute to realize what I'm feeling, the way things are all tangled inside of me with relief and happiness and sadness and bitterness and joy. There's something in there I haven't felt since before Mama fell off that horse and left me.

One deep breath, a gentle squeeze from my dad, and I realize then, what it is.

I feel safe.

I hug back a little tighter. And maybe I cry a little.

But that's okay. I don't think my dad minds. He's got plenty of clean shirts.

CHAPTER 14

One month later.

The sky really is bigger in Montana.

I thought it was one of those things people said like, *Everything is bigger in Texas*, which I guess could also be true. I've never been to Texas, so, honestly, who knows?

But the sky here is *big*. You look at it too long and you think it's going to collapse down onto you, so I try not to do it too much. Right now, though, I can't help myself. There's not a singular cloud anywhere in sight. The Beartooth Mountains sit directly in front of me, snowcapped even though it's September, which seems early as far as snow goes. That's another thing, it's cold as hell here—which, thinking on it, doesn't make a ton of sense as far as sayings go, but still. It's freezing. Thankfully Cecelia had insisted on a heavy shopping spree. I have new clothes, new toiletries, and new hair products for my new haircut.

That last one *I* had insisted on. It helped—with the people, I mean. No one really looks anymore. Maybe it's the time. Maybe four weeks was finally long enough for people to start thinking about something else, something that had nothing to do with me or him. Or maybe it really was the hair that now sat an inch above my shoulders. Either way, I'm happy with my hair, and happy with the lack of attention.

It most definitely is not a product of my heart-shattering breakup, as Charlotte keeps suggesting. The three of us FaceTime every single night, and she always asks how I'm doing. The answer? Complicated.

I'm happy in Montana. The program is better than I could have imagined. But every day, before my eyes are even open, I think of him. It's not even something I decide to do, my mind *does* it. One morning it's the feeling of his hand on my back guiding me forward. Another, it's the way he infuriated and infatuated me at the same time with his stupid smirk. Every morning, without fail.

He's thriving. I try not to look, I really do. But sometimes, I can't help myself. The need to see him, to know he's real and I didn't imagine everything gets so overwhelming that I search his name. He's filming again, this time a huge movie, one that will release in theaters everywhere and probably be nominated for some Oscars.

I had hoped I would be over him by now. But I am not over him. Not by a mile.

Maybe the Montana air will help. It's supposed to be good for sickness.

"Sorry," Chessie says, pulling me out of my sky hypnosis and back to the front door of our dorm. "Couldn't find my hat."

The great thing about Chessie (well, one of many great things, she really is the best roommate ever) is that, since she hails from Arizona, she hates the cold as much as I do. Our dorm room is always toasty, and we never argue about it.

"No problem, we're not that late."

We start the same walk we take every day, over to the stables.

"Making any progress with George?" she asks.

I groan. "No. That horse is the most frustrating animal I've ever dealt with."

She laughs. "Sucks you had to take one of the school horses."

Chessie is rich. Most of the people here are. They all came with their own horses. My whole class. Not me, though. Things are great between my dad and I. I think if I ask, he would probably buy a horse for me. But that's a big ask, especially when the school provides them.

"I'll figure it out," I say.

"No doubt," Chessie says. "Oh, hell," she murmurs. I follow her gaze to find Tessa watching us, her face pinched. Maybe we're a little later than I thought. Tessa points at me and makes a *come here* gesture.

"She's talking to you, right?" I ask hopefully.

"Definitely not," Chessie says. "Good luck."

"You're abandoning me?" I hiss.

"Yep," she says, unabashed. "Fill me in later."

I sigh and jog over to Tessa, wondering if tardiness was grounds for being kicked out of the program.

"You're late," she says, leaning against the paddock fence where Douglas is grooming his Andalusian—the most expensive horse I've ever seen in real life.

"Sorry. Won't happen again."

"Whatever. I'm more pissed about the horse you dropped on me today. Would have been nice to have a little notice. Had to find a new stall for George last minute."

"What are you talking about?"

Tessa scowls. "Let me know next time you're going to surprise me with something over six hundred pounds, all right?"

She pushes off the fence and walks away, leaving me there utterly confused. I head toward the stable that holds my horse and the other school assignments, wondering if this is some kind of joke. Mine is the very last stall, and I expect to look over the gate and see George standing there, looking at me with his stubborn expression.

But it's not George in the stall.

"Ethel?" I gasp. She huffs a breath and hoofs the ground, as excited to see me as I am to see her. "Ethel," I whisper again, throwing open the stall door and running my fingers through her mane. She huffs again, sending my new hair flying. I can't help myself. I gently wrap my arms around her neck and give her a soft squeeze, breathing in the scent of her. "What in the world are you doing here?" I ask, knowing good and well she can't answer me. I let her go and step back so I can take her all in. "You look so good, my girl."

She bobs her head three times at my shoulder, and even though she can't talk, I know exactly what she means. I laugh and say, "I got a haircut."

"It suits you," a voice says from behind me.

When I turn, my hand still on Ethel's neck, I see Alec standing in the open door.

His hands are in his pockets and he's wearing a flannel shirt that's a few shades darker than his hair.

Dreaming of him had seemed like enough. But with Alec standing here in front of me, as painfully handsome as he'd been the first time I'd seen him, I realize my dreams were soft echoes, tracings done from vague memories. They were nothing compared to the real thing.

We stare at each other in silence. My hand runs up and down Ethel's neck nervously.

"Most people send flowers, you know."

Alec breathes a laugh. "I thought you'd like this better."

I want to smile, tell him he's right. I want to throw my arms around his neck the same way I did Ethel's. But I stand there and wait, because I have no idea what he's doing here.

"I fired Sean," he says.

"Good."

"He admitted it immediately. Told me he'd do it again in a heartbeat. So I told him he was fired. Didn't take it well."

"What a surprise."

Alec nods. "It's been a really long time since someone's yelled at me like that."

I think he means Sean. Then he says, "You had hair and makeup buzzing for hours. Delayed production."

"Yeah, well. You kind of deserved it."

He smiles. "Yeah. I kind of did."

Then, the smile disappears. He looks at me and I'm reminded of the sky outside, how easy it is to take one look and get utterly lost in it.

"Every night, when I close my eyes, I see you standing in that alley. I see the look on your face after I said the most vile words that have ever left my lips."

"Alec—"

"It was my uncle and my pictures all over again. It was every friend who fell off one by one as they got an offer good enough to sell some part of me to the world. But the way I reacted, the things I said . . ." He shakes his head. "I can't remember ever being so ashamed." He stands up straight and walks toward me, stopping three steps away.

"But, in the beginning, at least I thought it was justified. I told myself you had betrayed me. Then you came storming on to the set and threw that money at my feet. I knew, right when I saw your face. You didn't have to say a thing, Nora. No one can fake that kind of hurt."

"Not even the greatest actress you know?"

"You're a terrible actress," he whispers.

He takes a steadying breath. "I don't expect you to ever forgive me. But I wanted to try to show you how sorry I was. When your dad told me where you were—"

"You talked to my dad?"

"Once filming wrapped, I sat on your doorstep for ten hours before he relented and let me in. I told him everything, and after he and Cecelia thoroughly reamed me for abandoning you, they told me exactly where to find you." He studies me with those green eyes that I had somehow forgotten the exact shade of. "They love you a lot, you know."

"I know."

He nods. "I'm sorry, Nora. Sorry for what I said. Sorry for leaving you in that alley, even if I had no intention of abandoning you. I should have known how terrifying that would be. Most of all, I'm sorry for not giving you time to explain."

I swallow my tears and breathe all my last bits of anger out. "Me too. What you said that night was the hardest thing I've ever had to hear. But you were right about how I shut people out. How I make a decision and power through without a thought about anyone else. I'm trying to fix all the damage I've done." My breath hitches and I find it harder to see the exact color of his eyes through my tears.

"But there are some things I'm not sorry for," I say. "I'm not sorry for how that changed things with my dad. With Charlotte and Bree and Cecelia." Tears stream down my face. "Most of all, I'm not sorry for falling for you when it was supposed to be fake. I tried to be sorry, tried to make myself regret it. But I can't."

He closes the distance between us, and I revel in the feel of his hand on my face—here, in real life, not in my imagination or my dreams. "From the first moment you said my name, voice full of irritation, I have been enamored," he whispers. I laugh, but he continues.

"You were the most annoying thing I had ever encountered, but I went to bed each night dreaming up excuses to see you the next day." His thumb runs across the edge of my lip. "I loved you when you almost knocked down my door to yell at me on set. I loved you every time you called me an idiot or a jerk or any of the very colorful names you have for me."

I laugh and sob at the same time, leaning into the hand he gently places on my cheek. He looks down at me, and I know what he's going to ask next. I nod before he even says the words, stretching myself up on my tiptoes in invitation.

Alec's lips brush across mine in a tender sweep. The barest touch. I forget how to breathe, but it's fine, because I'm not sure breathing is a necessity anymore.

His eyelashes flutter against mine, then he kisses me fully this time, in the way that you'd think Alexander Mathis would kiss his leading lady. I'm so thankful for every moment of longing, every second of heartbreak because it was all worth it to be here, in his arms, his extraordinary lips against mine.

It feels better than all my dreams.

We're interrupted by a horse neighing gently behind me.

I pull away, and Alec leans in closer, like he cannot possibly wait another second to kiss me again.

"I'm not sure Ethel enjoys so much PDA in her stall."

"Ethel. Right," he says, as if he completely forgot we were in a stable with a horse bigger than the two of us put together. He steps back and runs his fingers through his hair, and I resolve to reach up and do the same later, when he's least expecting it. I always wanted to know how it felt.

"How do you feel about a first date?" Alec asks, staring at my lips in a way that makes me blush.

"We've been on three," I remind him.

"Two *fake* dates," he says. "Two fake dates with *Alexander Mathis*, and cameras, and many ulterior motives. One terrible date on a red carpet that I refuse to count as real." His face softens a bit, and I see the vulnerability there. "I want to take you out on a real date, if you'd want."

I smile, reveling for a moment in how lovely it is to feel this whole again. Life ahead of me feels so open and wild and free. How it had felt to really ride a horse for the first time.

"Fine. But I get to pick where we eat."

He smiles and leans down again, brushing his lips against mine. "Anything you want."

EPILOGUE

One Year Later

Charlotte forces the phone in front of my face.

"It's right here, Nora. In full color. Photo evidence."

I sigh and push the screen out of my face. "Can you please not shove that thing anywhere near my mouth? I know you use it when you're in the bathroom."

"Everyone uses their phone in the bathroom," Charlotte shrieks, looking at Bree for confirmation.

"Well . . ." she says, taking a sip of her iced tea.

"Oh, come on," Charlotte says, throwing her hands up. "I know both of you—ugh, never mind. This isn't about me. This is about you," she says, aggressively pointing at me from across the table, "not telling us you broke up with Alec."

"Char, can you let me—"

She groans and looks up at the sky. We're sitting outside at our favorite brunch spot, where we meet up every three months. They're both busy with college, and flying in from Montana is an expensive pain, but it's worth it to see them in real life every once in a while.

"I thought we were past this whole keeping-everything-inside phase. You promised no more secrets. Yet we have to find out you're not dating Alec anymore through an Instagram photo?"

She shoves the phone in Bree's face this time, and I know she's looking at the same picture Charlotte showed me. It's Alec at a table with a redheaded girl a few years younger than him.

"You've shown me this ten times, Char," Bree says.

"I didn't say anything because—"

"Because you're still in this Nora-keeps-secrets-from-her-friends phase. You can't keep doing this. How can we help you if we don't know things are wrong? Breaking up with a movie star is a big deal, Nor. Also—"

She stops mid-sentence, her mouth hanging open as she stares at something behind me. From the way the heads at the tables next to us turn, and the noise around us grows, I know exactly what she's looking at.

"Okay, maybe I was keeping a secret. A guest is joining us for brunch," I say, biting back a smile. She doesn't look at me, her eyes still trained on Alec as he slides his hands on my shoulders and leans down to kiss the top of my head.

"Hello, Horse Girl," he whispers in my ear. I smile.

"Hello, Pretentious Jerk."

His laugh caresses my cheek. I turn to face him as he pulls out the seat beside me and slides in, ignoring the half dozen phones now pointing our way. He smiles softly and laces his fingers through mine.

I haven't seen Alec in person since he flew me out for Delilah's farewell party for the half of her thyroid they took out. It was a weird party, which was perfect for her because Delilah is weird in the very best way.

Alec and I stare, each drinking the other in. Then a cloth napkin hits the side of his face, and we both turn to stare at Charlotte.

"Seriously? You have the nerve to show up here after this?" Charlotte shoves her phone across the table at him this time. He glances down and then rolls his eyes.

"That's my cousin. We met up for dinner last week. Nora talked to her for half an hour on FaceTime."

"It's true," I say, taking a sip of my water. "She wants to learn how to ride, so I gave her some pointers."

Charlotte looks between us, the anger slowly fading from her face. "You two didn't break up?"

"No. I definitely would have said something."

"I told you," Bree tells her. Charlotte shoots her a look.

"Fine." She stares daggers at Alec. "Just know there are plenty of napkins to be thrown if you ever *do* break her heart."

"Noted," Alec says with a laugh.

We spend the next two hours catching up—Bree and Charlotte telling us about their second-year classes. Charlotte swears she's dropping out after sophomore year is over, but I don't buy it. Bree details her advanced classes, and I can barely decipher what she's saying it's so far out of my realm.

Alec tells us about his latest movie, sci-fi this time, and all the set drama.

The restaurant is well on their way to serving lunch by the time Charlotte and Bree have to go.

"I've got an early class tomorrow," Bree says. "Wish I could stay longer." I hug her tight, wishing I didn't have to let go.

"And my mom will literally disown me if I miss our nail appointment." Charlotte hugs me next. She gives Alec a look once we're done, and I wonder if she's ever going to warm up to him.

"Alexander," she says. It's more of a warning than a goodbye.

"Charlotte terrifies me," he confides once we're alone.

"More than my dad?"

He considers. "I think so. We still on for dinner with them tonight?"

"Cecelia spent the entire day marinating a tofurkey. So yeah, we're on, unless you want to face her wrath."

"I can choke down some tofurkey if it means staying on her good side."

Surprisingly, Alec and my parents get along great. And I'm glad for that, really. But there are these weird moments that happen between my dad and Cecelia and Alec.

When Alec's politely complimenting Cecelia on her new drapes or haircut, I can't help but imagine how things would be if he had met Mama. There would be a lot less of the awkward small talk and a lot more of my mom asking him why he's wearing khakis before the age of seventy, or her making him help birth a foal while he's dressed in them.

I'm happy. But I wish she knew him. I wish he knew her.

Maybe somewhere, she's watching. Maybe she likes Alec.

Maybe she's proud of me.

Alec threads his fingers back through mine, bringing me back to the present. He's staring at me.

"What?" I ask. "Something on my face?"

He laughs. "No. I have some news. I signed on for a new movie. Filming starts next month."

"Okay," I say, knowing there's more.

"It's a western. A remake of *Giant*. It's in the desert. Has guns and trains." He pauses. "And horses."

I raise my eyebrows. "Are you asking what I think you're asking?"

"Well?" He shrugs. "Have you had enough time under the Montana sky?"

"I could handle a few weeks away."

He smiles. "So, Alec and Nora, take two?"

I laugh. "Fine. But this time, I get my own trailer. And Ethel's definitely coming along."

His breath trails along my cheek as he laughs gently, lips pressed against my temple.

"Whatever you want, my horse girl. Whatever you want."

ACKNOWLEDGMENTS

TK
   TK